Ian Macpherson is UK Edi.
Agency, and he lives and work
Orient. He is married with tw.   ,ys the
sea, the grape and practicing ph   _-j. *Black Beach* is
his second novel.

Ian Macpherson

Black Beach

Matador
9 De Montfort Mews
Leicester LE1 7FW, UK
Tel: (+44) 116 255 9311 / 9312
Email: books@troubador.co.uk
Web: www.troubador.co.uk/matador

ISBN 10: 1 905886 42 X
ISBN 13: 978 1905886 425

Cover photograph and design © Andrew Farrar

Typeset in 11pt Stempel Garamond by Troubador Publishing Ltd, Leicester, UK
Printed in the UK by The Cromwell Press Ltd, Trowbridge, Wilts, UK

Matador is an imprint of Troubador Publishing Ltd

Prologue
Epilogue from *Invisibility*

That Christmas Bo could not help thinking that Lo Hi had gone a little overboard. He knew that in America they went in for that sort of thing, spray-on snow, drip-free candles, jingled-up shopping, but heavens above here they were in San Diego, of all un-Godly places, and Lo Hi had no more idea about the birth of the infant Jesus than she had about St. Nicklaus, St. Peter or St. Paul. Still, it kept her happy, and enthusiastic, and boy, was she enthusiastic. A freelance English/Korean translator by day, and housewife superstar by night, she had just started a company, her very first company as she kept reminding him, organising conferences for Koreans in San Diego, or maybe it was for Americans in Seoul, probably both, Bo could never quite remember.

Lo Hi had adopted America, and all it and she stood for, as well as the CIA had adopted PJ. It hadn't been such a bad deal for any of them. Bo got his hands on Lo Hi, Lo Hi got her hands on America, and the Americans got their hands on PJ. Kimiko had visited them recently in California as head of a Japanese cultural delegation, part of her new job as a member of the Diet. She said one day she would be Prime Minister, and they had all believed her.

No, it hadn't worked out too badly, but Bo was listless, had been for some time. It hadn't helped when his mother, the ever-upwards Miriam, phoned and dropped in to the conversation that his ex-fiancée Kelly Cuss was engaged to a Belgian doctor and they were both working for *Médicins Sans Frontières* in Mali, doing a little good for the world, having an adventure, she added pointedly.

Then she had called again earlier that week, said Bo had received a letter from Her Majesty's Government marked Strictly Confidential. It looked important; should she open it? He

1

supposed she should. She did. It was from Her Majesty's government, the Foreign and Commonwealth Office. He had been invited to an interview, at his convenience at Vauxhall Cross. What's Vauxhall Cross? she had asked. Bo was about to reply MI6, but thought better of it. Don't know mother. Shall I forward you the letter? Yes please. It was the letter he was waiting for now. And he thought he would attend, for Her Majesty's sake.

PART ONE

1
Dateline 25th

As is his habit, Sir Mungo starts the day at first light by moving backwards towards the darkness. What happens is this. Just as enough light creeps through the bars high on the cell wall to bring the space into view, he looks around, sees his favourite, darkest corner, the one behind the door, and wanders over and makes himself at home for the day. His cellmate, Gustavo Cortez, neither comments nor moves, just observes; he sleeps all day too. And then just as regularly as the dark of night takes over from the light of day, he strolls back to his spot under the bars and finishes off whatever is left of Cortez's gruel.

This has been Sir Mungo's routine for a while now. Cortez has been in here for one year and one day, Sir Mungo something like three months. Cortez is glad of the company. Sometimes Cortez is jealous of the exercise Sir Mungo takes; in fact to help waste away the time he, Cortez, has worked it out. Sir Mungo is four centimetres long. From the dark corner to below the bars is the length of the cell, say three metres. Back again makes six metres. So Sir Mungo gets the human equivalent of a three hundred metre walk per day. And that three hundred metres walk is per each pair of legs, so his real equivalent is twelve hundred metres. Twelve hundred metres! Cortez hasn't been that far in one year and one day. Now admittedly Sir Mungo doesn't break sweat when he takes his exercise, but at least he gets to stretch himself a bit.

Something else Cortez is jealous of is the pain, the lack of pain. Cortez is always in pain, in pain in his stomach. He often thinks it's funny how the only place they haven't punched, kicked or beaten him is the one that hurts the most. It's the food if that is what the food is, or the bits floating in the water. Or maybe an

3

insect bite, he might as well be in the jungle. Or the germs, the prisoners could hardly ever wash their hands, and he couldn't imagine the guards cooking or serving ever washing theirs. But all day, every day, all night, every night, there is the constant ache in the centre of the stomach. Often for hours on end he can think of nothing else.

There is nearly enough light to read by now this morning, expect there's nothing to read. His neighbour is a late riser for these parts, and it's another half an hour before he hears "Good morning Gus."

He replies as encouragingly as he can: "'Olà Big-K."

"And good morning to you too, Sir Mungo."

"He says that too," replies Cortez.

Cortez hates this place, hates the pain, hates what has happened to him. He is bitter that he has just been left to rot here, bitter about the uncertainty, bitter about the waste. He despises the guards, despises their corruption, despises their ignorance. He pushes himself up from the concrete floor. He prepares to bend back down again from the stomach pain, but it's not too bad today, that is it's still on his mind but he can at least stand upright.

"Sunday. It's Sunday today isn't it?" his neighbour shouts through the wall.

Cortez turns to look at this time scratchings on the wall. He already knows it is Sunday, but appreciates the task of checking. "Yes, Big-K, it is Sunday."

"Domingo."

"Domingo!"

Sunday is their special day, the weekly wash and the weekly visit from their lawyer Elisa Makepeace. Cortez thinks that Elisa is the only good thing about Nigeria. Elisa comes every Sunday with some food and the guards' bribe money, a gift and bribe money for the governor, letters and news from Spain for him and from South Africa for van Stahl. Cortez thinks Elisa is the only decent black in Nigeria, probably in all of stinking Africa. Cortez has been banged up with van Stahl for so long he is starting to think like him and now he doesn't like blacks in black countries any more and he is prepared not to be too keen on them in white countries either, that is if he ever gets to see a white country again. Van Stahl hates them all as a matter of course. Before Elisa arrives they have their weekly shower and change of string. Cortez is also bitter about the string, the fact that he, Gustavo Almunia Cortez, 33 years old, well born and well educated in Catalonia, that he is supposed to be grateful for a new piece of string every week with which to hold up his trousers, his trousers which are only too big because the filthy food has turned him into a walking skeleton and given him this stinking stomach ache, and that if it wasn't for Elisa bribing the idiot black guards there would be no food at all. He hates the way the string only lasts a week, and he hates that the trousers are so thin that he can feel the string move against his skin.

Cortez hears the sound of metal boots on concrete floor. This is not routine. This is far too early. Something unusual is happening. Cortez leans back against a wall and listens. The guard is now turning the corner and unlocking his neighbour's door. Cortez can hear the guard shout "Hey, van Stahl, you come w'me!" then walks the few paces to his cell, unlocks the door and shouts at him "You, Cortez, you come w'me!"

They walk behind the guard towards the Administration Block. They smell urine, shit, sweat, dirt, Africa, fear. They are afraid. "What's up, boss?" van Stahl asks the guard.

"Mr. Sunday, he wants see you both."

The prisoners look across at each other. This can only mean trouble, maybe a beating for some reason. Both have been beaten by Sunday Chukwu, Governor of Kirikiri Prison. He usually uses a blood smeared baseball bat, and aims for the arms, legs and back; he stops when he's exhausted. He's a big, well fed man. Now van Stahl is thinking that maybe Elisa's bribes are not big enough, it can't be for anything they have done because they never do anything. Cortez is worrying about his stomach, and planning to curl into a ball if he can as he did before, and cursing how things have worked out and the savages that have power over him. Now they are climbing the steps to the governor's office. They notice the fresh paint and easy door. They step into the air conditioning, turned down ostentatiously low. They see Elisa Makepeace sitting at the table next to Sunday Chukwu. The governor is leaning back in his chair and smiling; the lawyer is tidying up some papers.

"Ah, my terrorist friends Mr. van Stahl and Mr. Cortez,"

Chukwu gestures them to sit down. There is nowhere to sit down, they stay standing, and are now shivering from the sudden dry and chill air and from fear. "I have, as the British colonialists taught me to joke, good news and bad news." He looks up triumphantly, amused with his wit and enjoying the suspense of uncertainty he can see in their eyes. "Yes, good news for one of you, and bad news for the other. Now, I wonder which it will be and for whom?"

Krause van Stahl and Gustavo Cortez both know instantly what the good or the bad news is about. Ever since their conviction *in absentia* in December 2005 for conspiring to commit an act to terrorism, the ruling family, and therefore the government, of Fernando Po, had been trying to extradite them. At first everyone assumed the Nigerians would oblige their near neighbours, but the South Africans had leant on President Obasanjo to keep the prisoners in Nigeria and the Nigerians had responded for the chimera of African unity. Something must have changed. But only one of them was going. That was the good news for one and the bad news for the other.

"So, will it be you Mr. Cortez? A Spanish citizen being returned to his old colony, you will not be so fortunate as your colonial slave traders were in the past. And Mr. van Stahl, the ringleader, the great Boor marauder, the self-styled Big-K, caught red-handed swashbuckling around Africa as though it was still your personal fiefdom. You could join your co-terrorist Mr. Voorstmann, your bagman, there. I hear he is not too well."

Both men look at Elisa Makepeace, but she looks away uncomfortably. Chukwu is laughing again. "I hear it is bad, very bad in Fernando Po. They have a prison there called Black Beach, makes this Kirikiri here in Lagos look like a Girl Guide camp. A Girl Guide camp, that's very funny!" he turns to the lawyer for approval for his joke, the lawyer obliges faint-heartedly. "The prison sentence that waits one of you is fifteen years. Fifteen years of hell. Mr. Krause van Stahl here is already fifty-five years old, that will be the end of him. Mr. Gustavo Cortez is thirty-three, his best years ruined." He looks from one to the other, enjoying his moments to torment, wishing the moments would not have to end with revelation. van Stahl and Cortez stare at the floor, each attacked by private demons. Five and a half more years here. Survivable. Just. Or fifteen years of abuse and torture at Black Beach. They had heard about their friend Smit Voorstmann, a broken man in every sense, for whom death would be a blessing if they would only let him take it.

"But I said there was good news and bad news. So far you two fine European colonial gentleman have only heard the bad news." van Stahl and Cortez look up, curious. Both are convinced it is he who is going to Black Beach. "The good news. What can it be? An extension of your sentence here, because that is better than extradition to Fernando Po? A bigger cell, some books, some fruit? I will let the excellent Elisa Makepeace give you the good news."

The lawyer leans forward and moves the folders around the desk. "It is a pardon, an amnesty for some prisoners by President Obasanjo himself to celebrate his new wife's birthday. One of you is free and one is to go to Black Beach." van Stahl can feel his heart beating in his chest and the blood rise in his face. Cortez's stomach takes an acute pain attack and his eyes close. "I'm sorry," Elisa says, "but Gustavo it is you who will be extradited. Krause, in a short while you will be free."

"So, gentlemen, how will we celebrate?" Sunday Chukwu heaves his large bulk off the chair. "Maybe with a beating?" he laughs at all three of them.

"Governor, I must remind…."

"Relax Mrs. Makepeace; you will be far away. I cannot touch the one who leaves. From now on he will be fattened and cleaned. To make a good show to the outside world. But the one who stays, he should be beaten doubly, so that when he is beaten trebly in Black Beach he will remember the nice Governor Sunday Chukwu in Kirikiri Prison of Lagos who only beat him doubly." The governor laughs heartedly at his ruse, finds the baseball bat from behind the filing cabinet and points it close to Cortez's face. "Smell the wood, Cortez, next time my club will not be so still. Now get out. You two stay."

Cortez opens the door and is swamped by the hot, damp and sickly air. His stomach pain has become acute and he starts to bend double. The guard, who has been waiting outside, takes an arm and marches him back to his cell. The guard unlocks the door. Cortex sees Sir Mungo in the middle of the floor; he too must have broken his routine. The guard sees Sir Mungo too, and with one stride squashes him flat. "Cockroach no good!" he says, spitting onto the cell floor, smiling and pushing back Cortez into his own personal prison. Cortez notices for the first time that he is probably only fifteen years old, probably just trying to be helpful.

2
Dateline 1st

Bo Pett makes a vague gesture towards the new noise in the darkness, knocks the alarm clock onto the floor, realises what's happening, stretches, yawns, swings out of bed and fumbles around the floor until he can turn it off. He turns on the light, the light turns on the day. Today's the day, the day to contact his new life in London, the day for which he is up so early.

Bo moves to the kitchen in the half light and fires up the percolator. He looks outside; California is just waking up too. Another perfect day, but "enough of perfect days" he says aloud. He looks at the clock. Six thirty in the morning here, makes it two thirty in the afternoon in London. While the coffee coughs and wheezes he looks over to the two letters magnetted onto to the refrigerator door. He has rehearsed the telephone call more than a few times, at least his side of it, already. He pours the coffee and reads the letters again.

Foreign and Commonwealth Office,
Section 8/34.
Vauxhall Cross,
London
SE1 5UD.

Mr. Beaumont L. St.J. Flowerdew-Pett,
24, Rutland Gates Mews South,
London SW7 1 BB

Ref: IJH/LSD

28/08/06

Dear Mr. Flowerdew-Pett,

It has come to our attention that recent events in North Korea may have made you a suitable candidate for inclusion in our latest round of recruitment to this Section of the FCO.

If you would like to discuss this matter further, please contact the writer in the first instance to arrange an informal interview at your convenience.

If this is not the case, please disregard the letter and accept our apologies for your inconvenience,

Yours faithfully,

Colonel Ian J. Harding, CGC, DSC.

Bo imagines the scene in London. Colonel Harding, Conspicuous Gallantry Cross, Distinguished Service Cross, sitting at his shiny new desk in his smart new office, secretly wishing he was back where he was conspicuously gallant and distinguished in service. Maybe the Falklands. Goose Green. A bit of argy-bargy. Now back desk side, fielding phone calls from the field, looking around for bright young things. "Psst, Colonel, you heard about Professor Sung's escape from the North Korean gulag? Well I know the man who sprung him, went right into NoKo, whisked him out from under their noses. The boy was made for MI6."

Bo looks at his reply, and imagines Colonel Harding doing the same, maybe right now, wondering when his new recruit will call.

Bo and Lo-Hi Pett,
1653 Toyon Ranch,
San Diego,
California 92119
Tel: 619-7262-7403

Colonel Ian J. Harding, CGC, DSC.

Foreign and Commonwealth Office,
Section 8/34
Vauxhall Cross,
London SE1 5UD.

15/09/06

Dear Colonel Harding

Thank you for your letter to my London address inviting me for
an interview at Vauxhall Cross. Apologies for the delay caused
by it being forwarded to me here in California where I have
now finished recuperating from the exertions in North Korea to
which you referred.

I would be delighted to attend an interview and as suggested
will contact your office for an appointment in a couple of
weeks.

With kind regards,

Yours sincerely,

B. Pett.

Bo finishes off his coffee, waits for the mind and body to
respond, looks at the brightening hues of the beauty outside,
thinks he ought to get up early more often, sings the line "in the
land of milk and honey", tries to remember the rest of the song,
cannot, and dials the number.
　　"Section eight thirty four," a female voice, from the Estuary,
answers.
　　"Colonel Harding, please."
　　"Hang on, I'll put you through to someone who can help."
　　Then a new voice, male and more clearly spoken; "You're
looking for Colonel Harding?"
　　"Yes, please, he asked me to contact him."

"And who's calling please?"

"Pett. Bo Pett."

"I see, well it's a bit awkward, Colonel Harding has left the Section."

"Maybe I can speak to the person who has taken over from him?"

"That's me, but I know nothing about you. What was your name again?"

"Pett, Bo Pett. My full name is Flowerdew-Pett. That's how he wrote to me."

"Ah, Bo, like in John le Carré."

"I'm sorry?"

"Bo Brammel, you know, like in John le Carré, the boss."

"Yes, I think le Carré is the boss too."

"No, no not le Carré himself, his character Bo Brammel, he was the boss."

"Well, maybe, I didn't know."

"Flowerdew?"

"Flowerdew. It's the first half of a double-barrelled name. Flowerdew-Pett. Beaumont."

"Beaumont?"

"That my Christian name."

"First name," the voice corrects.

"Yes, sorry, first name," Bo replies. "Look he wrote to me on the twenty eighth of August. The reference is his initials stroke LSD."

"Ah, that will be the Section secretary Lynne Dunwoody."

"Maybe she knows about me."

"Maybe, but she's off."

"Off?"

"Yes, off. RSI."

"RSI?"

"Repetitive Strain Injury. Typing too many of Harding's letters," the voices laughs at some private joke. "Anyway, I'm very sorry but we can't help you. Maybe write to Colonel Harding and when Mrs. Dunwoody returns she will sort through his mail."

"Oh, alright, but when will that be?"

The voice sighs, "You never can tell with these modern conditions. RSI can last for months, she'll be on fully paid for months anyway. Look, I must go, just write to Colonel Harding is my suggestion, good-bye."

Bo hears the dead tone and replaces the receiver. He is too awake to go back to bed, still too tired to go for a swim. An empty feeling fills his chest and, becoming plaintive, spreads to his mind. Another long day in the endless summer threatens his certainty upon him.

3

Dateline 1st

Hernán Eboleh doesn't care less that he is being followed. From the moment he skipped down the stairs of the US Senate Library building, and now on his way to the First Virginia & DC Bank building, he knows he is being followed. By whom, well that was another matter, but he couldn't care less about that either. He knew about the distaste, the greed, the envy that the words Fernando Po conjured up in Washington these days, even if just a shuttle away in Wall Street corporate America was filling its boots with just as much greed as the members of his family that the hypocrites were always trying to nail.

He walks into a Starbucks, smiles and chats to the servers, slips his overcoat off, takes a seat by the window, and looks out. So, someone out there is watching someone in here. A journalist? Probably. A spook? Possibly. A tree-hugger? Maybe, unlikely. Not for the first time he thinks about having his British bodyguard Mike Tuffy come with him on these trips. Mike is smart, he'd outflank them, at least find out who they are. But no, this is smarter, in and out, under the radar of all but the most sanctimonious. Anyway, screw with them all, let them freeze out there, he's richer than all of them out together, and about to get a whole lot richer too. The CIA, Freedom House, Global Witness, Amnesty International, The Militant, Fair Finance Watch, Transparency International, Consumers Concerned, Human Rights Watch, Corporate Responsibility, they are all on the Fernando Po bandwagon. Maybe Al-Qaeda and the Daughters of the American Revolution will be next. One day, Hernán Eboleh smiles to himself, I'll keep my money somewhere else and then a different bunch of busybodies can bitch about that too.

He reflects on how things have changed. When he first came to America, first came to The First Virginia & DC Bank, ten years ago, when he was eighteen and his late father was the first Minister of Natural Resources, just after the first big oil discoveries, they were met personally by the bank's president Richard Rogerson III. Already trilingual in Fang, Spanish and English, he was on his way to the Université du Québec to study Economics and learn French. His father gave the immaculate Rogerson a suitcase full of three million brand new shrink-wrapped dollars fresh from one of the rig-building contractors. No-one had heard of Fernando Po, couldn't have cared less. Rogerson hadn't either until someone from ExxonMobil opened up a few bank accounts for them. Mind you, he chuckles to himself, hardly anyone back home had heard of ExxonMobil or The First Virginia & DC Bank either, but boy, do they all know each other now.

At Québec his thesis had been in oil exploration and exploitation in the developing world; he knew all about the US Senate committee investigation into the great Fernando Po/First Virginia & DC Bank/Big Oil scam, and his trip to the library was to see the Senate Report for himself, to look for one little detail in particular. The Report started with the background: the Gulf of Guinea could contain crude reserves of 115,000 million barrels, some ten percent of the world's total, and since the discovery of offshore oil reserves in 1995 companies like ExxonMobil, Marathon, ChevronTexaco, Triton and Amerada Hess have invested over $2.5 billion in his country, and as the Report mentioned that's a lot of $s in an island 40 miles by 30 miles, and with only 250,00 people to spend it. The Report investigated how The First Virginia & DC Bank had opened various accounts for the Fernando Po government's ruling Eboleh family, his family. They reckoned a total of $350 million has been stashed away by various of his relatives, including "gifts" of $200 million from ExxonMobil alone. And that was just the money that came to light in First Virginia & DC Bank. In fact, as he discovered for his thesis, the only reason that they nailed First Virginia & DC was because it was caught laundering money with Osama bin Laden's brother before and after 9/11. Before that the Bush family's financial links with the bin Ladens and the House of Saud, both of whom also banked extensively there, not to mention it being the CIA's favourite bank for slush fund for the likes of Pinochet and Marcos, had kept First Virginia & DC open when propriety had long since suggested it should have been closed.

Anyway, neuter The First Virginia & DC bank they may, but the money still flows like the oil, but now on an even bigger scale. The maths is simple and Hernán Eboleh knows it off by heart: the current production is 175,000 barrels of oil a day, and the annual income from oil is around $1.5 billion. The state receives 15% of the revenue, which is at the lower end of the scale, a situation Hernán Eboleh is going to rectify one day, but in the meantime that still amounts to $225,000,000 a year. He reckons his extended family cream off over $150,000,000 a year, and he knows he only has just over ten million dollars in his First Virginia & DC account, all put there by his father before the air crash ten years earlier, and now all sitting in an offshore shell company incorporated in the Bahamas. His branch of the family is seriously missing out on the bonanza, another situation Hernán Eboleh is going to rectify shortly. He snaps back into the present, tips back the rest of his cappuccino, looks outside for his follower again, sees none and heads off to The First Virginia & DC.

Halfway there his cellphone rings. It is his captain in the Fernando Po navy. He has just returned from today's missions and all is in order. Hernán Eboleh smiles into the phone, says good, well done, call me after tomorrow's runs, I'll be back in three days. He has a good scam himself with he navy, but it's peanuts compared with the big bucks flying round his relatives. When he returned from Canada his uncle Bolivar, the president, had told him his military service was to be in the navy. Their first ship, a US Coastguard Cutter, had just arrived, and the president needed a family member to be its captain. Hernán protested that he had never been on a boat before, but the president was adamant. His second cousin Alfredo had arranged for him to have a dozen African Portuguese mercenaries as crew, but it quickly became clear they didn't know much about the sea either. At first it was a shambles. Hernán Eboleh and half the crew were seasick every time they left the harbour, and when they returned the ship would crash into the harbour walls. But gradually he had learned to drive the boat, and the crew had learnt how to tie it up. Then one day he had fallen accidentally on the scam. Supply ships commute backward and forwards from the rigs. One day one of them had radioed for help with the steering. Hernán's naval cutter was nearby, they went over, tied up and one of his crew helped sort out the problem. In gratitude the supply ship's captain gave him a thousand dollars for the crew. Hernán Eboleh had pocketed the money, but now his naval patrol boat waits in the supply lanes and collects its service tax as the supply ships go back and forth from the capital Barbate to the rigs. Each delivery costs a thousand dollars, and there is usually one trip a day per rig, so he reckons on ten thousand dollars a day. After paying off the crew and the president he clears two million dollars a year. Until a year ago he would be carrying it in a suitcase to leave at First Virginia & DC, but now he has to stash it in the Banco Santander in Lagos just up the coast, and from there safely into the anonymity of the EU. The president is so pleased that he has made Hernán an admiral, and the admiral has made the best African Portuguese mercenary, the one calling him now, a captain.

The new manager at The First Virginia & DC, William Storey, with buckteeth and a mis-matched tie, greets him politely and formally, as though he is being taped, which Hernán Eboleh thinks he may very well be. They open the conversation with the exact state of the finances of Beverly S.A., Hernán Eboleh's Bahaman account. Eleven million, one hundred and thirty thousand US dollars. Tax free interest must have helped. The customer tells the manager he wants to invest a third of it in Mammoth Oil, who he happens to know have just out-bidded, in an unusually creative way, all the others for drilling rights in his country's Field 26. Another third he wants to transfer as a balance to his new account at Banco Santander in Paris, France.

The manager shifts awkwardly. It will be difficult to complete the transactions just now. Why? Well, all movements in and out of The First Virginia & DC are being watched, and new security safeguards mean that large sums of cash cannot be transported into quoted stocks or European banks. Hernán Eboleh feels a swell of anger, and demands to know what use the money is sitting in some lousy island in the middle of nowhere. The manager advises patience, it's just a hot time right now. The customer asks how he can turn the shell into cash. The manager advises dissolution and transfer to the Bank of Central African States in Chad, legitimised by France, and from there a million each to accounts in China,

Angola, Morocco, South Africa, the Cayman Islands and the balance to his father's dormant account in Switzerland, where a smallish sum like five million dollars would ruffle no feathers. The customer is not at all happy about this delay to his plans, but orders the manager to proceed. For the last time this particular member of the Eboleh family leaves The First Virginia & DC Bank, and once outside, looks round for his follower. No one seems to be there now, which disappoints Hernán Eboleh more than he can explain. He walks away towards the Wallace Hotel to rest and packs his bags before the overnight flight to Paris. His head is full of the adjusted planning needed after the session at First Virginia & DC. He looks up at an overhead sign: Time 12:08 Temp 25. He could never quite get to grips with Fahrenheit, but knows that 25 is way too cold for him.

4

Dateline 8th

"Well hi there again, folks, Cap'n Steerbacker here up front on the flight deck. OK, the local time in DC is eight minutes after twelve, and the temperature on the ground is a long way down from San Dee, a freezing 25 degrees. We expect to be on the ground in an hour, that's about half an hour ahead of schedule thanks to these bumpy ol' tailwinds."

Bo reaches out a lazy arm and presses the service button. An elderly, disagreeably faced stewardess eyes him with some distaste as she approaches. "A bottle of white wine, please," Bo says.

"Another wine, sir?"

"Yes, a bottle of white wine."

"Well OK, I'll have to check because we're landing shortly."

"Ah, I thought the pilot said not for an hour. Better make that two bottles while you're up there."

"Sir, really…"

"Only joking, the one will do."

She leaves as gracelessly as she arrived, and as Bo's eyes follow her down the aisle he sets to thinking about what might lie ahead for him at the British Embassy in Massachusetts Avenue, Washington. And what of the haughty but husky sounding Miss Anne FitzHerbert, with whom he has the appointment?

After the episode of responding to the Colonel Harding / Lynne Dunwoody invitation-that-wasn't, Bo had decided to keep on keeping on. He just liked the idea of working for MI6, he had had at least the beginning of an invitation to work for MI6, and the more he thought about MI6 the more determined he had become. A trip to Vauxhall Cross with the letter in hand and a demand for an interview had seemed to be the only solution, but then good luck paid him a visit. At a gallery opening in San Diego he had met the British Consul-General, Richard Hastings, based in Los Angeles. Bo explained the outline of his problem. Hastings had given him his business card and had told him to bring the paper-work to the Consulate on Wilshire Boulevard. Hastings was patriotic of course, and towards Bo paternalistic. He took notes "never photocopy anything, dear boy, could compromise your own side later on", bought Bo a lightly grilled seafood lunch with Muscadet and had him driven back to the airport. Two days later he called Bo in San Diego.

"All sorted dear boy. Had a word with Washington. Suspect London playing silly buggers. Washington far more useful to the world. Got a pen? Call Anne FitzHerbert at the Embassy, 1-202-588-7899, straight through private line, tell her Hastings passed on the message. Good luck."

Now Bo feels the plane touch down and he gathers himself for the afternoon ahead. He has no bags as he is booked on the 9.15 p.m. US Airways flight back home. He steps into a taxi, says British Embassy with a sense of small importance, is about to give the address and is told "no need, moth'fucka takes up half a block." His sense of small importance grows very slightly.

At the Embassy, at the mention of Miss FitzHerbert, he is shown through a swing door and down a brightly lit linoleum clad green passage, and then up in a service lift. Anne FitzHerbert is forty five, maybe edging fifty, slim, short haired, brunette, smartly dressed with matching reading glasses on a chain and is well prepared without being familiar. She fidgets with her glasses chain, and takes the glasses on and off more than is strictly necessary. She welcomes him into her room, gestures for him to sit opposite her, and from behind her desk picks up his file.

"You had a good journey, can I call you Bo?"

"Of course, and yes the journey was fine. Very early start."

"Good." She pauses to look through the file, but as though she already knows what is inside. "Harding was there all the time you know. When you phoned London. In fact it was Harding that you spoke to."

"Good heavens. How come?"

"The Firm is quite childish sometimes. Harding's little initiative test. He wanted to know if you were a stayer on the softer ground, as he would say."

"Do you work for him?"

"In a roundabout way."

"That's a roundabout answer."

"It's a roundabout world. Fewer straight lines these days. What you did in North Korea is most interesting. Brave too. Reading between the lines I would say you were in love." Bo notices her tone is half flirtatious, half accusing.

"Yes, yes I was in love. It all just seemed like a good idea. A good idea at the time."

She swings her chain again, puts her glasses back on, looks back down at the folder. Then she asks "Do you believe in anything?"

"Not if I can help it. I have faith in a few...you know, guidelines."

"May I ask about them?"

"Ten commandments type of thing. Myself, hands off. You mean England, Britain?"

"Not necessarily, but do you?"

"Strange, but I read on the flight this morning that Churchill once said we have a wise and kindly way of life. Probably not any more, I'm a bit out of touch, haven't been there for nearly two years. But wise and kindly sound good to me."

She stands up and walks over to the window. It's already growing dark outside. It looks colder by the minute. The noise from out there is insulated away. She says "I would like you to work on a specific project we have here. It requires a fresh face, courage, some luck." She pauses. Bo looks around at the soft dark furnishings, the worn book case, the worn sofa, and waits.

"You sound like you want to say 'but'", Bo says to fill the silence.

"Yes, the 'but' is first you must be cleared in London. They have already started. An hour ago they had still not found any skeletons. Not all skeletons are bad of course. Harding is waiting for you now. You will fly out tonight."

"I don't have my passport, clothes, anything."

"You're in the British Embassy, Bo. Passports are what we do for a living."

"Fine, when is the flight?"

"Nine thirty, British Airways. Economy I'm afraid for you. There'll be someone there to meet you, look for the name

21

Masterson on a board. There's one other thing you should know."

"Yes?"

"I have asked Colonel Harding if I can have you back. Having met you of course. Well now we have, and I do, want you back that is."

She walks over to the door and opening it, leaves him no choice but to leave. He holds out his hand to hers, they shake and say good bye, courteously, Anne FitzHerbert trying to hide her sense of discovery, Bo trying to hide his sense of excitement.

5

Dateline 8th

For the first time in months Gustavo Cortez feels no pain. Ever since the devastating news two weeks ago of his extradition to Fernando Po, things have been, most unexpectedly, looking up. The supplies which his lawyer Elisa Makepeace had always brought were now reaching them intact and unopened; Krause van Stahl has his Wilbur Smiths, complete works no less, and Gustavo has his painkillers, so although he can feel his stomach still contorting inside, the pain is now filtered away. His cell door is left open, his ankle chains have been removed and Krause and he are allowed to come and go as they please within their cell block. As Big-K had said, it was as if the news of his release and Gustavo's extradition had shaken everything up, and whereas before they were just rotting to death, now that they are making the news Kirikiri is having to put on a bit of a show to have them leaving looking more or less human.

The day after the extradition news Elisa had arrived to work out how they were going to stop Gustavo going to Black Beach. Elisa proposed to fly the following week to the Spanish Embassy in Pretoria, and, depending on when he was released, Krause would add his weight in Pretoria too. Not that white mercenaries could add much weight these days, but he could still make a lot of noise. They both reassured him that diplomatic pressure would have some effect; after all Fernando Po was once, and for a long time, a Spanish colony, there must still be channels that could be greased. The Eboleh family would sell their favourite aunts for a hundred bucks. Backing this up, and putting extra pressure on their efforts, they would start a publicity drive telling the world about the conditions in Black Beach. Elisa had left them a copy of the Amnesty International report, *Fernando Po: Trial of alleged terrorist seriously flawed*. "This is dynamite, Gustavo, the world will never let you go there once they hear about this," she had said on her way out.

Since then, Gustavo had been picking the Amnesty report up and putting it down, not reading more than a sentence or two at a time. He had not wanted to share his feelings with Krause, as they were too inconsistent, too confused. On the one hand what had happened at the show trial was so horrifying that he dreaded even more the slightest chance of going there, but on the other hand, because it was so horrifying, he felt sure that someone somewhere would stop him being sent there.

But now, on the evening before Elisa Makepeace's return from South Africa, as the dusk cools the early autumn air, he finds himself having to read the document in full.

A foreign national, Mr. Smithans "Smit" Voorstmann, a citizen of the Republic of South Africa, was sentenced to a lengthy prison term and hefty fine in Fernando Po after a grossly unfair trial ending on 30 December 2005.

"'Eh, Big-K," Gustavo calls out. Krause van Stahl struts in from the next cell. Gustavo sees he is looking healthier by the day.

"What's up, man?"

"We're famous. Listen to this: *Sometime in mid July 2005, Smithans Voorstmann, Krause van Stahl, Wickus Paulsie, all South African citizens, Gustavo Cortez, a Spanish citizen, and Phillipus Simonez, a Zimbabwean citizen, met in a hotel in the Sandton neighbourhood of Johannesburg to finalize the purchase of explosives, and to make logistic arrangements for their transfer to Barbate, the capital of Fernando Po. Voorstmann, van Stahl, Paulsie and Cortez were under financial considerations held by Simonez.* What the hell does that mean?"

"It means what it says, we were in the field, Simonez was back home counting on the money."

To this end they chartered 20 metre offshore oil rig supply boat in Port Harcourt, oil capital of Nigeria, for the transfer of the defendants and their explosives to Barbate with the intention of committing an act of terrorism.

Smithans Voorstmann would go ahead of the others on a trip of reconnaissance, and after reporting back would wait for the others to arrive by helicopter with further explosives. As paymaster Phillipus Simonez was not involved in the actual operation.

"Well, that's more or less right," said Krause van Stahl,

glancing back at his Wilbur Smith. Gustavo reads on, to himself:
After a tip-off from unknown intelligence sources Smithans Voorstmann, the alleged leader of the "terrorists" in Fernando Po was arrested at the central police station in Barbate in the morning of 24th September 2005. He was handcuffed and taken to Black Beach prison where he was placed in isolation for several months.

He was held incommunicado, handcuffed and shackled 24 hours a day. He did not receive an adequate diet, and only rarely received medical treatment for the many ailments that afflicted him in prison. These conditions, together with the minimal access by family members permitted while in Fernando Po, had a negative impact on the physical and mental health of the defendant. The detained did not have a lawyer present during interrogation or at any time when he gave statements, in fact he did not have access to his defence lawyer until two days before the start of the trial. In addition, the defence lawyer did not have sufficient time to prepare the defence. Furthermore, he was not served with the prosecution's evidence against his client.

He had earlier written a concise account of his torture on the back of a carton of cigarettes, which was smuggled out of prison. Below are extracts of his account:

"10/10 22h00-23h00 I was taken to the police station for interrogation. I had no lawyer. I was asked many questions. I had no answers for them.

1. *Handcuffs tightened and cut into my flesh, into bone of right hand. In the office.*
2. *I was beaten with the fist. I had no answers... Beaten on head and jaw.*
3. *They took me to a small dark room down the stairs into the police courtyard. Here I was put on the ground. A dim light was burning. I saw Paolo Rondoso hanging, face down, in the air with a pole through his arms and legs. The police guard started asking questions which I still could not answer. Every question a guard would stand on my shin bone, grinding off the skin and flesh of the right leg with the military boots. This carried on for at least 30 minutes. I was*

shouting, begging them to stop.

4. *Later I begged them rather shoot me for I could not take the pain and agony anymore…After no answers it stopped. I was taken back at 2 o'clock*
5. *20/10 about 15h00 I was tied to a bed with cuffs on my right hand. I was beaten and slapped…my right thumb broke*
6. *At my bed….I was beaten with a blow unconscious.*
7. *The same afternoon I was burnt with a lighter*
8. *At 17h00 I was taken to the police station and told to write everything I knew. Anything that came to my mind. I will have the same and worse treatment of the previous evening. I was terrified and wrote down as if I was involved in everything (which I was not) because they were to torture me again.*
9. *About six weeks later I had septicaemia…pus was running out of my wound…my ankle was heavily swollen of the infection…"*

Furthermore he said in court that he had been taken to the "torture room" and was tortured there and then he was taken back to the other room for further interrogation. He added that the person who tortured him was present in court and that this person had also taken his statement. On arrival to Black Beach prison he was shackled and chained to his bed and beaten on his backs and legs. For the first 10 days after their arrest, he was frequently beaten with batons by soldiers in the cells or outside in the courtyard.

"Gus," says Krause.

After a pause Gustavo looks up, "Yes, sorry."

"You've gone very quiet, my friend."

"My God, this Black Beach is mediaeval, worse. Bastards, they are worse than here, filthy blacks. I mean, listen to this piece: *No evidence was presented in court to sustain the charges against the accused other than his statement, which had been extracted under torture. The statements were presented in Spanish and without adequate translation into languages of the defendant, who did not speak Spanish. On at least two occasions when the defence counsel attempted to raise the issue of torture it was ruled inadmissible by the bench.*

About half a dozen weapons produced in court were not found in the possession of the accused but were presented in court as examples of what the prosecution claimed the defendants intended to buy in Nigeria.

Throughout the trial the defendant was referred to as "a terrorist", "a mercenary" or "a dog of war". He was brought to court and was crossed-examined, handcuffed and shackled. This constituted cruel, degrading and inhumane treatment."

"It's a black fuck nigger-rig business this Gus, and we all knew that. But you won't get there, really, between us we can get you out of there."

"Like your so-called friends Sir Mungo Nathan and Phillipus Simonez and all their well-connected buddies helped you?"

Krause van Stahl falls silent. Cortez doesn't know about Sir Mungo's hush money, doesn't know that Phillipus will be the fall guy. "Well, we don't know for sure that it was Nathan involved, remember that," says van Stahl.

Gustavo does not reply, but looks back down at the Amnesty report. *Despite the defendant's claims that he had been subjected to torture during interrogation in order to force them to sign statements, the issue of torture was not dealt with adequately in court and no doctor was called to examine the defendants. The court repeatedly ignored the allegations of torture made by the defendant. Whenever his lawyer raised these issues he was cut short by the bench and told that there would be an opportunity to expand on the issue later in the proceedings. That opportunity, however, never arrived. No investigation into the allegations of torture has taken place.*

Amnesty International delegates were informed that only the Presiding Judge had practised as a lawyer, and this was limited to one year's experience. Another judge had graduated from law school only six months earlier, while the other judge had always worked in a Ministry. Amnesty International delegates were further informed that two of the judges were related to President Bolivar Eboleh.

The defence lawyer was not given adequate time to prepare his defence and, despite repeated requests, was not allowed to see his client until 20 December, a Friday, three days before the trial began with foreseen Christmas interruptions. Moreover, they did not have access to the whole indictment, and only received the charge sheet and the statements in Spanish signed by his client.

The charges bore little or no relation to any evidence presented in court, and seemed to be geared to demonstrating that there had been an attempt to cause an explosion which would have the effect of overthrowing the government and killing President Eboleh, all orchestrated abroad, in connivance with foreign governments and carried out by foreigners.

No evidence was presented in court to substantiate the charges. Importantly, the prosecution failed to produce in court the key piece of evidence it deemed most vital, on which most of the case rested, namely, any from of contract between Smithans Voorstmann and Krause van Stahl. The prosecution claimed that the original contract was kept in a safe in Zurich and that only a photocopy was available in Fernando Po. However, not even the photocopy was presented in court.

After the trial, the prison conditions of the prisoner so deteriorated that for a few months the only food he received was a cup of rice daily and that their lawyer has not been allowed to visit him. Since early May the prison conditions for all the prisoners in Black Beach prison had deteriorated further and all the prisoners have been kept inside the overcrowded cells 24 hours a day and have not been allowed to bath. In addition, any foreign prisoners such as the defendant have gone without food at times for several days.

Neither the verdict nor the sentences were translated, and the defendant left court with no knowledge of his fate.

The man they describe as the "ringleader", Smithans Voorstmann, was sentenced to a total of 34 years in prison while his alleged South African and one Spanish co-conspirators were each given 17 years' prison sentences in their absence.

Gustavo puts the report down, reflects for a minute, then picks it up again and says: "What do you make of this: *The South African and Nigerian authorities alleged that the "terrorists" were en route to overthrow the government of Fernando Po with the assistance of the British, Spanish and USA secret services.*"

"Not exactly assistance, but Smit knew that they knew, we all thought that they knew, wasn't that a big part of the whole fuck-up? We only wanted to blow up an oil installation and half a harbour, they hoped it would lead to a full scale overthrow," asks Krause.

"We all thought we had their approval, at least their connivance. MI6, CIA, the South Africans. Everyone hates the Ebolehs. How about this: *One of the striking aspects of the case was the number of foreign lawyers acting on behalf of the Fernando Poan government. All were seen speaking to the Attorney General during the trial. A British lawyer asked for Smithans Voorstmann to be recalled in order to obtain further evidence about Sir Mungo Nathan. The South African newspaper the "Mail and Guardian" in an on-line article dated 27 December stated that the foreign lawyers – who refused to be identified – at times presented themselves as orchestrating the trial, which is playing out in a done-over convention centre. One day the British lawyer used a journalist to pass a note to a French colleague reminding the prosecution to introduce photos of Nathan as evidence.*"

"No surprise the French are in there, trying to fuck it up for everyone else," replies Krause. Outside they can hear a small commotion. Elisa Makepeace has returned earlier than expected.

"Elisa," says Gustavo anxiously, and standing now close to him asks "what news from Pretoria?"

"Bad news, Gustavo. Only bad news. I saw the Spanish ambassador and the Minister for Intelligence Services. I saw them together, that is why I am early. They had just seen someone from the Ministry of Foreign Affairs. Simonez is going to take the rap, put there by Wickus Paulsie. He's going to co-operate to save his own skin. No-one is going to help you, at least not until you are there. The ambassador wanted them to insist on your extradition to South Africa, but they have no grounds. He wanted them to lean on Nigeria, but you are a pawn, just a pawn. This is what they said to me later. These words. I am sorry."

"So what can we do?" pleads Gustavo.

"It may be easier to put pressure on the Spanish and South African governments there once you have arrived, plus we can make a hell of a fuss with Amnesty, Human Rights Watch, even the UN," replies the lawyer.

"Why? How?"

"We are going to run a campaign, a public campaign to get you out of there."

"But Elisa, I am a terrorist, at least that is what they think I am. Who will help?" The room falls silent, suddenly the air feels cold, they look awkwardly at anywhere except each other. Gustavo gestures them both to leave, and he closes the cell door behind them as they do so.

6
Dateline 8th–9th

From the passport office at the British Embassy in Washington DC Bo calls home in San Diego. Lo Hi knows all about his MI6 interview saga and is keen for him to make it work; she likes the idea of him being a secret agent as much as she dislikes him lolling about the house or splashing uselessly around the pool. Her life has become one big business adventure, and California has become her natural ally in life; Bo's life has become a series of listless moments and California is driving him nuts, or nutz as the locals would have it. He tells her he is flying to London tonight, British Airways no less, being met at the other end no less, limo to London no less. She worries about his clothes and passport, he tells her not to, and she stops fretting, reluctantly.

He collects his shiny new passport, the similarity to his real name being apparently co-incidental, thanks to all concerned, hails a taxi, arrives at Dulles airport, asks for a receipt, finds the BA check-in, sees the long queue and joins it. Foot by foot the queue shuffles forward until he is in front of the lady at the desk. He gives her a big smile and hands over his new passport. He nearly says no when she asks if he is Ernest Pitt. She smiles back and asks where Mr. Pitt would like to sit. He says that he is rather tall with long legs so an aisle anywhere would be great. Then she tells him there are only middle seats left. He replies that in which case he will take one of them.

Now, eight hours later, Bo thinks back to that conversation and wishes he had asked for a later flight. He tries to turn again but can only wriggle back to where he was ten minutes ago. He cannot see the screen because he is too far back and there are too many heads in the way, and there is a lot of local noise from the baby on his left which has screamed more or less constantly all the way from Washington; for some amazing reason of evolution its mother seems unable to hear it. From time to time Bo had thought about asking the stewardess for a bottle of milk for it, but then thought he had better not interfere. Then he thought he might suggest to the mother that she might feed it, but he thought that might be a bit rude. After the meal thing had been cleared he had kept behind the yoghurt with the thought that he might offer it a spoonful when it cried again; but then it had fallen asleep and he was stuck with the yoghurt. He ate it, and then it awoke again. The minutes stretched the one into the other. Behind him was another baby, which does not scream but kicks, kicks the back of his seat. Once he had turned around to say "excuse me madam..." but found that the parent was a he and as fully wrought as Bo. They had smiled helplessly at each other. Four rows behind are the lavatories and in the aisles either side of him people are waiting to use them. The seat in front is reclined and so he cannot read today's Telegraph which he bought with such enthusiasm from the W.H. Smith in the airport. Like being back in England already he had felt rather proudly. Now on his tray are the remains of something they announced as breakfast, and which is still not cleared away. And he is tired, his eyes are stinging. It has been a long day, an eighteen hour long day, and not unexciting at that. He moves a little sideways again and feels the relief of the first nudge of the descent, then another little kick to reality from behind.

He looks out of the window as best he can, but it's a long way away and turning heads are in the way. The descent and whirring sounds go on forever; when he can see outside all he sees is grey, more grey. Suddenly there's a bump; they are down. Bo wants to stretch but can't. The babies scream and kick together.

He approaches HM Immigration and right on cue a small balding man in a purple cardigan walks up to the desk, excuses himself to the officer sitting and checking, and takes Bo's passport. He thanks Mr. Pitt for the passport, wishes him a pleasant day in London, gives him a Home Office card, showing him a reference number hand written on the back. "Call this number," he advises, showing Bo the front of the card, and turning it over says "and quote this reference when you want to leave. Give us 24 hours." And then he is gone. Bo goes downstairs and sees his flight number and the notice that his carousel is number four. He waits; and waits. Passengers are becoming restless, but Bo appreciates the space and peace, and finds a quiet chair from which to watch. His eyes close and he dozes. He awakes, has a momentary panic about missed luggage and is reassured by the same milling masses milling around the same carousel. Then it comes to him, he has no luggage. He is about to leave when he decides to repeat the dozing exercise, and when he awakes this time he sees movement. It has been fifty minutes, but he feels more refreshed than frustrated. He walks through Customs rather conspicuously with only hand baggage, but no-one seems to mind.

Masterson, that was the name. He is confronted by a sea of placards. He scans them all as he walks past, but none say Masterson. He walks back to a wall from which he can see them all. No Masterson, no doubt about it, no Masterson. He changes twenty dollars, goes to the train, is surprised that twenty dollars won't take him to London, changes twenty more and, feeling less than totally impressed, waits for the train to Paddington which itself is "experiencing delays caused by previous cancellations". Bo allows himself a wistful recall of California, but tells himself to pull himself together.

7
Dateline 8th–9th

"I am so sorry, Mr. Eboleh, it is really embarrassing, we understand your dismay, but the computer has made a mistake and overbooked the flight. I can of course offer you business class, and the other gentlemen it has overbooked have accepted a free return journey to Paris at their convenience, but I simply do not have the first class seat you desire, and that I must say you have reserved." The head of Air France ground crew at Dulles is having a bad day, is flustered beyond his training, and he folds his arms, lets out a puff of cheek and shrugs.

The tall, thin, softly spoken man from West Africa leans onto the desk, pushes his head forwards and says discreetly: "There is no need for embarrassment. In my country we must also pay local taxes from time to time. I am sure this will help?" he says, and opening his brief case, turning it sideways on the counter against prying eyes behind, places a wedge of crisp new hundred dollar bills, maybe ten thousand dollars worth, in front of the manager.

"But, monsieur, I assure you it has nothing to do with, with…with local taxes. We really do not have available seats. It's certain."

Hernán Eboleh swivels back his open briefcase, reaches into it, pulls back the newspaper, and puts another equal amount of dollars back in the fold and pushing it forwards again says "I am sure someone can be persuaded to help me. You see I want to be in Paris tomorrow morning fully rested, and I need to be in first class." He looks across at the manager, who is looking fixedly at the fold in the newspaper.

"Please wait here, monsieur, I have one idea, it may work, it may not, but we can try."

Behind Hernán Eboleh a small line of first class passengers, unused to waiting, is shuffling impatiently. He turns to say to them with hands spread wide: "Please excuse the delay, there has been a computer glitch. Shouldn't be long now." The faces in the line smile back, nodding with some sympathy, surprised by his courtesy.

"Well, monsieur, we are in luck. One of the seats was reserved for a training captain flying home, but I must report that he has absolutely insisted that these local taxes go to a charity."

Hernán Eboleh smiles and pushes the newspaper right over. "Of course, the training captain and you yourself must deploy them as you see fit."

The manager smiles obliquely, "Your ticket, sir."

Hernán Eboleh thanks the manager profusely for his under-standing, apologises once more to his first class colleagues waiting their turn, and heads for the washroom. He has one more task before the checks and boarding; he enters a cubicle, stands on the seat, takes the Smith & Wesson 686P 5-inch .357 handgun out of his left overcoat pocket, takes a glove from his right overcoat pocket, presses the flush button, opens the cistern, lets the gun drop in, replaces the cistern, puts his glove away, climbs off the seat, opens the door, washes his hands and leaves. Best thing about America as far as he's concerned, well second best after the dollars, the guns. He is a member of two guns clubs in Washington, and is grateful he doesn't have to bother with that sort of nonsense in Africa.

Two hours later Hernán relaxes in 2A; not his favourite seat, too much wind noise on the front curve of a 747; he prefers row 6 on the Air France, the back row from which to observe the comings and goings. He has spent many happy hours in first class placing his fellow passengers in this situation or that. An outrightly effeminate mixed race steward leans over him, and asks for his drinking requirements. Eboleh bristles; he does not like effeminate men, or mixed race men, and he certainly does not like this steward. "Diet coke, ice and lemon, not too much ice."

"Would monsieur like to inspect our wine cellar on wheels, that's what I call it, for a little *fantasie du vin* with his meal."

Eboleh remembers himself, and merely says "No thank you, I am fine. And let me sleep through breakfast."

He rinses a texplokn down with the diet coke, he reclines, reclines fully on his single bed, he sleeps, sleeps soundly with his ear plugs and eye mask. Only when they are near to landing is he disturbed and made to prepare himself and his seat. He lands, quite refreshed if still a little drowsy.

At Charles de Gaulle he heads for the Terminal One Air Crew fast track. It's not exactly official but anyone with a Diplomatic Passport can use it. He shows his passport and says in perfect French, "I want to speak to your superior, please."

"But, monsieur, what is the problem, you can go through?"

"There is no problem, I just need to see him, if you don't mind," Hernán replies, noticing again an impatient queue gathering behind, this time air crew, and then looking obviously at the officer's lapel and number adds, "immediately would be most convenient for everyone." The officer presses a buzzer and waives the others through.

Two minutes later the superior arrives, adjusting his jacket, looking dapper and in a hurry. He nods, waives without courtesy for Eboleh to follow him and shows the young West African into a small room and asks how he can help.

Hernán passes the superior his passport face down across the table. "You can tell by my name, my passport, my country something about me."

The superior picks it, leafs through quickly and expertly. "The passport is diplomatic, the country is Fernando Po and your family name is Eboleh, as is the President's, in fact the whole government. No disrespect, Admiral Eboleh."

"Exactly so. I have some information which will be of value to your country. I want you to make me an appointment with the head Africa Francophone of the *Direction Generale de la Sécurité Exterieure.*"

"But, monsieur, the *DGSE* is the secret service, I know nobody from that department, no-one at all, no-one does, it's all secret," he smiles to himself, certain the West African will not see his cleverness.

Eboleh smiles encouragingly. "Of course you will not know immediately. You will have to phone your boss, who will have to phone his boss, who will then phone his boss. This one will make a sideways call to the head of DGSE who will make a downwards call to the head of the Francophone. It is well before lunch, it should not take more than, I don't know, two hours. I will wait here. And your name, please?"

"I am Inspector Didier Cressuil of *Direction Generale des Douanes et Droits Indirect*. Well, it's not everyday…"

"Can you arrange for some coffee? Café au lait. And a croissant?"

"Yes, monsieur, of course, right away," and with that he got up, whirled away and went on Eboleh's errands.

8

Dateline 9th, am

"'ey, Big-K!" Gustavo shouts through their wall. His stomach hurts again from the exertion of raising his voice.

"Si, amigo," van Stahl replies jauntily.

"You remember the time that President Bush greeted us at The White House?"

"I do," replies Krause laughing, and now ambling through their open doors and into Gustavo's cell. He adds: "and as we both know it wasn't *the* President Bush, but *a* President Bush."

"So you always say, but for me he will always be just plain President Bush. What was he President of again?"

"He was President of Anglo-Argentinean Exploration and Mining. Probably still is."

"But it was in the White House."

"It was in the White House, Gus, that is a fact."

"Sir Mungo's White House.'

Gustavo can feel van Stahl tense at the mention of Sir Mungo. Always does. "It was The White House, but not *The* White House. Full address: The White House, Constantia, Capetown. In the republic of South Africa," replies van Stahl. "That once great country. South Africa, it will go the way of this hellhole. Look at it this stinking place. Arsehole of the world, armpit of Africa – and that's not easy! – they've completely fucked it up, idiot kaffirs couldn't run a bath, and that's in plain Springbok speak, my friend."

"OK, it was the wrong president and the wrong White House. But I can say, when I am rotting to death in Black Beach, I can say," and Gus puts on an important voice, "When I met President Bush at the White House..."

"Come on Gus, man, we're going to get you out of this mess."

"Like the great Sir Mungo...never mind. How did you meet the great hero anyway?" Outside the cell a commotion is starting down the passage, then they hear raised voices, becoming louder as a prisoner is being dragged by two guards toward the office block. Gustavo and van Stahl both know that means: one of Sunday Chukwa's baseball bat sessions. The whimpering and already bloodstained prisoner knows it too. Gustavo shudders and thinks of Black Beach. van Stahl shudders and hopes nothing goes wrong, that he is soon out of here. They both turn back to talk to each other as the screaming turns the corner and climbs the stairs.

"Sir Mungo and me, we were neighbours, in Constantia. You came to my shack, the Famous Officer's Mess, The White House was just round the corner. It was also twenty times bigger."

"Is everything they say about him true?" asks Gustavo.

"Well, if everything they say about him is true, that depends on what you've heard. What've you heard?"

"That from the roughest beginnings he owns, more or less, sub-Saharan Africa."

"He was born in Rhodesia before the second world war, to poor shopkeepers, importers really, in Salisbury. That's what the idiot kaffirs call Harare now. He made his first million in that war, black racketeering in Southern Europe. The Rhodesians kept him out of the front on account of his being Jewish. After the war he stayed on for a few years making more money from breaking rations."

"Stayed out of Africa then?"

"He told me that he didn't come back to Africa until 1950, when he was thirty, and then only to bury his mother. His father died of something or other in the war years. And he fell in love with Africa then and there. The space, the opportunities. Now he was rich, he could buy what he wanted, and what he wanted was land. It was cheap enough, and productive too, not like now the niggers have fucked it up. He says he was put on God's planet to make money."

"Is he religious?"

"Not likely, Gus. Not at all. He's not a very nice man. Never married, if he wants to fuck he sends for a whore. A white or brown whore. Jews won't fuck a schwartzer, not unless they're blind drunk. Not many friends, I mean I only met him because one of his houses, one of his smaller houses, was near mine. Even

39

Phillipus, his number two, doesn't like him."

"How did he get involved?"

"Phillipus? They met in Zambia. Both Zimbabweans. Simonez was about to lose his shirt on a mining contract, a mine with no copper, a paper mine. He's a lawyer, not a digger. But he's greedy, just like his little piggy eyes tell you he is. I'm not sure exactly of the circumstances, but Mungo, he wasn't a sir back then, bailed him out in return for some legal loopholes Phillipus had dreamt up. Anyway, they've been tweedle dum and tweedle dee ever since."

"Then what?"

"Then what, what?"

"With his life, his career? Nathan's."

"Yes, well land led into mining, as he said almost by accident. One day he buys another farm, and under the farm is ore. Not much, but enough to give him a taste. Then he goes international. He buys mining shares in London and mines in Africa. His inside information fed on itself. Buy now Africa is splitting up as the Brits give them their independence. Rhodesia and Nyasaland became Zambia, Malawi and Zimbabwe. Once again he was in the right place at the right time. Owned large chunks of all of them, plus was often the biggest monkey in the banana tree in any one of them. He practically owned Zambia. Then he moved south into South Africa, and west into Angola, took over gold and diamond mining there once he'd cornered the shares in London. The man is a rollercoaster Gus."

"I heard he made his most money from oil."

"No, that's not true, at least I don't think it's true. Oil only came along more recently. He was backing the good guys in Angola, UNITA, in fact at the time he was paying my wages in a manner of speaking. Then they found oil there. That's when he got a taste for it, so quite recently. After independence he made sure he was in with the new in-crowd. You know, someone once told me he was ideally suited to the old and the new Africa. In the old days you owned the land, and in the new days you own the politics. Greed is the uniting factor."

"And Fernando Po?"

Gustavo sees van Stahl take a deeper breath as if about to say something, something extra. But no. "Sorry, forbidden subject," says Gustavo.

"Gus, listen to me. We've been through a lot together. We'll be going through a lot more if not together. I don't know everything you think I know. I was the leader of our little expedition, but I only know what they thought I needed to know. I treated you on the same basis. It's for everyone's benefit. I'm sorry it's worked out like this. It's costing me a lot of money," he tries to make a joke of it but that falls flat. "It's best if we leave it there. I don't know a lot more than you do, but the difference in what I know to what you know is going to keep you safe. Forget Sir Mungo, even if he was the biggest bastard on the planet and cooked all this up for fun, he has enough bottom to stop anyone believing you. Do you follow that?"

Gus blows out his cheeks, and shrugs, then nods. "I know. What a total fuck-up. If I ever get out of here I'm going to buy a bomb and drop it on the first bit of Africa I see, boor-style."

They both laugh aloud. "Not bad Gus, not bad at all. I see our years together in this S-H-one-T-hole have not been wasted."

Without quite knowing why, Gustavo and van Stahl meet in the middle of the cell and hug each other as men, tapping each other on the back. Then Gustavo starts slowly to cry, and van Stahl can feel tears welling in his eyes too, and still holding each other in their filthy clothes in their filthy cell, they stay hugged together for another minute.

9

Dateline 9th

Big Ben tells Bo it is 11.30 a.m. as he looks to his left walking across Vauxhall Bridge. It is a beautiful early autumn morning, ambient in temperature, with clear light which sparkles off the Thames from behind the new MI6 headquarters in front of him. Bo finds that most, practically all, modern buildings in London are hideous, a city betrayed by architects, but Vauxhall Cross is rather handsome and certainly imposing. His mother, Miriam, hates it passionately as a mish-mash of unrelated shapes and styles, but she probably hates what she thinks goes on inside more than what she can see goes on outside. For an organisation that was not, at least until very recently, supposed to exist at all it certainly had a stand-out statement for a home.

Ever since receiving his invitation to an interview, Bo had imagined a cloak and dagger entrance to the building. Nothing could be further than the truth; in fact from the main entrance at the back of the building he is reminded of the entrance to the Bank of America building in San Diego, with people coming and going brandishing swipe cards around their necks, belts and handbags.

Behind the desk he finds perched an equally imposing commissionaire, with braid and medals shining from his dark blue uniform. Walking up to him, Bo half expected him to morph into a Regimental Sergeant Major and yell at him to Get Yer 'air Cut You 'orrible Little Man, which reminded Bo that he did in fact need to get his hair cut.

"Yes, sir, can I help you?" the commissionaire asks kindly.

"Yes, I have come to see Colonel Harding."

"Colonel Harding? I don't think we have a Colonel Harding here, sir."

Bo reaches into his top pocket and, producing the letter inviting him here, hands it to the commissionaire.

"Do you have an appointment, sir?"

"So he does work here?" asks Bo in return.

"That depends. But your appointment?"

"Not exactly at a particular time, but he knows I am here this morning. Please try him, my name is Pett, Bo Pett."

"I am sorry, sir, without a firm appointment no-one is allowed in. I'm sure you understand. All very hush-hush, if you see what I mean. Best is to write to this person at this address and ask if you can come at a certain day and time, and with the reply come back and then you can enter. That's the normal procedure." He hands Bo back the letter. "Another day, sir."

"No, maybe I haven't explained myself properly," insists Bo, but he notices the commissionaire reach under his desk and press a buzzer. Bo decides he better leave before he is arrested and then come back later with a Plan B.

Bo leaves the building and walks briskly away. Big Ben tells him it is 11.45 as he looks to his right re-crossing Vauxhall Bridge. He is thinking: is this another of Colonel Harding's initiative tests Anne FitzHerbert told him about? Has Colonel Harding spoken about him to Anne FitzHerbert and has he been fired before he has even started? Maybe Colonel Harding really was not there?

"Well," says Bo slightly aloud "time for a walk". He has the idea to call Anne FitzHerbert and ask her what to do, after all this is her plan. Then he thinks maybe they are trying to make him dependent on her. Then he thinks that's pretty stupid. Then he thinks the whole thing is waste of time, then he thinks what else is he going to do? Washington is five hours behind, so in two hours they will open. Then he seems suddenly tired from the dreadful flight and feels the jet lag and a sleep coming on. He walks up to the Hilton Metropole in Victoria Street, goes in, blends with the tourists, finds a quiet chair and nods off.

He dozes for three hours instead of two, wakes feeling groggy and goes off in search of a coffee and a phone card. Ten minutes later he is on the phone to Anne FitzHerbert. She explodes. She advises him, orders him, to go back and guarantees that Colonel Harding will meet him personally at the front desk; and asks him to call her afterwards for a debrief. He says he would, but is not so sure he should.

Once more he enters Vauxhall Cross's imposing portals, and

this time finds the commissionaire smiling and telling him to go straight up, that Colonel Harding "himself" is waiting for him in 1007 "that's right, tenth floor". The lift whooshes up faster than his stomach and stops on the tenth floor as his stomach catches up. The doors open and standing in front of him is a tall, smartly dressed upright man in his mid-fifties with surprisingly thick black hair, creases around his eyes, a neatly trimmed salt and pepper moustache and a friendly, outstretched hand.

"You must be Bo Pett, I am so frightfully sorry for the mix up."

"And you must be Colonel Harding, very pleased to meet you, sir."

Bo follows him into a large office with minimal furniture and an open view down the Thames to the Houses of Parliament. Bo feels excitement and latent loyalty; looking at Colonel Harding reminds him of an old family photograph from somewhere, and the words "military bearing" cross his mind.

"So?" says Colonel Harding. There is a silence.

"I have been trying to respond to your letter, inviting me here for an interview."

"You've been wonderfully persistent." Another silence. Bo is aware of Colonel Harding's eyes dissecting him.

"This morning, you not being here, was that another initiative test?"

Colonel Harding laughs a bit too jollily. "No, no, we just thought you would come tomorrow that's all. You showed too much initiative if anything, caught us all unawares, on the hop as it were."

"Persistence pays," says Bo, smiling awkwardly, and wondering if this was indeed the longed-for interview.

"Your interview, we have these set procedures, all very civil service I'm afraid. You'll have to take a psychometric test, do you know what that is?"

"Slightly."

"Answering a lot of silly questions for the shrinks. Don't worry, everyone passes, say you admire motherhood, like Americans and have nothing against organised religion." He picks up the phone and asks the other end to bring up the "category three physco-test" and then says "no, for Bo Pett. Oh, alright in that case that's what we'll do." He turns back to Bo and says, "It will be on Monday, they are ordering some more from FCO HR HQ. You must be tired anyway." And right on cue Bo does feel another wave of tiredness coming over him.

"Look, never mind, you've made it so far, well done, first step and all that," says Colonel Harding, and Bo feels suitably encouraged. "Pop in on Monday," and with that Colonel Harding stands up and shows Bo out.

10
Dateline 9th, pm

Propped up in a corner of the cell, his mind on his stomach pains again, Gustavo Cortez hears two sets of footsteps approaching, but the sound no longer provokes the fear it once did; since the news of his extradition to Fernando Po and Krause van Stahl's release from Nigeria, life has become easier. As Krause said, "they're fattening us up to show us off."

The two men enter his cell. One is the young guard who used to kick him on the shins, almost as part of his job, every time he entered the cell. Now he just says, "this is Doctor Mumpatha."

Gustavo smiles, "Ah, thanks for coming" and hoists himself up as best he can. He has been asking for a doctor for the last three or four months, but now they have allowed his lawyer Elisa Makepeace to find one for him. He feels relief through every bone in his body to see the doctor.

"What seems to be the problem?" asks the young African doctor.

"I just hurt all the time, right here," says Gustavo pointing to the centre of his stomach. "The painkillers Mrs. Makepeace brought last week helped for a while, but not any more. Maybe there's an ulcer."

"An ulcer?" the doctor looks confused. "Why do you say that?" The thought dawns on Gustavo that maybe Doctor Mumpatha is not a doctor at all, at least not of medicine. Maybe he is an orderly. "Let me feel." Gustavo lies back down on the floor, and the doctor passes his hand over his stomach. "It's not an ulcer, they normally are in the mouth. We are short of medicines here in Nigeria right now, but we local people take these remedies for stomach cramps. I think you have cramps." Gustavo knows he does not have cramps. The doctor takes a bottle out of a bag, unscrews the top and empties the liquid into a small plastic cup. "Take this, it will make you feel better. I will leave the bottle. When you hurt, take more. Mrs. Makepeace has paid. OK?" Without waiting for a reply the doctor gets up and packs his bag.

Gustavo thanks him and swallows the medicine, nothing to

lose in hoping for the best, anything to stop this crap rotten pain all the time. The doctor and guard leave, as they do so Krause van Stahl walks in, asks how that went, hears there's been no change yet.

"Maybe not a good time to ask Gus, but when I get out of here I'm thinking of writing about the whole adventure, maybe make a film. Of course everyone will be called someone else."

"It would be a great film," Gustavo replies uncomfortably.

"I was in one once. *Suicide Pact* it was called. It was about some domestic cock-up in Natal a hundred years ago. I was an extra, an overseer in charge of the kaffirs. I was almost playing myself then, you know what, I could play myself now? Anyway the book first. Can I ask you something?"

"Sure, what?"

"About you. I mean I met you at the beginning of all this. We never talk about the past, no questions, no names, no details in case of torture, but now I'm not, you know, about to be tortured, not any more and I'm wondering what happened before, with you?"

"Well, I can tell you that thirty-three years ago I was born in Spain, in Andalusia..."

"I thought they all looked like Arabs up there."

"Well no, my parents are from Catalonia, both dead now, but I grew up in Malaga. My father was in shipping. I went to university in Granada, studied English and Philosophy, then went into property."

"What kind of property?"

"Residential, selling property, villas and apartments around Marbella in the boom years. I was young, ambitious, there was construction everywhere, I spoke English, hard to go wrong. I did that for five years, was making a lot of money, spending a lot of money too. Then I got really lucky. I met a guy who was also in property, but in timeshare in the Canaries."

"You were selling timeshare?"

"No, investing in it. Krause, you would not believe those times. It was the two years before the Euro introduction and everyone needed to rinse their old cash. The whole of Spain existed on cash pesetas which would be worthless. And Deutschmarks. I tell you there was more German cash than any other. And lire. Oh my God, they brought it in suitcases! Timeshare was perfect, they could buy in ten or twenty thousand hits depending on how much old currency cash they needed to get rid of. And they had something to show for it. A property, you know what is timeshare, some of a property, some of the time but when they sell they have Euros. For us it was amazing, five, six, seven hundred percent profit because we could sell each one so many times. And all legal. We were selling off plans almost at the airport. In the three months before the Euro I was working twenty hours a day. All of us knew this was a once in a life time bonanza. Spanish word, bonanza. The day after the euro, I remember it was New Year's Day, four years ago, I had a nervous breakdown."

"What a real breakdown?"

"Yes, really, I was just exhausted. When everything was settled and converted I had twenty, just under twenty, million euros in the bank."

"And then?"

"And then I went to Martinique. For six months. Did nothing, really absolutely nothing. But slowly one day I became a little bored. And the next day a little more bored. The summer started there, hurricanes, humidity, so I went back to see friends in Andalusia."

"What's wrong?"

"Bloody pain, it's almost worse, comes in waves, God knows what that shot was. Anyway, in Marbella I met a few South Africans. Some knew of others who wanted to leave, but couldn't because of currency problems, whereas they had beautiful properties, and really cheap by our standards. Like where you and Nathan lived, Constantia, what were they, twenty, twenty-five percent of Med prices, and better built. Cheap gardeners, maids. I thought I could go there with some Marbella introductions, legal cash, agreed purchases and they all call it – facilitate."

"Gus, you're an old fashioned property spiv! Now I like the sound of that!" says Krause laughing.

"You can talk, you're a lousy mercenary! Then I met your friend Wickus Paulsie, Wicko. Fernando frigging Po, the so-called FP, sounded like the second bonanza. Unluckiest day of my life, the day I met that bastard. I'll tell you the full story about that too one day, meeting him. What a joke." Gustavo starts to laugh too, but the pain catches him short.

"So you became a terrorist too. What a fucked-up pair we are," says Krause.

"Yes, but I was never going to blow anything up if you remember. I was just an investor, like before. Someone else does the dirty work, in Canaries selling the boxes, in FP blowing the bombs. And you needed my money Krause."

"I did indeed, and I'm not complaining, not judging. You're a good man Gus. So am I, but as they say shit happened. When I'm out I'll help, you know that. I've said that. Hey, you OK?" Krause moves over towards Gustavo, now doubled up and writhing and wincing. "I'll go find the doctor," he says springing up to leave.

"Forget that fucking doctor, fucking witch doctor. What is in that bottle?"

Krause van Stahl walks over, picks up the bottle and unscrews the top. He smells something like disinfectant mixed with herbs. "Smells OK," he says, but sets to thinking if they're trying to poison Gus for some reason. And why, now? "Let me try to reach Elisa."

Gustavo can barely make words. "Hurry, Krause, I'm dying here."

11
Dateline 10th

Hernán Eboleh wakes up just before eight, a few minutes before his alarm clock is due to go off. He has slept fitfully, partly through jet lag and partly through concerns about the interview with the DGSE at 10 o'clock later this morning. He does not need to remind himself that this is the riskiest part of his plan, when he has to share it with outside influences, especially foreign governments with agendas unknown to him. As he washes and shaves the image of a giraffe at a watering hole comes to mind: it needs to drink, but it's on full alert to the dangers as it does so.

Downstairs breakfast is waiting for him, as is the ebullient Madame Pinot, mother of his Université du Québec friend Alain, who runs an unofficial B&B here in the 14th. The arrangement works perfectly for host and guest; the former takes the cash and the latter takes the anonymity. Hernán Eboleh is not particularly worried about his own government, his own family, knowing what he does and where he does it; they don't have the capacity or suspicion to keep him under surveillance, but as a general principle he can't help but feel the fewer people who know about his movements the better. Even Mike Tuffy doesn't know he's here, and Mike is his personal protection. Always paying in cash, the diplomatic passport and disposable phones all help, as does staying with Madame Pinot here in Paris and at Señora Morente's B&B in Madrid.

"Good morning, Mr. Eboleh, you slept well?"

"As always here, thank you, Madame Pinot."

"Dreadful about the strike. That'll be the second time this month. Whole city shuts down."

Hernán Eboleh looks up from his breakfast "What strike, Madame?"

"The transport strike. Till nine o'clock this evening. Bus drivers, Metro drivers, then inspectors, guards, they all come out in solidarity. All of Paris is clogged up by cars, but they are not going anywhere, it's terrible. But you're not leaving today, for the airport, that's tomorrow, no?"

He hurries up his breakfast, "Yes, tomorrow, but I need to be at the far side of the 2nd at 10 o'clock, I was going to catch a taxi at 9.30."

Madame Pinot advises him to start the long walk now, he does and with long strides and some knowledge of the city arrives only ten minutes late. He is not concerned, he is sure they will understand, he even considers stopping for a quick *café crème* just outside the building, but considers he'll be offered one inside anyway.

He enters the swing doors and passes through the metal detector. He has no brief case for them to x-ray, what he needs to know and say are fully prepared in his head. "My name is Hernán Eboleh and I have an appointment with Commandant Claude-Michel Michaux."

The North African female receptionist looks up wearily and asks him to sign in, and then asks, "Is that the Michaux in African Francophone, section chief? We have two Michaux here you see."

"I believe so, he is Claude-Michel Michaux."

"Ah, you should have said, that will be him. Wait over there."

Hernán Eboleh sits on the plastic chair. It is hot, surprisingly hot. He touches the radiator, on full blast. The black and white squared linoleum floor needs replacing, the floor is uneven and his chair legs won't settle, the windows need cleaning.

After ten minutes a small and pale man in his mid-fifties, with a tartan waistcoat and strands of hair brushed over his balding pate walks up to him, introduces himself as Gerard Montpasseux and sits on the chair opposite him.

"I am sorry, Monsieur Eboleh, but Commandant Michaux is not here. The strike you see, he has taken the day off, like most of the bureaucracy. I myself am only here because I live with my mother who has a small apartment nearby. But he will be here tomorrow I am sure, the strikes only ever last one day, up to nine o'clock."

"That's no good I'm afraid, I'm flying out tomorrow. Why don't I call him at home, maybe we can meet tonight at his home when the strike is over? Can we go to his, or your, office to do this?"

The clerk puffs himself up to look important, "I am sorry, monsieur, your appointment is with Commandant Michaux, and you can only go through these doors with his appointment."

"Very well, then I will speak with him at his home," replies Eboleh producing a mobile telephone from his top pocket.

"I am sorry, monsieur, we are not at liberty to give you such a home telephone number."

"Very well, you dial the number on your mobile phone and when he answers give it to me."

"I am sorry, monsieur, that will also not be possible, we are not issued with mobile phones. Maybe I can help you instead? I work for the Commandant, what is your meeting concerning?"

Hernán Eboleh has no intention of sharing any information with this *petit fonctionnaire*. He turns around, looks him straight in the eyes and speaking softly says "Monsieur Montpasseux, it is Montpasseux if I remember correctly, my advice to you, my sincere advice to you, in the interests of your own and your country's security and prospects, is to find a telephone so that a diplomatic representative of the government of Fernando Po can speak directly to the Chief of Section, African Francophone department of the *Direction Generale de la Sécurité Exterieure* of the Fifth Republic."

The clerk moves uneasily in his chair; Eboleh can see the cogs turning in his head. "Wait here please." Three minutes later he reappears with a mobile phone, and holds it out to Eboleh, "Commandant Michaux."

"Good morning Commandant Michaux. I'm sure Montpasseux has briefed you to some extent. I would like to meet before I leave tomorrow morning."

"Of course, of course, my dear Mr. Eboleh. I am so sorry, the transport strike, Paris is log jammed, please accept my apologies."

"That's fine, Commandant, we need to talk man-to-man, can we meet for dinner tonight?"

"Any other night of the year, Mr. Eboleh, any other night, it's my wife's birthday and we have a small family gathering here in the apartment, she would certainly kill me, and slowly, I am sure you understand."

"Completely. Then we'll meet for breakfast. Somewhere anonymous."

"Of course, that will be fine. There is an Ibis Hotel in Saint Denis. It is near my apartment and on the way to the airport. There is nowhere more anonymous in all of France. What time would you like?"

"Nine o'clock would be fine. I will be waiting at reception. I am African, just on two metres, late twenties, thin, grey suit."

"Until then, Mr. Eboleh, I look forward to it."

"Until then Commandant Michaux," and pressing the red button and handing the phone back to the clerk "and thank you Monsieur Montpasseux, you have been most helpful." Eboleh leaves the stuffiness of the overheated office for the cool chic of the Paris streets, a tourist for the day, except he will probably find a library to do more research, especially into the most recent activities of TotalFinaElf in West Africa.

12
Dateline 13th

"And so, here you are, take your time, call me if you get stuck," says Colonel Harding passing the psychometric test paper over the desk to Bo. "By the way, if you...."

"Sorry to interrupt Y, there's an urgent call from 101 in Baghdad," a newly poked-in head says from just inside the door. Colonel Harding excuses himself and follows the head through the open door.

Bo looks at the test paper. He has been looking forward to this, always did like a personality test. He had even stopped off at the Scientologists once, lured inside by the "Free Personality Test" board outside. They said he needed help, and no doubt they were right, but he had passed up the opportunity. He picked up the Foreign Office test, and leafed through it keenly. Twenty-two pages, but he sees twelve of them are Explanatory Notes, then notices that half the notes are in gobbledygook and then recognises what he assumes must be Welsh. He looks at a random question: *You are standing at the front door, and see your mother approaching one hundred yards away with the shopping. Suddenly she is mugged, and the attacker runs away. Do you A) run after him, ignoring your mother, B) go and look after your mother, C) call the police?* Bo feels a little dread, puts that to one side and starts with the easy part:

Full name: Bo hated doing this. His father was a mad keen sportsman and while his mother was in Queen Charlotte's, Hammersmith, recovering from "your difficult birth", he had registered his name after the first names of his favourite rugby, cricket and soccer players. Bo sighed and wrote: *Beaumont Lloyd St.John Flowerdew-Pett,* and cheered himself up by remembering they all thought the Bo part of him was named after the John le Carré boss.

Address: Should he give the London one, where lives his

fearful mother Miriam, Rutland Gate Mews South, South Kensington, or his home address in San Diego? He taps his pen and knows he wants his mother kept out of this and writes *1653 Toyon Ranch, San Diego, California 92119, USA*

Sex: that's easy *Male*

Date and place of birth: still easy *4th April 1980, London*

Native language: *English*

Additional language(s): *Spanish, Italian*. More pencil taps, he studied Classics at university, not particularly brilliantly he has to admit, but still writes down *Latin, Ancient Greek*, and remembering his nine months for Amnesty International in Tokyo, adds *moderate Japanese (not written)*

Ethnic origin: Hell's bells, Bo thinks, it's one of those tricky ones, I can't say white, better say *Anglo Saxon* and hope for the best.

Religious belief (if any): well C of E by birth, but they probably don't want to hear that, but after his time in the far east he wants to say Buddhist, which is what he does consider he is now, but then again they don't want to hear that either, so he writes *Nothing in particular*, and remembering Colonel Harding's advise adds *Tolerance*.

Education and qualifications: Now he knows this is a minefield, he had read in California how they are discriminating against privately educated people nowadays. In the US they have positive discrimination, in the UK negative discrimination, that was the gist of it, like rich people in US soap operas versus poor people in UK soap operas. But he thinks they probably know anyway and are bound to check, so with trepidation he writes the truth: *Westminster: Five A levels (English, Latin, Spanish, History, Philosophy). Cambridge University: Classics 2:1.* He wants to add cricket and squash blue, but thinks he should stick to the questions.

"Sorry about that," Colonel Harding walks back through the door "how are you getting on?"

"Still on page one," answers Bo "the easy bit about mother's maiden name etcetera. By the way, why did that man call you Y?"

"Oh that," replies Colonel Harding chuckling, "old Firm tradition. We controllers are known by letters. Mine is Y."

"Oh, so will I have a number like that man in Baghdad, 101? If I pass of course," asks Bo.

"You will, I'm not sure what yet. I think it will be 108, somewhere around there."

"One–oh-eight," says Bo, testing the sound out on himself. "Does that mean there have only been one hundred and seven secret agents before me?'"

"Good heavens, no. We leave off the thousand to keep them manageable, you will actually be nine thousand one hundred and eight."

"So there are only ever less than a thousand in circulation?"

"It's a job, 108, with a high mortality rate." His pager bleeps; he says "Bloody thing." He reads the message, is annoyed, apologises and leaves again.

Bo says he sees, about the mortality rate, and returns to the questions. But the first feeling of dread he felt after the mother-mugged question grows worse. Each question has three options, so he hopes that 33% is a pass, as all the answers to all the questions seem to him quite valid. *Your dog wakes in the night and barks ferociously. Do you A) go back to sleep with a pillow over your ears, B) go and investigate what the dog is barking at or C) tell the dog to be quiet.* Or how about: *You are at a Diplomatic luncheon with a sensitive government and are served raw sea slugs as the local delicacy. Do you A) eat them anyway, B) discreetly try to loose them in your napkin or C) say you are vegetarian.* Well, Bo thinks, yes and no to all of them. What am I meant to say? He looks back through his previous answers and sees they are probably all wrong. *You are asked to help in a pagan festival in a developing country in which a virgin is symbolically sacrificed. Do you A) join in enthusiastically, B) try to tell them it is not an acceptable practice or C) make you apologies and leave.* Bo had wanted to answer A), but they probably want to hear B) and he had already answered C). He tells himself that this was not looking good as Colonel Harding reappears. "Finished yet?"

"More or less, how important is this test?"

"Old hands like me think it's a lot of baloney, but the pooftahs and lezzos in HR think it's all they need to know. Thumbs up or thumbs down, kind of thing."

"I've got that thumbs down feeling," replies Bo, handing over the paper. Colonel Harding looks disappointed, and a little worried, and harrumphs his good-bye. Before leaving he hands Bo a slip of paper. "This is my pay-as-you-go, incoming only, one in the Thames each week. Call me tomorrow afternoon, we'll see how you've done."

13
Dateline 14th

"Is he any better?" asks Elisa Makepeace.

"No, not really, Elisa, he is not better at all. He's still very weak is what he is, just lying down there. This water helps, I make sure he drinks and drinks," replies Krause van Stahl, swatting away more flies.

The lawyer passes him another five litre plastic jug of Cape Spring. "Expensive stuff here water. But at least you can get it, unlike medicines."

"I thought it was a plot to kill him. What was that the doctor gave him?"

"It's an old local cure for stomach ailments, a cure-all. It's the best he could do. There are no modern medicines," he says, then lowering her voice "unless you are part of the clique. Look, Krause, I have bad news for Gustavo."

"Go on."

"We won't tell him now, sounds like he's still too weak. There is a date set for his extradition now, on the 28th, in a couple of weeks."

The prisoner and the lawyer stay quiet for a while. They both look from the interview room over to Gustavo's cell across the passage. Outside they see dirt and dust and dilapidated buildings and rusty bars but they know this is a million times better than Black Beach. Krause van Stahl feels another fly walking on his arm and slowly lowers his hand to cover it; he squashes it dead slowly without looking and flicks it onto the floor.

After a while Elisa says quietly, "I have an idea."

Krause says "so do I, but it involves guns and mercenaries, yours will be better."

"Don't laugh. Wickus Paulsie."

"Jesus, Elisa, I'm not laughing. Wicko!" van Stahl considers for a while, stands up and says, "let's take a walk."

As they shuffle up and down the shaded part of the yard the lawyer explains her plan. Wickus Paulsie just turned state's evidence against Phillipus Simonez, and it was the former's declaration that eventually sunk the latter. Paulsie had been an insider from the very beginning, in fact, as Elisa reminds Krause just now, the very first "military" person that Krause had turned to when the was planning the FP job. Paulsie's evidence had nailed Simonez, and it hadn't played too kindly for Smit Voorstmann, but he was already on a long, "and let's face it, probably terminal" incarceration in FP anyway. But Paulsie had been easy on Krause "as easy as he could be, seeing as he's your friend" and had said very little about Gustavo, just mentioned him a few times as a late-coming investor "which is quite a constructive way to look at it you see."

Krause kicks some dust, sees it drift slowly away from his shoe. "So you want Wicko to help Gus in some way, is that it?"

"I haven't told you the worse news yet. You remember they sentenced Gustavo, and you too for that matter *in absentia* to half Smit Voorstmann's term, seventeen years, but that was before Paulsie's affidavit against Simonez. Now I hear they plan to use Paulsie's evidence in a new trial after Gustavo arrives – to re-try him. Of course, it's just for show, but they want to make their point, as we know they're paranoid about coups. See them everywhere, with good reason I should think. Now if we can persuade Paulsie to issue another statement saying, as close as he can, that Gustavo was just, I don't know, along for the ride, didn't realise there was a coup being planned, less guilty than Simonez, whatever we can get him to say, so much the better. If we handle it right, proper international outcry, we could use his deposition to cut out the whole extradition. At the very worse we could put a stop to the show trial."

Krause looks across the yard to Gustavo's cell. "Not such a bad idea, if we could get him to help. I've known Wicko for years, maybe twenty years. Fought a lot of battles together. I suppose everyone would be down on him after his confessions, but they don't know him like I do. Prison would strangle him. He's an old African, Afrikaans, adventurer, likes to sleep in the open, he'd do, say, anything to stay out of gaol. Plus Phillipus was bloody rude to him always, the way he talks down to everyone that was just his way, but Wicko took it personally. Not too subtle a soul our Wicko. Brilliant pilot though, I'd go anywhere with him. He'd fly anything, fly into danger for fun, always came out the other side. Once in Angola we captured some old UNITA prop job, some old Antonov I think it was, twenty seater, you know it had two different engines on it – one short stubby one and one long thin one. Wicko took it up by himself, pronounced it fit and we all clambered in, flew us up to Npepe till the juice ran out and it started coughing. It's probably still there. That's what he was really, the best bush pilot in Africa. Brilliant bomber, instinctive."

"They say he ran your air force, when you had Security Matters."

"He did run my air force, we called it Morse Air International. We had quite an operation going with Security Matters, my own private army, best fighting outfit in Africa. Sorry Elisa, didn't mean to offend."

"You didn't offend, Krause. Everyone fights in Africa. Those were different days, and you never fought against Nigeria, like I fought against apartheid."

"No, we never fought against you guys. Our air force, which Wickus ran, we had 727s, four Mi-17 helicopters, we had a couple of Hind Mi-24 gunships, surveillance planes, a whole bunch of air taxis and transports." Krause chuckles at the memory. "We almost set Smit Voorstmann up with a navy for Angola, that would have been something," then becoming serious again "of course not much use in Namibia, even for Smitty."

"You did business too, with Paulsie I mean?"

"Yeah, yeah, we were both directors of Stone International, that was our holding for lots of mining pick ups, gold, oil, diamonds. Whatever. We made a lot of money." They walk on, Krause looking at the ground, smiling to himself, Elisa scanning the barbed wire along the prison walls, waiting for more memories. "We didn't do it for the money Elisa, not in the end. You know, like mercenary, sounds like life is just a payday, some kind of job. It wasn't like that, not for people like Smitty, Wicko and myself. We loved the adventure, we all knew Africa was the last place anyone would have a chance to do this. There we no governments, no civil servants, no idiot do-gooders. If it was there you fought for it, if you won you mined it. You made up the rules every day, whatever was needed."

"What went wrong?"

"Peace. So-called progress. The media, in our faces all the time. They all went wrong. But as you say, when this FP deal came on the table, Wickus was the first person I called. Air support. We needed to get from Port Harcourt to Barbate, and then out of there before anyway knew we'd even arrived."

"And so who's behind Phillipus Simonez? Simonez is just a lawyer."

"Well, firstly he's a lot more than just a lawyer, and secondly I suspect you know the answer to your own question, and I'm not going to comment. Let's keep it as it is. If Phillipus is to be the fall guy...well that's what fall guys are for."

"Will Wickus help Gustavo?"

"Wicko got lucky, don't forget that. If he hadn't gone for a shit when we got busted he would have been rotting away with us in here now. Two minutes either way would have done it. On the other hand he may blame Gustavo for some leak in the buying chain, a leak that meant we all got busted, except him of course. No leak, no bust and we would all have flown down there as planned. Picked up Smitty at the target, blown his boat as well on the way out. All be tucked up safe and rich in Constantia by now. He's a proud man Wickus Paulsie. I don't know. He'll be embarrassed to meet me again, I know that, even hear from me. He'll think that I think he chickened out. But I can see it from his side. Prison or Simonez? Has to be the lawyer gets stuffed every time. It's worth a try, for Gus's sake, we've got to try. So what do we do?"

"You write to him, write to Paulsie, we'll work on the letter together, I'll go and see him. I know how to find the Minister in Pretoria, he'll know how to find Wickus."

"Yup, good thinking, Elisa, let's get to it."

14
Dateline 14th

Commandant Michaux and his only departmental boss, the much decorated but little known General (retired) Maurice Lainé, pull their chairs up at their favourite lunchtime restaurant, *Le Pilot Ancien* on Rue de Tivoli, just around the corner from DGSE's offices at 141 Boulevard Mortier. After the usual friendly greetings and banter with the owner, the formidable Madame Trintignant, they both order, as usual from the menu du jour; as the General, as he still likes to be called, remarks, the menu du jour at Le Pilot Ancien is the only acceptable lunchtime compromise between eating well and eating quickly.

"I had an interesting breakfast on Saturday," says Michaux.

"Yes, tell me more."

"With the nephew of the president of Fernando Po, a certain Admiral Hernán Eboleh."

"But Fernando Po is not one of ours, not Francophone."

"Exactly so."

"And what did he want this Admiral Eboleh?"

The potage arrives, they stop talking briefly, not out of suspicion of Madame Trintignant, but out of habit.

"That's the funny thing, General, nothing, he wanted nothing. I was expecting he wanted money, they all do down there, money for spying, or to sell us some information. But, no, just to make contact, to stay in contact. For one day in the future. He is a cautious young man."

"And his uncle is the president?"

"Yes, the country is run by the one family. Before that the president's uncle was the president, until the current president, his nephew, assassinated him."

"Dangerous affair, being an uncle in Fernando Po. What do we know about this nephew and his family?"

"I have been in contact with Gabon, which is one of ours and next door, and the station there sent me some information." Madame clears away the potage and immediately serves the *côte du porc*. Michaux pulls three sheets of paper from his inside pocket. "Well, the president is Bolivar Eboleh, full name Brigadier General, retired, Bolivar Eboleh Nguru Musagoro. Born on 05 June 1942 into the Esangui tribe in the Akoakam-Esangui district of Mongomo; he was the third of ten brothers to father Nguru Eneme Obama and mother Mbasogo Ngui. The fourth brother, Carlos, was the father of my breakfast companion this weekend, Hernán Eboleh. So the president, Bolivar, is his uncle.

"Then what do we have? In 1950 Bolivar commenced his schooling at the School of Mongomo. Carlos followed a year later. Then comes the military part, of course it was still a Spanish colony and General Franco himself took a big interest in the place. In September 1963 Bolivar attended the General Francisco Franco Military Academy in Saragossa, Spain. Graduated from there in '65. Then he became Lieutenant of the Territorial Guard and then worked his way up from there. His brother Carlos followed the same pattern, always one year later."

Michaux puts the papers down to catch up with General Lainé, still reading as he eats, then he says "Da-di-da-di-da, jumping ahead, by 1969 Bolivar is Lieutenant of the National Guard responsible for defending the capital Barbate. Also in charge of the infamous Black Beach prison.

"So, on to 1970; Spain had thrown in the towel. That year Hernán Eboleh father's uncle, Francisco Solomon Nguru, was in power and his own uncle Bolivar, the current president, had joined the Ministry of Defence and his father Carlos was a captain in the National Guard. And it says that after this point, with their uncle in power, both brothers' careers took off with numerous promotions.

"By 1979, the year of his coup, Bolivar was a Field Marshall and the Minister of the Armed Forces and his younger brother Carlos was Commander and Secretary General of the Armed Forces."

"I can just picture it Claude-Michel," laughs the General, "them all lined up, Bokassa-style, magnificent uniforms, not a soldier who could shoot straight amongst them."

"Yes, but the coup took some planning, backed by our old friend King Hassan II of Morocco. He sent 600 of his special forces. That wasn't organised in a day."

"Mmm," says the General slightly more impressed, "they were good boys, the Moroccan specials, trained by us. And what about our young Hernán, any news of him yet?"

Michaux looks ahead to the last page. "Gabon says the first time he comes on the radar was aged 16, so in 1994, he was recognized for his outstanding studies, and was granted a scholarship to the Mission School of the Priests of "Claretrados de Bata" and was baptized a Catholic then too."

"Probably had to be," says the General between mouthfuls.

"Probably. But two years later, in 1996, his father died, killed in a plane crash. By then it was the usual one party state, and his father Carlos was Minister of Mines, Forestry and Natural Resources. A double tragedy, reports Gabon, because a year before that ExxonMobil had found oil and he was the Minister responsible, so he not only died but missed out on the main bonanza, most of the subsequent oil revenues going straight to the direct Eboleh family."

Madame Trintignant takes away their plates, and confirms they would prefer the *mousse au chocolat* to the *plat du fromage*. They would and then the General asks "this plane crash, was it deliberate?"

"Not as far as we know. It seems to be a genuine accident, African pilot."

"And this Admiral you met on Saturday, Hernán Eboleh, he just wants to be our friend, or what?"

"He is smart. Speaks perfect French, went to the Université du Québec, studied economics. Speaks Spanish too of course, and Gabon say English and Fang, I suppose that'll be his tribal language. He is cautious. If we want to communicate with him, we must do so through his ex-landlady in Québec, a certain Madame Laforge, no doubt an alias. She is staunch French nationalist, and his family assume, if anything, that she is an old white girlfriend from his university days. He is next in Europe at DefEx, that's the International Defence Equipment Exhibition in London next week."

"I can tell you are enthusiastic about enlisting your new find Claude-Michel, but I am less so. The fact is that although Fernando Po may be becoming an American colony, it is still surrounded by our ex-colonies, where our influence is profound. I'm not sure it is worth upsetting the Americans over this; they may have set your admiral up to embarrass us. They still have scores to settle. Don't forget the recent Nathan coup, I think the British and Spanish terrorists are still in prison. There are many sensitivities."

"But a chance meeting in London, at an international show, can it hurt?"

"The bill please, Madame Trintignant," says the General. "My turn Claude-Michel." When it is quiet again he says "alright, go to London, see your admiral, but not at the show. Arrange to meet wherever he suggests, and when you arrive insist on talking outside, along a busy street. Be careful my friend, as the English say 'I smell a rat'. In our case a big American rat!"

15
Dateline 14th

Y, K and B have fallen into the habit of holding their triumvirate morning meeting in the canteen. The rectangular table is suitably hierarchical, the usual distracting Thames view here non-existent and, most importantly, there are no other distractions like telephones and secretaries. Colonel Harding knows both K and B very well, of course. K is Commander Sir Derek Scott-Smith, ex-Royal Marines, the head of London Sections, the husband of his, Y's, wife's best friend, also his neighbour, mentor, golfing partner and godfather to young, well not so young now, Patrick. K is old school, knows the ropes, and is due to retire in eighteen months. B, on the other hand, apart from being Y's rival for K's job and knighthood, is the next generation, mid-forties, never did National Service, never polished an officer's boots, never actually killed anyone. There are lots like him these days, pen pushers, balanced only by a chip on each shoulder; Y and K often speculated on the 19th if he wasn't really a sleeper for Amicus.

"And so," says K pushing his drained coffee cup and saucer to the centre of the table "AOB?"

"I have some any other business, yes," announces B finishing off his mug of tea. B, and Y for that matter, being only heads of Sections, have to rub along with mugs. "The potential new recruit," he picks up the file and reads snidely from the cover "Beaumont Lloyd St.John Flowerdew-Pett, well he screwed up the psychometrics. I'm not sure we can use him."

"Look, we all know that's mumbo jumbo," says Y. "Anne FitzHerbert is practically begging me to send him to Washington."

"But that's precisely the point," replies B. "Imagine if something goes wrong in America. There's bound to be an investigation. They'll be asking all sorts of questions. How come we sent this Flowerdew guy? What are his qualifications? Can we see his physco-tests? Knowing this, and you still sent him, we'd have every lawyer in Washington suing us. The publicity, the cost would be ridiculous."

"What does Anne want him for?" asks K.

"Industrial espionage?" replies Y.

"Details?" asks K.

"Yes, you remember the Al-Yamamah arms deal?"

"Not that bloody thing again," replies K

"I thought we'd buried that," adds B.

Y leans forwards and lowers his voice, although they are the only ones left in the canteen, "well, it was twenty years ago and lot of the stuff we sold the Saudis is due for replacement. Last time the Jewish lobby scuppered the Americans, but this time their defence contractors are so multinational it will harder be for the Jews to knobble them. So, on the one hand British Aerospace should have a clear run, but on the other all these proxy Yank outfits will be sniffing around."

"Frogs will want a bit of it too," says K.

"*Bien sûr*. Now, Anne wants him to find out what the Yanks are up to?"

"In Seattle?" asks B incredulously.

"No of course not," says Y. "In Washington, that's where the deals are done, where the lobbies fight it out."

"How come she's so keen on him?" asks K.

"She heard about his exploits in North Korea, reckoned he was just the sort of go-getter to do a bit of industrial espionage," replies Y.

"What on earth did he do in NoKo?" asks B.

"You've heard of Sung Pi-Jam?" asks Y back to B. "No, you wouldn't have. Well they, the North Koreans, were convinced he was spying for the CIA. He was on their nuclear weapons programme. He wasn't, spying that is. Anyway, he was banged up, and our Mr. Pett went and sprang him from prison."

"Well that wasn't the work of a moment. How come?" asks K.

"He was working for Amnesty International, I know, I know, but he's not a commie, in Tokyo, fell in love with this chap Sung's daughter, she persuaded him to get him, and her, out before the gulags closed in."

K stands up abruptly and walks over to the till. Y and B watch this unexpected development in silence and interest. "Mrs. bin-Quadi, if you are there?" No response. "Hello, Mrs bin-Quadi?" A tall and erect English woman with a head scarf and too many bracelets appears from nowhere behind him and says "yes, Commander Scott-Smith." K, Y and B all wince at the mention of his name. "Another round of teas and coffees if you don't mind. Any maybe we could run to some biscuits?"

K walks back to table. Y and B look up expectantly. "This Pett. I've got the perfect job for him. The Spanish African job."

Y and B look back blankly. K notices. "Sorry, you wouldn't have known about it, only came in yesterday. I don't know too much about it myself. The Foreign Secretary himself called yesterday. Seems his oppo in Madrid has asked him for the loan of one of our agents for a job they can't do themselves. 'Can you have a think about it?' the minister asked. 'Any more details?' I asked. 'Only that one of their citizens is in trouble in Africa. In prison. They want him out, but can't do it themselves in case it goes tits up. It wouldn't do us any harm to help them, Gibraltar negotiations a bit tricky etcetera'. That's as far as we've got, but if this Pett can spring someone out of gaol in NoKo, Africa should be a doddle."

Mrs. bin-Quadi arrives with the tray. "Here you are gents, no milk chocolates today I'm afraid Colonel Harding." They wait till she is out of earshot.

K lowers his voice. "Listen Y, this boy Pett is yours. I'll find out more from the FO about what the spics actually want. You get Pett in here and gen him up. B is right about the yank lawyers. I'll call Anne and keep her happy. If he makes a hash of it, no harm done, at least we tried to help our Common Market ally. If he ends up with their man safely tucked up in Madrid they'll owe us a favour. It's a win/win as the Yanks say."

B shakes his head and raises his eyebrows. K and Y nod with satisfaction to each other. Mrs. bin-Quadi wipes the tray stack again.

16
Dateline 16th

"Is Wickus Paulsie there please?" Elisa Makepeace is struggling to hear back from the buzzer over the rasps of barking dogs. Her feeling of pride of having located the great pilot here in the middle of nowhere is diminishing.

From the house across the lawn the door opens and four German Shepherds rush towards the gate. White man's dogs. Their owner comes after them and when he's close enough to talk to Elisa through the security wire shouts above the barking, "Who are you?"

"I'm Elisa Makepeace. Remote place you've got here. Took me a while to find."

"I like it like this. OK, I am expecting you. Just checking, you can't be too careful these days with the crime rate out of control like it is. Max! Trudy! Shut up! Fritz! Enough! Steffy! Be quiet now!" and one by one the dogs slink away, their job done. Elisa follows him into the modest hallway. She is not offered any hospitality and instructed to sit on a chair just inside the door.

"Now what can I do for you?" asks Paulsie sitting on the chair opposite her. Elisa notices Paulsie is framed by game trophies, and without looking up knows she will be too.

"I am Krause van Stahl's lawyer in Lagos, and…"

"I know you who are."

"And Krause asked me to give you this letter," says Elisa handing it over.

"OK, now you have."

"Krause asks that you read it, and tell me what to bring back to him."

"OK, but the answer will be 'no'." says Paulsie and he reads the letter. "The answer is no."

"Gustavo Cortez is going to Black Beach prison in Fernando Po. We think, Krause thinks, you are the best hope of stopping it.

69

A simple affidavit from the witness whose statement they plan to use."

"Mrs. Makepeace, I couldn't give a flying fuck about Gustavo Cortez now, pardon my French. My friend Smit Voorstmann is already there, in your shithouse Black Beach..."

"It's not my Black Beach, Mr. Paulsie, it's in Fernando Po."

"I know very well where it is. OK, I'm sorry, not your Black Beach then. Look, if I change my statement in any way it may, and I only say may, harm Smit. I'm not prepared to do it, especially for Cortez whom I hardly know and don't particularly like anyway."

"Mr. Paulsie, will you excuse me just running through some facts about Mr. Voorstmann. For my own clarity I just want to see how helping Gustavo can harm your friend. Then maybe I can, as a lawyer, suggest a situation where no harm comes to Mr. Voorstmann and yet we can help my client Mr. Cortez. Is that alright?"

"You can go ahead, but the answer will still be no."

"From the point of view of the court, if you can call it that, in FP, the facts leading up to the attempted act have been established. Krause van Stahl was the ring leader, and yourself and Mr. Voorstmann his lieutenants. You were in charge of air support, getting them all in and out, and Mr. Voorstmann local ground support, reconnaissance, with the boat as cover, that sort of thing."

"That's right so far."

"Krause van Stahl gave Smit Voorstmann a budget of one million US dollars, not all the cash up front, but the budget. The plan was for him to go the FP as a bridgehead. This is the FP court speaking now, Mr. Paulsie, not me. Smit Voorstmann himself went to Barbate with the front of owning an oil rig supply vessel looking for charter work so he would have an excuse for the boat being there, a boat that would bring in half of the explosives, and would in fact later be blown up in Barbate harbour when moored next to various other oil supply vessels. You would then fly in Mr. van Stahl, blow up an oil installation, pick Smit Voorstmann up from the same spot and fly them out. Meanwhile Mr. Cortez would just leave Nigeria by normal means, unconnected with any of this. Not quite as simple as all that, but in effect what would happen".

"That's how I remember it, yes."

"On the night in question, in the very early hours of the morning, once all three are safely back in the helicopter, you denote the first explosion and then flying low over the harbour denote the second, blowing up the boat.

"OK, all that is right."

"So, with these facts before them, the court in FP has already sentenced your friend to thirty-four years, and all the rest of you to seventeen. Any help that you give my client Mr. Cortez cannot make that worse."

"Yes, it can."

"Why? How?"

"Because the bastards will re-open the whole case given any new opportunity. I know Africa as well as you do Mrs. Makepeace. Better. Also I know Smitty's wife and family, know them very well. My only obligation now is to them. You should know that my statement to the police Scorpions here was not just cobbled together at the last moment. It took many drafts to get it right. The first aim was to shaft Sir Mungo fucking Nathan, but they had to settle for Phillipus Simonez. Nathan is too smart, and Simonez would never squeal. In the end they are happy enough to nail Simonez, especially because everyone knows Simonez doesn't even fart first thing in the morning in the privacy of some whore's bed without Nathan's prior instruction. I was particularly careful to say nothing at all, or the complete minimum, about Smitty, and Big-K too for that matter. The final version was seen by Smitty's lawyer and family before I signed it. There are a lot of unhappy people in South Africa right now Mrs. Makepeace, and I am one of them. We are unhappy about Smitty's and Big-K's treatment too. OK, you could say he knew what he was doing, he was playing for the big pay day, and he lost his trousers. That's true. But he was, and is, a South African citizen like me, but our government did not support him by extraditing him from FP when they could have done, no, they almost wanted a show trial there to show the other Africans how squeaky clean they are these days. If I changed my statement to help Cortez and there were any repercussions for Smitty, even ones we cannot think about now, any change at all, and it will be for the worse, I could never look Smit's friends or family in the face again. I'm sorry about Cortez, but he knew what

71

he was doing too, buying arms in Nigeria. Not the brightest thing to do either considering how our government and Obasanjo's cowboys are up each others' arses. But that, as they say, is a different story."

Elisa Makepeace reflects for a few moments, but she too has been in Africa long enough that you don't change a Boor's mind. "If you reconsider, here is my card. If you want to write anything to Mr. van Stahl, or pass a message I can deliver it."

"Big-K will be out soon. I hear he has a comfortable life in prison now, novels to read. Nathan and Simonez were his friends not mine. Tell him…no, don't tell him anything. When he gets out we'll meet for a drink again. Tell him the answer is no, and if he thinks about Smitty he'll understand. Don't forget Big-K is an African like you or me or Smitty." Paulsie stands up and holds the door open for his visitor to leave. "I'm sorry to have not been able to help, but you know my reasons. Good-bye Mrs. Makepeace, and good luck with your Mr. Cortez."

17

Dateline 16th

After five days London's Indian summer reverts to mid autumn and Bo wakes to hear rain driving into Simon Lister's windows. He twists again on the sofa, tries his legs back over the arm, gives up on comfort and gets up. It's still dark outside, and he tiptoes into the kitchen, puts on the kettle, and shivers. That was his last night here as Simon's brother is due to take over the sofa from tonight. Still, Bo is pleased to have got together with Simon again, after all it was his recommendation to go and see his father Jeremy in Tokyo before the jaunt to North Korea, and this same father, who Bo presumed worked for MI6, that Bo gave as a reference.

Bo sips his tea and reflects. He hopes the job offer from Colonel Harding comes soon as apart from having nowhere to stay he has no money, hardly any clothes and someone else's passport – not even that – and on the phone from San Diego yesterday Lo Hi had made it very clear she was unamused when she went online to check their credit card. She was even less sympathetic to hear he had not even asked for, never even claimed, any expenses from the Foreign Office "for heaven's sake Bo, they are rich, rich". Now looking into his mug he supposes that she is right, and he'll have to broach the subject with Colonel Harding later, over lunch at the colonel's invitation at the Cavalry Club. At least that will be a free lunch, as it were. Bo realises how badly he wants, needs, this job, whatever it might be.

Six hours later Bo walks up to another immaculate commissionaire and asks for Colonel Harding. This time there is no obfuscation, and Bo is sent straight up to the Members' Bar. Colonel Harding is standing by the window, deep in thought, looking out on to Piccadilly below.

"Colonel Harding."

He snaps back into the present. "Yes, Bo. Good afternoon." They shake hands, and the colonel orders Bo a gin and tonic, and a refresher for himself. Bo notices he looks concerned.

"There is a slight security issue. Your mother is setting alarm bells ringing. Now there's nothing illegal about her activities, but she's what you might describe as a busy North One lawyer." Before Bo can explain about his mother, and he scarcely knows where to start, the colonel anticipates him: "I'm sure she and her causes are worthy, but the Firm tends to look at the big picture, what's right for HMG in the larger sense; we are more concerned with the treading foot than the trodden toes. Anyway, I was hoping for your final clearance before we met, but my pager is on standby, which reminds me I must put it on vibrate, they don't like bells and whistles going off in the Cavalry Club. Anyway, how have you been getting along? Staying with Lister *fils* I see."

Bo cannot help but look surprised, and before he could answer the colonel apologises and mentions the word security. A vibrating sound arises from his hip. He reads the message, looks up and says "well, it seems your mother has survived our checks, she is not, contrary to first impressions, planning a *coup d'etat* against her Queen and country after all." Bo smiles with relief, a smile deeper inside than the one the colonel sees on his face. "There'll be formalities now, the Official Secrets Act, various types of specific Non-Disclosure Agreements, and this new All-Purpose Media Confidentiality Agreement, presuming of course you still want to join. Shall we go in?"

Colonel Harding orders the Club Lunch du jour, tomato soup followed by toad-in-the-hole, and a bottle of Berry Brother's Cavalry Claret. Bo follows suite. After some pleasantries about tinned food, school food and club plonk the colonel asks: "have you heard of FP?" Bo looks blank and apologises, and the colonel says "Sorry, Fernando Po."

"Yes", replies Bo "in West Africa. One of only two of Spain's African colonies I seem to remember."

"That's the one. Complete disaster area as you would expect. The Spanish left in 1968, bit like the Portuguese colonies they bled it dry, then just upped sticks and went. Not for publication these days, but we were the only ones who did it right. There wasn't an African left who could read and write. Needless to say it immediately fell into anarchy, and a particularly unpleasant maniac called

Francisco Solomon Nguru took over. Thought he was a God, or God, but he was more or less an illiterate cannibal. One Christmas he rounded up a hundred and fifty of his opponents, stuck 'em all in the football stadium, and while the band played Those Were The Days My Friend he had them all mowed down. He was on one of the guns himself. A third of the population died or fled, diplomats at the time saw people actually crucified on the road into town from the airport. A role model for Pol Pot you could say. That sort of place."

"Charming."

"Then it got worse, or at least no better. In '80 Solomon's nephew, a particularly nasty piece of work called Bolivar Eboleh Nguru Mbasogo, Eboleh for short, staged a coup, killed his uncle, ate his testicles, and has been in power and milking it ever since."

"Ah," says Bo " this is about the Krause Stahl/Mungo Nathan mess, been in the papers."

"*van* Stahl and *Sir* Mungo, but yes that's the one, if not quite yet. Anyway, back to the 'nineties and friend Eboleh gets lucky. Nigeria, that's another complete hellhole, had already found oil, lots of oil, and one of the southerly fields goes south, all the way into Fernando Po territory. MobilExxon go drilling and bingo! Ever since '95 wealth beyond their wildest dreams, all of course straight into the Eboleh family coffers, but instead of stashing it offshore or in the Alps like everyone else, they bung it in a cowboy bank in Washington and all of a sudden hares are running this way and that. You get my drift?" Bo does and says so.

The soup arrives. The colonel tucks his napkin into his collar and tilts the bowl away. Bo, who would not normally do the former, but would the latter, does both. "Of course all this does not go unnoticed by various sharks swimming offshore. It sounds like you've heard of Sir Mungo Nathan?"

"Only what gets out. He's supposed to be paranoid about privacy."

"That's one way of putting it. Secretive to the point of paranoia. Frightful little shit Nathan, got a place right here in Chelsea, sodding great mansion, I met him once at a reception at the Nigerian Embassy. Typical Jewish trader, if you get my drift, will buy and sell anything, up to every trick in the book. He's made many fortunes but his most recent one was in Angola with the oil. Was there right from the start, sort of chap who is always in the right place at the right time. He still trades of course, not just in oil, but generals, politicians, anything really. Only got sniffed out once, a few years back paying off the Nigerian dictator Abacha, now there's another real crook, but used French government money pertaining to come from Elf Aquitaine, maybe he forgot it was nationalised. Frogs promptly arrested him, but couldn't make it stick, a surprising lack of Nigerian witnesses – funnily enough. Nathan has friends, not social friends like you or me, and some of them with pips on their shoulders. Lots of pips on their shoulders."

Bo does not answer so that the colonel can catch up him up with the soup; when he does, Bo then suggests that he presumes Nathan wanted some of the Fernando Po action too. The colonel readily concurs.

Before the toad-in-hole arrives Colonel Harding continues to brief, as easily as he had done a hundred times before. "There's more to it than that. Another FP bandit, this one holed up in Madrid, called Adolpho Stobo, reckons he should be the president. No one can quite work out why, just one of those things. Anyway, needless to say Sir Mungo is chums with him too. Good chums. They cook up a plot. Nathan rustles up a few million dollars, three or four comes to mind, gets some old white African pros, mercenaries in the popular parlance, to cause an explosion. A particularly clever wheeze because it has two beneficial side effects. Firstly it frightens off the Americans who are scared of even a whiff of terrorism so that Nathan can front the next round of concessions for them, and secondly in the ensuing chaos there's a good chance he can bung Stobo in as president and it's divvy-up time all round for the foreseeable. Everyone is happy, well, rich. But as we know it all goes tits up." They pause while the toad-in-the-hole is served.

"So do I fit into this somewhere?" asks Bo.

The colonel picks up his knife and fork, spears a toad and says, "Yes. That's the plan. We're not quite sure yet why, but the CNI have asked us…"

"Sorry, CNI?" asks Bo.

"Sorry, *Centro Nacional de Inteligencia*. Spain's version of us. MI6."

"They've asked us for help. A Spanish citizen called Cortez is about to imprisoned there, they want him out. Don't know why, don't know how, you'll have to go to Madrid, on secondment. They'll brief you there. It's too sensitive to do it themselves, being an ex-colony and they being the most sanctimonious bunch of tearjerkers on the planet. But that's another story."

After coffee Colonel Harding suggests Bo comes to HQ in a couple of days to go through the job formalities; relax a bit until then. As Bo leaves he says, "Thanks a lot for everything Colonel Harding." Colonel Harding suggests Bo calls him Y from now on, and says in turn "until Friday then, 108".

Feeling at one with the world, Bo remembers he forgot to ask about expenses, but checks into the Capital round the corner anyway. "Chap needs a treat, 108," he says to himself, mimicking Y.

18
Dateline 17th

Commandant Claude-Michel Michaux is walking along Sussex Gardens in London W2, a street of seemingly endless Bed & Breakfasts and one or two star hotels between Hyde Park and Paddington Station. He does not have a house number, just a name. He looks at the buildings as he walks along the street: the Regency Hotel, Connaught Rooms, Clarefield Hotel, Hampshire Hotel until eventually he arrives at the Capital Hotel, with a sign underneath announcing Bed & Breakfast vacancies.

He walks in and asks the owner, he presumes the quiet little man must be the owner, for Mr. Slater, and is directed to Room 6 on the third floor. He knocks, and Hernán Eboleh opens the door and welcomes him in.

"An excellent choice of venue, Admiral," offers Michaux.

"It's nothing. I found it when we arrived, it was the first one with a vacancy sign, and they like the cash. Everyone likes cash."

"Well, I did not think you were staying here."

"No, no our delegation, well that is just the two of us, myself as Admiral and one of my brothers from the Defence Ministry, are at the Dorchester. Many of the delegates to DefEx are staying there, so we can easily broaden our circles. And you are staying in London, or just came over for our meeting?"

"I just came for this time together. By train, it's quicker now the English have some French track. But time, as always, is tight, and we should talk. I hope you don't mind if we talk outside, in the street."

"Of course not," replies Eboleh, "and I hope you don't mind if I quickly search your clothes for sound. You are welcome to do the same to mine."

They both pad down each other's jackets and trousers, and overcoats, for mikes and transmitters. There are none. They nod smilingly at each other; they understand each other perfectly.

Out of the hotel, as they turn left then right for the bustle of Praed Street and towards the anonymity of Paddington Station, Hernán Eboleh explains his starting point: that the only certainty in Fernando Po is that there will be a coup, "not if but when." His uncle Bolivar, the President, is suffering from prostate cancer, and in spite of the best treatment he can buy, he is known to be slowly dying. There is no clear successor. His uncle's preferred solution would be his elder son, Augusto, but "he is just a playboy addicted to Lamborghinis and showgirls" whose only interest in money is how quickly and ostentatiously he can spend it. The youngest son, Jorge, now the Minister of Information, is brighter and more responsible, but has no personality. The successor will certainly be from the Esangui tribe, and unless the family let it slip away, from the Eboleh family.

"And, my dear Admiral, you think another solution could come from the navy, with the backing of a certain European power?"

"The future is uncertain, but what is sure is that you would say 'no' immediately to any such suggestion. As things stand now."

Michaux nods approvingly, and asks, "So what now?"

"You have heard of the Gulf of Guinea Guard?"

"Of course."

"And were you at the Gulf of Guinea Maritime Security Conference?"

"Not personally, no, but some of our friends from the region were there."

"So let me recap for you. Africa produces let's say twelve million barrels of oil a day, and let's say half of this, a growing half, is from West Africa, that would be Nigeria in the north, down across the Gulf of Guinea nations like ourselves, and down to Angola. The US's stated policy is to import 25% of its oil from the region."

"Agreed," says Michaux

"So the US military, through their European operations, EUCOM, starts up the Gulf of Guinea Guard, and we are all invited to attend. Of course I attended myself in my official naval capacity. The idea is that EUCOM will assist countries in the Gulf of Guinea with security to protect supply lines, and for America's idea of stability. They want to provide us with additional naval vessels, radar, surveillance, coastguards, training, all that sort of thing. All for free. And it is not all about the sea, an equal or bigger part of this is to control, what they call protect, the airspace. Let's face it there are no controls at all now."

"And how do you interpret these developments Admiral?"

"From the Gulf of Guinea countries it is good news and bad news. Of course all the cliques want stability and protection, what the US calls *pax americana*, but we will eventually be dependent colonies. Colonialism is sensitive subject in Africa, Commandant Michaux."

"I believe it is. There will be less room for, shall we say, free range financial activity, less room for commercial creativity."

"Exactly so. Now in the nations of the Gulf of Guinea, so we have Nigeria, Angola, Chad, Equatorial Guinea, ourselves Fernando Po, Gabon, and Sao Tome and Principe, France through her Francophone connections and those of TotalFinaElf has been highly successful. There are three exceptions, Fernando Po, Equatorial Guinea and Sao Tome and Principe. It seems to me you could use some influence, at least in Fernando Po, before we become an impenetrable US colony."

"I agree with your analysis, we have reached the same conclusions. We cannot compete with the Americans militarily that is for sure, but our oil companies can certainly compete with theirs. So what are you proposing, if I may be so blunt?"

Commandante Michaux steps onto the road looking only to his left. Within an instant Eboleh grabs his arm and pulls him back as a black taxi dives to halt and the cabbie slams on the horn in anger and relief. Without pausing Eboleh says, "I can provide you with inside information on the exploration bidding contracts. Whom to pay, how much. For example you will not know that Mammoth Oil have just won the drilling rights for Field 26, although I am informed that TotalFinaElf had a higher potential on the table bid."

"And you have in mind a percentage for helping in these negotiations?" asks Michaux.

"Nothing so vulgar as a fixed percentage, Commandant, but a consideration from time to time if we are successful together. No, I want something else."

"Which is?"

"I believe you have the technology to monitor mobile telephone calls?"

"With a difficult approval process, yes."

"I want you to monitor the mobile phone calls of three individuals in my country. I will give you the numbers, you give me the transcripts. That's all I want."

"How do we know the Americans are not monitoring yours?" asks Michaux.

"I collect disposable mobile phones. I dispose of them. I think you know by now I am a cautious man on one side, and a ruthless one on the other."

"And whose numbers would we be monitoring, for my permissions?"

"Family members," replies Eboleh.

"Anyone in particular?"

"My dear Commandant, let's keep this simple. I give you access to the bonanza, I give my country a second front, and you give me some transcripts. A good deal for each of us in our way."

"It seems to be so, Admiral, it seems to be so, and for us a small price for us to pay, but the ways of the world are not always logical. But I am sure somehow we can do business. Let's leave it there. I can take a taxi to the Eurostar from here. I will call your Madame Laforge in Québec."

They shake hands, always looking the other in the eye, and each parts contentedly as co-conspirators in a bigger game.

19
Dateline 17th

Krause van Stahl waits patiently in the interview room for his weekly meeting with Elisa Makepeace. It is the high point of his week; actually it is the high point of the lawyer's week too. Circumstances had thrown them together, two people who are much more intelligent and far better educated in the ways of the world than the forces railed against them, two people who actually like each other and who one day know without having to say so that they will be friends for a long time after they have sorted out this present mess. Two people who, uniquely for both of them, don't care if the one is black and the other is white.

Outside the room van Stahl can hear an unusually quarrelsome amount of noise and movement, and he knows by now that any variation from the norm in Kirikiri prison means unwelcome developments. The door opens and his lawyer walks in breathlessly. "Sorry I'm late, problems getting in here today, there's been a big round-up overnight, Obasanjo's ex-wife's first cousin's family no less, so the rumours go. They're all arriving here at once. You got my message about Wickus?"

They both sit down on the stools either side of the old school desk. "Yeah, I'm not surprised. Wicko and Smitty go back a long way. But it was a worth a try, well worth a try. So he's just keeping his head down, eh? You got the expenses back OK?" asks van Stahl.

"Yes thanks, all the expenses came through as usual. Now, how's Gustavo today?"

"He comes and goes. It's like there's a switch in his stomach. He's bad today, that's why he's not here."

"Well I've got good news, tell him to act ill all the time."

"Why, what have you managed now?"

"I've got him a hospital bed. Real medicines too. Well, I was pushing on an open door is the reality of it. The ruling clique knows that when he is extradited to FP he will be in all the media, and they want him to look healthy."

"And I hope I've got good news of him too. Elisa, will you take the case, act for him in FP? I mean, I presume there's going to be some kind of trial? I'll pay for it of course."

The lawyer does not reply but stands up to look out through the bars. Six men are standing to attention in the sun, still in civilian dress. An officer with a clipboard is going through the motions of taking notes, but the lawyer suspects he is illiterate. He walks back to the stool and sees his client looking at him patiently. From upstairs, from the prison governor's office, there comes a sudden loud scream. Then another. Then the sound of furniture scrapping across the floor, then a crash, then three of four thuds, then more cries, pleas.

Elisa says, "It has started, the questions. Sunday Chukwa style. I feel sick staying here, these thugs are worse than animals. Where else can we go to talk?"

van Stahl says there's nothing wrong with animals, but waves his lawyer to follow him. The lawyer picks up her briefcase and they walk in silence together to the far end of the yard and sit down in the shade on the dust of the dirt ground. They can see the six men still lined up, now one hundred metres away. The guard has left them standing in the sun, and they are trying to stand to attention. Almost like children trying to please, van Stahl reflects to himself.

"I'll take the case, of course I will. I know what happened off by heart. Official and unofficial versions too. We both know he's guilty, we don't have to pretend anything to each other, or to him, and I know you'll take care of the expenses."

"Well, Elisa, so far so good," says van Stahl clapping his hands together and smiling "Gus has got himself some proper hospital treatment and the best lawyer I've ever met, what can go wrong?"

The lawyer does not answer, they just both sit there ominously looking at the prisoners lined up in the sun. One of them drops to his haunches and covers his balding head with his hands. From nowhere a guard rushes out and hits him across the back with a sjambok. The man falls to the ground screaming. The guard kicks him, shouting at him. The man staggers back to his feet.

"God help Gustavo in Black Beach," whispers Elisa. "Just when some parts of Africa are starting to behave like the twenty-first century we have to deal with Nigeria and Fernando Po. It's not easy loving your country sometimes. I'll tell you what can go wrong." She opens her briefcase and shows van Stahl a sheath of paper. "This is the deposition against him just issued by the court in Barbate. It doesn't make good reading."

"Why, what have they got?"

The lawyer skimmed quickly through the papers again. "Well, they've got the contract between Gustavo Cortez and the Nigeria Defence Industries Limited. Gustavo's shopping list. It says that on August seventeenth he flew to the Sibbolek Airbase in Port Harcourt and paid ninety thousand US dollars cash...."

"To Obasanjo's brother–in–law, I don't suppose it says that."

"No mention of that Krause, no. Gustavo paid for what the court will see as an arsenal."

"It was an arsenal, that was the whole point."

"And now as his lawyer I will say not a very helpful point. What do we have here? Three hundred pounds of nitroglycerin, two hundred pounds of Pentolite, twenty pounds of guncotton, thirty waxed cartridges, forty pounds of sodium nitrate, forty pounds of ammonium nitrate." Elisa shakes his head, and then laughs "how many countries were you planning to blow up?"

Krause van Stahl laughs too. "Just the one. I know it sounds a bit excessive, but you can't have enough high explosive for a job like this. That boat has got to blow too don't forget, and take a few others with it, as well as the pumping station."

"But seriously, this does not make good reading. Then there's the end–user certificate."

"What end-user cert? There wasn't one, that's why we paid cash," insists van Stahl.

"Exactly. Like the dog that didn't bark, what is missing is what is important. I remember from my training an old English expression 'bang-to-rights', have you heard it?"

"Of course, it means you're stuffed, caught with the smoking gun, caught with your pants down, take your pick."

"Well, Krause, between you and me, Gustavo is all of these. With this evidence against him he's in big trouble."

"If it ever gets to court."

"Yes," replies the lawyer pensively. "If it ever gets to court."

20
Dateline 17th

Bo had had a bad day so far and it was still only 4.30 in the afternoon. Lo Hi was on the warpath from Seoul: she had been online with the credit card again and had gone ballistic about the £210 night at the Capital Hotel. Actually Bo had thought it was a bit steep too, should have checked first really. But since then he had moved to a B&B in Sussex Gardens, which, confusingly, was also called Capital Hotel. Lo Hi had jumped to the conclusion that he was in the same Capital Hotel, and with a girl the first night. He had tried to explain about the hotel names, that there had been no girl on the first night, but had omitted to admit that there had been one, but not on the credit card, last night. Anyway, there was no stopping her new travel plan to return home to San Diego from Seoul westabout, via Europe, so that they could have a few days together. Worse, she "really, really looks forward to finally meet your mother Miriam, yes". Bo shuddered, and said he was more than likely to be in Madrid by the weekend; "no problem for me, I come to Madrid instead, and maybe Miriam can come too".

Then Colonel Harding, who was on the phone across his desk from Bo at the moment, had raised the issue of "political complications, well, situations, really." Since the Spanish request he, Y, had been digging up some more background as he "would be running you on this one, 108." Seems the Spanish had not been so squeaky clean as they pretended: this Adolpho Stobo was "thick as thieves with ex-Prime Minister Aznar when Aznar was in power and actively encouraging what was going on, telling him to hurry up and be ready before the elections and quite right Stobo was too, because Aznar then lost the election, but only because the Spanish caved in to the towelheads after the Madrid bombing and went for the lefties instead." The Spanish had been losing out on the oil bonanza in spite of "well, probably because of" being the "sitting tenant, colony-wise". The previous year their major oil company

Repsol-YPF had acquired the prospecting rights near the disputed island of Mbagne. This island was given by the Spanish to Fernando Po at the time of independence in 1968, but was sold to Gabon by the first President of the newly independent country, the "self same maniac Solomon I was telling you about over lunch. Now there's oil FP wants it back. Of course there's no paperwork about the sale." Adolpho Stobo had done a deal with Aznar to settle the dispute, presumably for a healthy sum of future cash, plus looking more favourably on future Spanish prospecting bids.

Then the Americans were involved "all the way to the top." Y had picked up some handwritten notes. "Apart from ExxonMobil and ChevronTexaco, various lesser players were at it. CMS Energy, now part of Marathon, major, early Bush contributors. Likewise Ocean Energy. Triton, now with Amerada Hess who are also there, turned a soft Bush investment of $600,000 into $15 million when they sold the Texas Rangers. Halliburton, that's Dick Cheney's outfit, is the major subcontractor to Vanco, based round the corner in Houston. Vanco are the principal license holders of underwater rights in West Africa." He put the folder down and told Bo "this spells protection, influence."

Then there was a local dimension too. It seems that twice in the months leading up to the plot, Jacobus du Randt, a South African spook working in the area, had tipped off MI6 and the CIA. "We ignored both warnings. Feeling around the campfire was that if the Spanish and Americans knew about it and were relaxed, so should we be too, not exactly our corner after all. After it all went wrong it came out, about the tip-offs. The FO denied it all of course, operational discretions, usual guff."

"Sorry about that," says Y putting the phone back. "Domestic issues couldn't wait. Where was I? Oh yes, the minefield. Be careful 108. What started off as a simple request to help an ally with a citizen abroad has deeper currents. Hidden agendas. Governments involved. The South Africans too I wouldn't be surprised. Anyway," he announces standing up with a broad gesture "let's get you kitted up."

They take the lift down to the basement, and go through two security swipe doors. In the centre of the room, eyes down at her desk, is a formidable looking woman, short died black hair, stocky, in a grey trouser suit that struggles to cope.

"Miss ffinch, this is 108. 108, may I introduce you to Miss ffinch." They shake hands, Bo politely, Miss ffinch warily. "What have we got for him?"

"Sit down Y, 108." They both do. Her voice is deep, almost resonating. She takes some papers out of a folder. Bo notices a letter from Manchester United. "I understand you already have a passport issued in the name of Ernest Jasper Pitt?" Bo agrees. "I know, we've decided to stick with that. Your cover is as a scout for Manchester United FC." Bo winces inside, he can't stand ManU and their whingeing manager, but says nothing. The Spanish will arrange for you to fly in to Barbate locally, maybe from Nigeria, maybe Gabon, that's up to them. Madrid will also take care of your visas, that sort of thing. You are looking at football matches, scouting for young talent. You look like a sportsman yourself 108, it's a totally believable cover." Bo had to agree with her on both counts; he would have preferred to be a cricket scout, but would readily admit to the limited opportunities in FP.

"Y here tells me you are going to release a prisoner without permission, and so you will need a diversion. Come over here." They follow her to a table in the corner. She picks up a boxed tray of inch high candles in tin holders. "This might look like a boxed tray of night candles to you, but each one is in fact troxophoron plastic explosive coated with wax. The wicks are real so don't light them. The candles are triggered by this mobile phone." She hands them a perfectly normal looking Nokia 8210. "This is a perfectly normal Nokia 8210, but with two SIM cards, a regular one inside and this one which will be hidden in the heel of this shoe. You dial 999 then from 001 to 024 to set off each candle. Any questions?"

"What happens if the 999 connects to the police?" asks Bo, he thinks intelligently.

"Do try to act your age 108. You'll be in West Africa," Miss ffinch replies scornfully. "Now I am assuming you will be stopped and searched and probably robbed at Customs. If they steal your phone don't worry, the SIM card in your shoe will work in any phone. There's no point in giving you a GPS videophone watch, that's bound to go. You should get away with this torch." She hands Bo a cheap looking slightly rusty but large torch, which would indeed attract little envious attention. "It's a little too large to avoid all suspicion, but battered about quite a bit. It's large because it's really a taser. Do you know what that it is 108?"

"Yes, Miss ffinch, a kind of electronic stun gun."

"Nearly. It works on EMD – Electro-Muscular Disruption. It will temporarily override the central nervous system, taking over all the victim's muscular control ability. It has laser sights. If you press this switch a normal torch light appears." She flashes a beam across the ceiling, "but if you press and hold the switch, then pull it back it becomes a taser. It will give you an effective range of two metres for disabling an opponent, much further for pinpointing any object of course. Theses candles and this torch should be sufficient. Forget anything the Spanish give you, they never work. Try the taser now."

She hands it to Bo. He presses the switch and pulls it back. A deep sharp red beam shoots out across the room. "Zap, zap." Bo says enthusiastically.

"Do try to act your age 108," says Miss ffinch again with a withering stare.

21
Dateline 18th

"Hey Gus, I didn't recognise you in civvies," says Krause van Stahl as Gustavo Cortez walks into van Stahl's open cell. "So, today's the big move, off to the nurses, you my friend are the first one out of the world famous Kirikiri Prison, torture capital of the world, Obasanjo's private playground. Congratulations! If we had champagne, now would be a good time to open it."

"No chance of that. I know, I think the clothes look good, apart from being five sizes too small. I am amazed the bastards had not sold them already. These are expensive clothes, from *Corte Inglés* in Marbella if I remember correctly. After the rags we've been wearing all this time, it's good, feels good. And no more string. Look here is a real belt," he pulls the belt and trousers several inches out from his concave stomach.

There's nowhere to sit except the floor, but Gustavo is reluctant to get his tan chinos dirty already and so he props himself up against the wall. He looks down on Krause on his mattress and says, "It almost makes me forget where I'm going after the hospital. I'm still sure it's an ulcer, not that I know anything about medicine. With a bit of luck it will take them ages to figure it out while I eat three good meals a day. Maybe pull a nurse."

Krause van Stahl moves up to squat, "Forget it, there are no white ones there I'm sure of that. If there are they'll be fucking missionaries, and even you won't get to fuck one of them! So you've no idea how long you will be there, in the hospital?"

"No, just long enough for me to be fit to travel. Not that they care too much about me, they just don't want to look like the barbarians they are if I have to crawl onto the plane on all fours like I feel now. How about you, any idea how long you'll be stuck in this shithole?"

"No, Gus, no idea. It's doing wonders for my patience. Elisa is working on it, but it's at the whim of Obasanjo. He'll want his max from this one, first time for the decision to release me, which I guess he's already got, and once again for the big day itself. Could be six weeks, six months, a year. But I'm sane again now, well quite sane considering."

"I'll be thinking about you, half dead in Black Beach for the next twenty years. Not that I'll survive that long. I'm not even looking forward to seeing Smit Voorstmann, he was never friendly company like you."

"Smit's OK, he's just a merc. Not too much up top, no airs and graces. And I'll be working on your case too. We've got Elisa on board, there's no-one better. That twenty mill euros you've got stashed away, make sure Elisa and I have power of attorney, not for her fees, I want to make that low life fuck Simonez take care of that, for the goons in FP. You know this whole episode we're in now, it's the first time in Africa I haven't been able to buy myself in or out of a situation. I can't believe it's a trend." They both look away from each other, and after a while van Stahl says "but we had some fun though, didn't we? The set up, the planning, the meetings at the Sandton and the Butchers in Jo'burg? Hanging out with Wicko, Smitty, even that bastard Simonez? President Bush, The White House? It wasn't dull. We had a go. We had good times too, Gus. Even the night we got busted."

"Si, I remember, they nearly fucked that up too. Arrested the wrong guys loading up. Ten minutes later we'd have got away with it. You remember that big commotion with the Twin Otter, regular tourists? How these gooks could confuse an unmarked Hind helicopter with two terrorists standing around it with a Twin Otter plane full of fat American oilmen I'll never know."

"And lucky old Wicko went to the shithouse at just the right time, luckiest shit of his life. But you know I don't think we could have bought our way of that one. I think it was too high level by then. Someone tipped them off. I have my suspicions. Next thing they're on board the Hind busting our arses. I think it's still there, the chopper, at Port Harcourt, isn't it? The Hind, Wicko's Hind as it happens."

"Probably, and what have they done with my explosives apart from sell them again?"

"Plus they took our second hundred grand cash dollars off the chopper."

Both men look at the floor, in their private thoughts: van Stahl thinking about the past, the betrayal by Günther Koekemoor which must have led to the tip off, like he had thought a thousand times before, Gustavo thinking about the future, about finally feeling well in the hospital and then the horrors of Black Beach to come. They hear footsteps, then two unfamiliar guards in unfamiliar uniforms, and one of them says "Come on, Cortez, you come with us now."

Gustavo pushes himself upright, and van Stahl stands up. "Well, Big-K, good friend, this is goodbye. One year and twenty four days here together."

van Stahl walks over and takes both his hands in his own. "No, Gus, it's not goodbye. You will go to different places, but I will always be with you, working for you. I'm not a religious man as you know, but in my own way I'll be praying for you, no, doing something more useful than that."

"I know you will, and I will remember the good times too. Don't forget me, Krause."

"You have my word Gustavo. Go now, be brave my friend. Adios."

"Adios. God bless you," says Gustavo with a breaking voice, as he is lead away.

22
Dateline 18th

Bo saw the ashtray flying towards him, had just time to duck and think thank God it was empty, but still ducked he doesn't see the mug coming right after the ashtray. It hits him hard on his left eyebrow and the coffee inside spills down his fresh white shirt and new Gap khakis. Lo Hi is looking for something else to throw and still screaming "you fucking fuck you fuck!" as she picks up the waste paper basket and bowls it over to him.

"That's a wide," says Bo.

"Bloody cricket. That's all you talk with!" Bo had noticed that her excellent Californian Korean becomes scrabbled when she's excited, which in all fairness isn't that often.

"Where you keep that whore, you fucking fuck?"

"Now not again, Lo Hi, I promise, there've been no whores."

"So you admit girls not whores!" she's really screaming now.

"No, no whores, no girls."

"So why now you go, because I come!"

"No, I tried to explain when you were in Seoul, yesterday, day before, whenever it was, I have to go to Madrid. I've got a job, you wanted me to have a job, now I've got one, but I have to leave. You said you'd come to Madrid but you wanted to surprise me in London, wonderful, it's lovely to see you, but I've got to go, like now. I'm sorry. Don't throw that, it'll only break."

Lo Hi sits down shaking, but quieter. Bo knows she's distressed, exhausted, plain angry. He also knows she's a completely different type of woman than the one he fell in love with in Tokyo, the one he risked all for in North Korea. Money, or to be more precise greed, had done the damage, and the heady freedoms of California had rained down on her too.

"Now look," says Bo, sitting down next to her, and putting his arm around her shoulders, on the edge of the tiny bed in the tiny B&B room "I have to leave now, really now, there's a flight to catch, my passport to collect at the airport, someone waiting to meet the flight. I'm sure you can stay here if you want. You'll be back home in San Diego tomorrow, later today if you come to the airport with me. There's something else." She looks over suspiciously. "You know the work I'm doing, my new job?"

"You secret agent, MI6."

"Yes, and secret is the word. You mustn't tell anyone, it could be dangerous for both of us, you understand, don't you?"

"So what do I say?"

"I work for Manchester United, as a talent spotter."

She almost smiles. "Manchester United, they are famous." Then she puts her head back in her hands. "What are they like?"

"Always whinging. The pretty one has left, now there's a thug. American owned by the way."

"MI6?"

"Ah, no, I thought you meant Manchester. No, MI6, well between you and me, they seem to be fairly amateurish, not what I expected. My boss is easy enough, it's just that everything's a cock up."

Now she starts crying again. "Cock-up! That's all that's on your mind since you're a secret agent. No, you go now you bastard!"

Bo stands up, picks up his packed case and shoulder bag and goes quietly down the stairs.

"Everything all right Mr. Pitt?" the landlord asks timidly, anxiously.

They hear a quick movement from upstairs, and now she's shrieking again "What you mean Pitt, he is Pett, Bo you give false name I know you have whore here!" They hear more movement from the room.

"Thanks for everything, I'm all paid up. I think I better leg it."

"Yes, maybe for the best." he replies with the beginnings of a smirk.

Bo stalks quickly to Paddington and takes the Heathrow Express, and now he is at the airport. Time is a little tight due to the domestic diversion, but he's not quite late yet. He goes to Terminal One Enquiries and, as instructed, asks them to dial the ICC, the Immigration Control Centre, where the passport he surrendered on the way in ten days ago will be waiting for him. miss ffinch has arranged for Ernest "try and get used to Ernie, 108" Pitt to have a driving licence, a credit card, a bank account, even with a £2,500 float in it, but as she said "why waste money on a new passport when a perfectly good aliased one already exists? When you get through to the ICC, say the collection is for Captain Dunbar, that's our code with them."

"Captain Dunbar, passport collection, please," says Bo into the phone.

"Fine. Come up to Room 4/272, ask enquiries to point you in the right direction."

He asks and they do, point him in the right direction. He knocks on the door, hears "Enter!" and enters.

"Hello, yes I called about Captain Dunbar."

"Yes, you spoke to me'" replies the officer as Bo looks around the otherwise empty room, "would have to have done as I'm the only one here. Take a seat." He opens a drawer and takes out and looks at three passports. "None of them for you by the look of them. What was the name to be?"

"Pitt, Ernest Jasper Pitt. I flew in from Washington on the 31st. Here's the card the officer gave me, the reference is on the back."

"Oh, OK, and you called him to say you'd be collecting today."

"I didn't, no, but Captain Dunbar or his office did. I suppose. I was just told to come and collect it like this."

"Well, there's been some kid of snafu. Not for the first time, why don't these people just stick to arrangements? When's your flight?"

"At a quarter to two, so in just over an hour."

"You'll be lucky. Hang on here." He goes next door, and Bo can hear his side of the telephone conversation. He seems to be talking, yes he is talking, to the officer on the business card. Bo hears the reference, then a series of grunts, the name Captain Dunbar, more OKs, then the officer returns.

"OK, the passport is in the safe in Terminal Four where you arrived. No-one told us you were due here. He's going to get Dunbar clearance and if OK bring it over, but you can forget the 1345. Why don't you go downstairs, work something out with BA and come back in an hour?"

Bo does as suggested, finds the ticket is non-changeable and so opens the bowling on the Pitt credit card for a new one, and an hour later collects the Ernest Pitt passport. He tries to call Y, but can only leave a message which asks for him, Y, to text Bo the hotel name as he presumably will no longer be met in Madrid three hours later. He buys a new white shirt, stuffs the old one in his shoulder bag, thinks he can just about get away with the coffee stains on the khaki trousers, boards the later plane. As the steward brings him a Scotch and water he says "nice shiner you've got there, sir" and Bo asks his Spanish neighbour in Spanish if he has a black eye. The neighbour concurs and jokes he will not ask how.

Bo collects his bags, the Pitt passport goes through Immigration unchecked and in the arrivals hall he turns on his mobile to collect the hotel name text from London. He is waiting for the screen to fill when a voice off his shoulder says "Señor Flowerdew-Pett?"

He turns round in surprise and sees wonderful green eyes, framed by thick and rich shoulder length jet-black hair. She is only a few inches shorter than him. She is smiling, and two little dimple creases show up either side of her mouth. The traces of freckles are sprinkled around her face. Bo immediately thinks of his back eye, and now she is staring at it. "No problems, I hope?"

"Er, no, no," says Bo, "um, it's really good of you to wait, did anyone get you a message?"

"Oh, you speak Spanish, very well. No, but it's OK, is my job. I was lucky you were late as I was late too, office delays." She holds out her hand "'Onorita Rosca, without the aitch. Spells Honorita, says 'Onorita. I am to be your collaborator at the CNI."

Bo shakes her hand, aware he is staring like a fool at her, "Oh yes, Pett, Bo Pett."

"Not Flowerdew?"

"No, no, it's like your aitch, there but not there."

"Very fine. I will get you a taxi to your hotel. Because of the lateness I cannot take you myself." Damn, Bo thinks, sounds like she's got a date. "But I collect you in the morning. Ten o'clock, is alright?"

"Wonderful," says Bo, and to himself, "oh boy, and so are you."

23
Dateline 19th

Even by the doldrums standards of the Gulf of Guinea the air is dead and the sea is lifeless. Humidity hangs like a wet curtain over Barbate harbour. Hernán Eboleh, his bodyguard Mike Tuffy and his crew of the Fernando Poan naval cutter *Nguru* are pleased just to have some forward motion as they leave the harbour, and not even the most lily-livered of his African Portuguese crew will be seasick today. They open the throttle to 75% and head out to the first rig to collect their first supply boat passage tax. A new sense of enthusiasm has joined them on board since they accidentally intercepted some cigarette smugglers from Baku, and now the smugglers too have to pay their passage tax. On the bridge the internal telephone rings. Eboleh picks it up.

"Admiral, there is a radio massage, you better deal with this one." Eboleh walks back the radio room and asks the caller to go ahead.

"Yes, *Nguru* this is *ChevronTexaco Shuttle 14*, over." Eboleh hears the usual supply vessel broad Texan folksy drawl.

"*ChevronTexaco 14, this is Nguru*, the captain speaking, over"

"Captain, we got ourselves a swimmer here, found him paddlin' away south east towards Gabon in an inner tube. We've hauled him on board, didn't want to come too much. He's pretty scared. We're heading back to Barbate, you want us to hand him over to the port police there?"

Eboleh does a quick calculation. On the one hand it makes sense for the supply boat to do just that, because that is what *Nguru* would have to do anyway when they returned from their day's tax collection. But you never know what opportunities might arise. He could be important, this escapee, valuable, some credit attached for his capture, you just never know where things might lead. Eboleh replies, "No, captain, we'll come and collect him. We've got you on the squawker; see you in a few minutes. Out."

The sea is so flat that the two slowing boats hardly have to protect themselves from each other with fenders. The supply ship puts the swimmer and his inner tube in a net and cranes him onto *Nguru's* foredeck. Eboleh goes down to inspect him. He can tell immediately he is from the Kirange tribe and likely to be a petty criminal. He looks ragged, dishevelled and frightened. Eboleh calculates a visit to Black Beach would do him no harm, and that that was almost certainly what he was trying to escape from. As a capture he is probably worthless, but a personal hand-over to his mad cousin Julio, the Governor of Black Beach would do him, Hernán, no harm either. Might even join in the questioning, word of that would soon spread and do him no harm either. Eboleh tells his new prisoner to follow him to the bridge deck; the prisoner reaches down and collects his inner tube but Mike Tuffy snatches it from him.

As he enters the air conditioned heaven on the bridge one of his mobile telephone rings. He looks at the number, 418-613-9832, Québec, Madame Laforge and the call he had been waiting for, six a.m. her time. He orders the helmsman and duty officer to leave him alone on the bridge. He points the wheel at a rig on the horizon, flicks on the autopilot and turns down the throttles and the noise. "Hey, Michelle, good to hear from you. Has there been any contact?"

"Yes, the tiger has called," she replies in her thick Québécoise accent. The tiger is their code for Claude-Michelle Michaux. Eboleh's excitement rises, and he can picture his ex-landlady in her living room, surrounded by *Québec Libre* posters as they speak. The image causes him to smile in memory and anticipation.

"Was he a positive tiger?" he asks.

"No, not positive. He himself I believe to be hungry, but his superiors are frightened of upsetting, of upsetting...." she is thinking of the way to put it, "certain parties to the south of here."

"Shit!" he snaps.

"But he would like a chance to meet you again when you are near his territory. He wants to explain some aspects to you man-to-man. I have the contact details. What shall I tell him?"

"Tell him his superiors are idiots. No, better, not. Shit, I cannot believe they would reject such an offer. What is their problem?"

"We all know what happens when a bully is throwing his weight around. The timid ones become more timid. It is happening here too with our movement."

"Tell him, no, tell him nothing. If he calls you again, insist it is a wrong number. When I am ready I will call him. Idiots. Anyway, thank you again Mar…," he nearly says her real name, "Michelle. Money OK?"

"Yes, money is good. Until the next time."

Hernán Eboleh stomps from port to starboard across the bridge. "Fools and idiots! No guts, no spine, just office boys!" he shouts to himself above the engines. Outside he sees the helmsman and duty officer waiting in the shade and the prisoner standing next to them. He cannot believe the DGSE have rejected his offer. He opens the door and waves the crew back in. Outside is the prisoner. "What are you looking at?" Eboleh shouts at him in Fang.

The man does not answer and looks down on the deck. "I said, Kirange cockroach, what are you looking at?" Again there is no reply and Eboleh strikes him hard with the back of his hand across the man's face. Then he hits him again with his forehand, and now shouting, "I'll tell you what you're looking at, you're looking at the sea!" and grabbing hold of the remains of his shirt he hauls the prisoner over the side. The prisoner strikes his head on the bulwark on his way down. Mike Tuffy on the foredeck sees it all, and above the noise of the boat points to the inner tube, gesturing if he should throw it after the man. The admiral waves his finger 'no', Tuffy waves his thumb up back, smiles, pierces the tube with his knife and, chuckling to himself, throws the piece of dead rubber over the other side.

PART TWO

24
Dateline 19th

"Thanks for having me collected, Honorita," says Bo on being ushered into her panoramic office.

"I'm sorry I could not come myself," she replies standing to greet him with a handshake and the beginnings of a pre-dimple smile, "domestic affairs, I sent the driver instead. Sorry we are running so late, I hope you got the message." Bo notices she looks more formal, more, well, severe, her hair tied back and no jewellery except an engagement ring. She is wearing a trouser suit, plain and dark grey.

"No problem, I went for a swim. What a limo, there I was sitting in the back like an eastern potentate."

She laughs, "And how do you like our new offices?"

He looks around the bright and light freshly built room with carpets soft on colour and foot. He looks back at her and for some reason the words 'shag pile' come into his head, but he says, "Espléndido! If only they could see this in London."

"But Vauxhall Cross is a fine new building too, no?"

Bo has to admit that it is fine and new "but they thought I was coming to some hardship posting. I have the impression that they think anywhere abroad is a hardship."

"Have you been to the CIA building in Langley?" she asks. Bo admitted he hadn't. "I have, twice. Not as fine as this, smaller rooms and no views by and large, but quantity. My God, so many rooms, you need a guide. And all work, everybody rush-rush-rush. But first, some coffee, or tea, English tea?" Bo tries to concentrate, hoping she's flirting, but fears she isn't.

"Lovely," says Bo looking at her as she brushes a strand of

stray hair to one side and agreeing about the coffee. She presses a buzzer on the desk. A maid appears almost immediately and takes the order, and finishes with "Si, Capitán."

Bo says he is surprised that she is in the military. She says she comes from a military family and that she is still a captain in the army intelligence corps; this secondment to the CNI is a regular career move. She is surprised in turn that Bo is not in the military and never has been; she says she assumes it was an integral part of the job. Bo decides now is not the time to mention any pacifist tendencies.

"I said at the airport that I was to be your case worker," she says pouring his coffee.

"You make me sound like a hooligan," Bo replies, settling comfortably into the luxury executive chair, running his hand along the new oak conference tabletop.

"Well I meant we should work together on this case, this case of Teniente Gustavo Cortez. Teniente is Lieutenant in English. How much do you know about him?"

Bo pushes himself up again. "Can you adjust this chair just to stay upright?" She shrugs; he heaves himself out and turns a wheel on the side. "I'll try that, that's better. Cortez you say, no, sorry never heard of him. Lovely coffee."

"So what have they told you at MI6?"

Bo thinks back to his lunch with Y at the cavalry Club. Seems like months ago, but not only half a week ago. "Only that one of your citizens is about to be transported to Fernando Po, to Black Beach prison, and they want me to help you guys, or maybe do it on my own, to spring him from there. That was it really. Don't know why, don't know who. Is that more or less the sum of it?"

Honorita leaves the table and walks over to a cabinet, opens the door to reveal a large television. He sees her bend her knees to lower herself to insert a videotape into the machine below the television, straighten up again, pick up a remote controller and sit down back at the table opposite. Bo watches her every move and curve and tries to stay focussing on what she is saying, "You have heard of *Canal Verdio*?" He regrets that he hasn't. "It's a subscription cable channel in Barcelona. Lots of alternative programmes, art, politics, religion, philosophy." She smiles the two dimples back again, "definitely no game shows or reality TV, sitcoms, no repeats."

"Maybe a bit like BBC4?" suggests Bo.

"Oh no," she replies, "it's completely independent, not a government channel. The opposite. Anyway, in December last year, after Gustavo Cortez was sentenced to six years in prison in Nigeria, they made this video, broadcast it on March 20th."

Bo watches her flick the remote and tells him "You'r Spanish is good enough to understand Catalan."

"My Latin was quite good so I'll probably be OK, Catalan maybe a struggle." He sees a quixotic look in return. The screen is flickering odd images before the feature starts. "What did the programme say, more or less?" he asks.

"It declared," he notices her leaning forwards and tries to keep his eyes level with hers "that Teniente Gustavo Cortez was a Spanish spy working for us, the CNI, and was actively involved, with our knowledge, blessing and encouragement, in trying to overthrow the democratically elected government of Fernando Po. Of course we denied it."

"Is there any truth in it?" asks Bo.

"Well it's half true. We didn't try to stop what we knew possibly was about to happen. We were passive rather than active. We were deniable," she says matter of factly. "That's why you're here. Because it's half-true."

The image on the screen comes to life. Bo turns around to see the video. Honorita has seen it many times before, and goes across the room to make a telephone call. Bo is watching her out of the corner of his eyes and is trying to listen to two conversations in the different forms of Spanish at once. On the screen he sees images of a tropical African town, can make out the words *Barbate, cuidad capital de la República de Fernando Po,* various oil rigs out at sea, then it cuts to Washington, to the Senate in session, to The First Virginia & DC Bank, to Sir Mungo Nathan, various shady looking characters "that's Wickus Paulsie, one of the ringleaders," Honorita says with her hand over the receiver, then a man being interviewed in prison, and again from Honorita "that's Smit Voorstmann, and that's Black Beach." The picture changes to a scratchy battle scene, and a soldier firing a machine gun in the jungle. Honorita stands up and says "There's Krause van Stahl, aka Big-K, the boss of all this." Now the picture stayed on a stocky man of medium height, broad shoulders, with the build of a gym enthusiast, flat and trim moustache, Latin dark hair, in different scenes but always well dressed and in a bit of a hurry.

"Cortez?" Bo asks over his shoulder. He receives a thumbs up from the telephone goddess. The pace of the voice over is breathless but he can make out the key words easily enough: *gobierno Español.... Espionaje....José María Aznar.... Subterráneo.... Implícito....Adolpho Stobo.... junta exilio.... Británico....co-conspirator Krause van Stahl.... ilegal armas.... Centro Nacional de Intelligencia.... Black Beach....Presidente Bolivar Eboleh.... democrático elegido...."*

The tape finishes, and Honorita says "So? What do you think?"

"The government of Fernando Po was not democratically elected, they got that wrong."

"That's about all they did get wrong. Although he has been elected twice, once with ninety-six and then with ninety eight percent of the vote."

"Popular tyrant. So our Señor Cortez is not quite the Spanish tourist on safari, bad luck, wrong place, wrong time, surfer dude London hoped he might be."

"No, Bo, he is not. He's a bit like you. And me. He's a secret agent. A spy."

"Ah!" says Bo. She passes over some files, and stands up to leave. She asks him to make himself at home while she's in another meeting and then lunch, and tells him to meet her back here after lunch, say 3 p.m. if he would be so kind. He would.

25
Dateline 19th

"I'm sorry I'm late," says Honorita Rosca absent mindedly, "traffic. It just gets worse. Even the driver, who knows Madrid like a taxi driver, could not find a shortcut through it."

"Do you always have a driver?" asks Bo

"Yes. He is in my regiment, the First Mountain Brigade, and followed me here. He is my batman. He is meant to be for the section, but I'm the only one who uses him. The boys prefer bicycles or motorbikes, *La Coronel* public transport and long walks. Anyway, where were we?" she asks and for the first time after lunch stops moving around, settles in her chair and looks at the young British spy that London has sent to help them. She was expecting someone older, a bit more...more...more physical, more beefy, more, she doesn't know, typical; a bit less...less, she's not quite sure, well, less nonchalant. But he's tall and handsome, blonde – not that that will help in Africa, and she can tell he's more interested in her than the poor Gustavo Cortez he has been sent to rescue. Honorita is used to the attention of men, she is still just about single in spite of several proposals and a long engagement, but this one is forward for an Englishman. She has seen that when he walks he stalks, he walks almost like a jungle cat, and now looking again she can see he must be a good athlete, but then again a bit young for this, and a bit young for her too. One day when he's a man, maybe, but why they sent this boy, she is not so sure.

"You were briefing me," he replies, "about our assignment. Fernando Po. Gustavo Corto."

"*Cortez*. Gustavo Cortez," she corrects forcefully. 'Can't even get his name right' crosses her mind. "Yes, well, he works for us, we have established that."

"Right," says Bo sitting upright and paying attention.

"He had just been stationed to our embassy in Pretoria, the usual thing, Cultural Attaché, nearly two years ago now, when we received here in Madrid a report by someone called Jacobus du Randt. You've heard of him?" He replies that he had but only vaguely, she continues, "Jacobus du Randt is what is called a Political Risk Analyst. They go around sniffing out trouble and advising governments or corporations, whoever is paying them. Anyway, this du Randt has first class connections to the world of mercenaries, mostly through his former colleagues in the Thirty-Two Buffalo Battalion of the old apartheid era South African army. The officers were white but the soldiers were black, mostly of Portuguese, well Portuguese African origin. They are as hard and tough as soldiers can be but with the new black regime, unemployable, because of their past apartheid association. So, whenever there's any mercenary activity, anywhere in Africa, it's the Thirty Twos who sign up first. You with me?"

"All the way," says Bo smiling.

"The man you saw in the video from Black Beach prison, Smit Voorstmann…"

"I remember."

"He was one of them, an ex-Thirty-Two man. We think the leak to du Randt came from, or via, him. The other guy, Krause van Stahl, is too professional for that. Wickus Paulsie, possible but unlikely, too antisocial. The third one, Günter Koekemoor, dropped out early. van Stahl is as secretive, he would say discreet, as Sir Mungo Nathan who paid for it all. Well, however, through his grapevine, this Jacobus du Randt hears all about the FP blow-up plan four months before it was due to happen, and he tipped off all the governments concerned. The South Africans because the plotters were operating from their country, the Fernando Poans for obvious reasons, the CIA because of the three billion dollar oil investment, MI6 because the paymaster Nathan and how you say, bagman, Simonez are British, well their passports are British, and ourselves because the previous government of Jose María Aznar was, we could say, more than usually well disposed to an FP political exile and would-be president called Adolpho Stobo. We wanted Stobo in and Eboleh out, but not via a coup d'etat. Too unseemly. Chaos after an act of terrorism suited us better. Their Madrid bombing. Our Madrid bombing caused a change of government, albeit democratically, so why couldn't the FP regime change too? With a little, shall we say, push. You would think that as an ex-colony our interests would be favourably taken care of, as happens in the French ex-colonies, but the FP mentality is to annoy or embarrass us wherever they can. And then there is the oil. Our oil company Repsol is drilling in territory disputed by Gabon and FP, and the Aznar government's plan was to send some warships down there, sort out the Gabon problem, legally, and install Stobo on the back of the ensuing fracas. You may have heard that the warships had actually left Cadiz for the area when this whole affair went wrong."

"So this Jacobus du Randt set some hares running," says Bo, and she notices for the first time he is more interested in the plot than in her.

"Yes, and he did not tell any of the governments involved that he had told any of the others, so all the agencies thought they alone had the knowledge. Clever. Even the CIA and MI6 did not tell each other, which is pretty unusual." She stands up to look out of the window.

"So you wonder why we were not too concerned about two big Brits, Nathan and Simonez, being involved?" he asks.

"It's a mystery to us."

"Well I don't know, I'm not taking that kind of interest, or disinterest. It could be because they are not really British. Lots of people have got British passports, doesn't make them British. As in British-British. I mean, as far as I know Simonez is South African and Nathan is Zimbabwean. Somewhere along the line they stumbled across British passports. They are both big boys, so I'm not surprised our guys gave them a damn good leaving alone."

"What doesn't make sense is that over the years both Nathan and Simonez have been helpful to western intelligence. At least Simonez has, there's never been any direct contact with Nathan as you would expect. But you speak to Simonez as you would to Nathan. I'm not saying they were out and out spooks, far from it, but if MI6 ever wanted information they would try to find it out. If they came across helpful intelligence, for instances in the Kenyan or Rhodesian independence struggles, they would be on hand to deliver." She closes the files, and says, "I think Simonez got busted because he assumed that we all knew about their little plan and because we knew about it and did not try to stop it, we must be approving it. But he didn't reckon with the new South Africa. His stance was only logical, but too logical."

"Logic confused with wishful thinking," says Bo. "And here, here at the CNI, how did you react to this du Randt's report?"

"It came as quite a bombshell, messed up our bigger picture plans pretty conclusively. We wanted to know more. Luckily we had just sent one of our guys to his new posting in Pretoria, of course that was Teniente Cortez. We asked him to investigate."

"And?"

"And he did such a good job that he became a terrorist insider. Friends not just with Krause van Stahl, but also with Wickus Paulsie and Smit Voorstmann. This Günter Koekemoor had left by then. He was so far on the inside of this deal that when the arrests came he was actually at Port Harcourt airport and caught red handed next to the helicopter full of explosives on to their way to the coast."

"He was too good," says Bo

"Yes, he was too good, too good a spy," she replies leaning forward and closer to him now, until both realised how close she is and move back at the same time.

She stands up and says "do you know what a bridge is?" and before he could reply she says ,"You won't, it's when there is a national holiday on a Tuesday or Thursday, and people can take a day's holiday on the Monday or Friday and make it a four day break. We've got one this weekend. I'm going to give you this file, and some others, and that video, and actually another one now I think about it, and see you back here Monday morning. Then you can meet my boss Coronel Molistán from the Spanish Legion itself too, she's back on Monday." Then she senses he is about to ask her about meeting over the bridge, and says, "I have to leave town, to spend it with my parents in Saragossa," then smiling warmly to him, because she is warming to him, goes over and pecks him goodbye on both cheeks, and is quite glad to find his hand on her shoulder as he bends down slightly to do the same to her. "Now I must go, I'm late, see you Monday."

26
Dateline 19th

Commandante Michaux knocks three times on General Lainé's door on the top floor of the DGSE headquarters, 141 Boulevard Mortier. He hears 'entrez!' and enters. The room is small and dishevelled, a mystery to all that worked there why the lower ranks had the spacious rooms downstairs, albeit shared, while *les grands fromages* had to work from a garret. The only consolation was the view of the Parisian rooftops, and it was over these that the general was musing as Michaux enters. They are not alone, a smartly dressed and well coiffured man in his mid forties was sitting in the chair opposite the general's desk.

"Ah, Michaux," says the general turning back into the room, "let me introduce Monsieur René Montrachaud of the *Quai d'Orsay*. And Monsieur Montrachaud, this is Commandante Michaux, head of the Africa Francophone section here at the DGSE" They shake hands cordially, but Montrachaud does so with the ease of someone who wants it to be known he outranks the other.

"This affair falls under Security Classification C8, Michaux," announces the general, and Michaux nods his head as if familiar with the sensitivities, and pulls up the old wooden chair from the wall.

"Commandante Michaux," says Montrachaud, "does the name Gustavo Cortez mean anything to you?"

"Not immediately. I could check the files if you need to know."

"Oh, we know, we know," says Montrachaud. "Does the name Krause van Stahl mean anything to you?"

"Only the name, the South African mercenary turned terrorist," replies Michaux warily, then "ah yes, wasn't Cortez one of the other plotters? The Fernando Po bomb, or non-bomb? They're still in prison in Nigeria."

"Exactly," says Montrachaud. "Now, a situation has arisen which has the potential to embarrass us considerably, very considerably, especially in Africa. Cortez was due to serve his time in Nigeria, may have been released in four or five years or so, all depending on Obasanjo's whims. All the while the Fernando Poans have been trying to extradite him, mostly as far as we can see because he is Spanish, and they believe, rightly it would seem, that the previous Spanish government, the old colonial power, was promoting the interests of a leader in exile in Madrid, one Adolpho Stobo."

"And now they have succeeded I hear, in the extradition," replies Michaux.

"Yes, it's been on/off on/off for three weeks, but now there seems to be a timetable, the 28th. Cortez has been ill, they have been treating him in a civilian hospital, we hear he has responded well and is now quite fit considering that he has been in Kirikiri prison in Lagos. anyway fit enough to travel. A charter flight has been booked."

General Lainé leans forward at his desk. "Commandante, in view of the sensitivities I have told Monsieur Montrachaud about your meetings with Hernán Eboleh, and the possibility of, shall we say, change, in FP."

"And may I know of the sensitivities?" asks Michaux.

"I'm afraid not," replies Montrachaud quickly. "Security Classification C8 mentioned earlier."

Before Michaux can protest, the general says, "We want you to contact Eboleh. Find out if there's any situation, any situation, in which Cortez's extradition can be stopped from the FP end."

"I don't believe my Eboleh has that sort of influence," says Michaux. "It's not a lobbying type of country. Bribes? The ruling family are so rich, with the prospect of only becoming richer, why should they take money to stop embarrassing their old enemy?"

"Nevertheless, we must try. It is our best option, in fact right now our only option," says Montrachaud. "How do you contact him?"

"Through a number in Québec."

"Please call and say you will be visiting FP, as, I don't know, you said he is in the navy?"

"He is an admiral, the admiral," says General Lainé.

"Very well. Tell him you will be visiting FP in the next days, as a naval equipment representative. Radar systems, something like that? You must have an appointment. Please go ahead."

"Now?" asks Michaux.

"Why not? I have to report upwards immediately after this." says Montrachaud.

"Very well." Michaux looks in the address book at the back of his diary and dials the eleven digits to Québec. "I hope she is an early riser, ah it's ringing. Yes, Madame Laforge, hello, sorry so early, this is uncle Remus. Yes fine thank you. Well you know what they say about Paris in the fall. Yes, yes, me too. Now, can you please send a message to Sylvester? Yes, that will be fine. Tell him that I will be in his office in two days, no make that three days, with some equipment he might want to buy. Yes, for his work. Yes, anytime. You have my incoming cellphone number? That's it. Good bye Madame Laforge."

Montrachaud rises and puts on his overcoat, and says, "thank you and goodbye General Lainé, goodbye to you Commandante Michaux. You will report through General Lainé, and he will be our contact too. Just find out what they want, there's always a way in Africa." The general holds the door open, wishes him goodbye too and closes it behind him.

"Good heavens Claude-Michel, this one you will not believe," says the general shaking his head. "Bloody civil servants and their stupid clearance levels. There's no point in you going to meet Eboleh if you don't know what's going on, and believe me, my old friend, you won't believe what's going on. I'm afraid they are sending you on a lost cause."

"It won't be the first time, General," says Michaux bitterly, "that politicians and civil servants have interfered with the smooth running of Intelligence. I can feel a major waste of everyone's time coming on."

27
Dateline 22nd

Bo arrives at the CNI building ten minutes early, at ten to nine on Monday morning. He says hello to the receptionist, who recognises him and suggests he goes straight up to Capitán Rosca's room and wait for her there. Bo contrasts the security here to Vauxhall Cross, and casually finds his way into Honorita's office. He notices a connecting door is a quarter open, enough for him to hear a rather gruff sounding woman on the telephone. When the call finishes he can hear the sounds of her moving around the office, opening and closing drawers, pouring a drink, coughing, talking, mumbling to herself. He sits quietly and waits for Honorita. After twenty minutes he hears a knock, three taps, on the neighbour's passage door, then her raised voice "Enter!"

"Coronel, I am sorry I am late, the neighbours were ...." he recognises Honorita's voice.

"You are late too often Capitán Rosca. It is sign of poor self management. Please be more punctual in future."

"Yes, Coronel."

"Sit down. Now I am back from Morocco. This English special agent they have sent us for the FP job, what's he like?"

Bo, startled, leans forward in his seat to hear the nuance in every word, not that he has to. "Coronel, he is not what I expected. He is not military and is only 26 years old, not strong, physically, he is tall, thin, I would say in good condition like an athlete but not in tough condition, in training, like a soldier. He has limited experience in special operations."

"Limited to what?"

"A break out in North Korea, so I suppose they thought he could do another."

"From Black Beach! Daydreamers! So they have sent us a loser, a chancer. Never trust the English. Remember Drake. Shall we send him back and get a man, a commando like they should have sent us?"

"We could, yes."

Bo could hear La Coronel moving around the office. "It's your case, Rosca, you decide. Personally I would swap him, we cannot risk this going wrong." Then Bo hears her voice rising, "in fact they are idiots in London, the reason we asked for someone special in the first place was because we dare not risk anything going wrong!"

"I'll send him back then, get a new one." says Honorita. Bo senses the conversation next door is coming to an end and quietly stands up, glides across the thick carpet and silently opens and closes the passage door. He walks along the corridor and back, twice, and then knocks as if for the first time there today, is told to enter, and enters.

"Good morning, Honorita, sorry I'm late, there were travel delays."

She points to her chair and says a little awkwardly, "Sit down, Bo."

Before she can say anything more Bo gets his retaliation in first. "I have been studying the files you gave me, and watched the videos several times, and I think you are making an important mistaken assumption."

She looks up surprised, and asks him what it would be.

"This Gustavo Cortez, you say he is one of yours."

"Yes, it is certain, he works for the CNI, no question."

"Well, I think that is just his day job."

"Meaning?"

"Meaning that there is no way he could become so involved in all this without being an active insider, an investor probably, almost certainly, minimum the bomb buyer. You have assumed he was an insider because he is such a good spy. But if you look at the facts objectively there has to be more to it than that."

"And what makes you say all this? What proof have you?"

"Over your bridge weekend I spend pretty much every moment studying what happened. I went to London." This was not literally true, but Bo did have four long conversations with Y, and had spent most of the weekend in his local Internet café, "and now I think I know as much about the case as you do."

"But Cortez, Gustavo, he has no money to spare for investing as you put it, he is paid like we are as soldiers and civil servants."

From the side wall they both hear the open connecting door open further, and Bo sees a squarely built short haired dark complexioned woman, at first sight around fifty five but probably younger than that, in a smartly pressed uniform enter. "Good morning. I am Coronel Molistán. I was overhearing your conversation with Capitán Rosca. Please proceed." Bo starts to stand up. "Stay seated," she instructs.

"Gustavo Cortez did not get to hear about the plot until after you had tipped him off following Jacobus du Randt's report."

"So?" demands La Coronel.

"He organised for himself to be introduced to Wickus Paulsie through an embassy contact."

"Very possibly, nothing wrong with that."

"Nothing at all. But van Stahl is not the most honest of men. His trade is a mercenary. His record speaks for itself. When he's not killing he is swindling. The plot was well financed by Simonez acting for Nathan, at least we can safely assume it was, it's not Nathan's style to do anything by halves. But van Stahl has been around a long time and he would not be too worried about selling the same thing twice. There is no other reason for Paulsie to get van Stahl to fly up from his home in Capetown the next morning, a Sunday morning, to meet Cortez unless Cortez had given Paulsie the impression that he was a potential investor in the success fee. I'm guessing here but let's say Nathan promised van Stahl three million dollars up front and three million on completion. An investor in the scheme would have said I'll put a million in now and take out two if it works. It's a high risk for the new investor but at two to one a well calculated risk. He would sell it to van Stahl, and to himself, on the basis that it flattens the plotter's risk. But van Stahl doesn't think like this, for him it's just a free million, as I'm sure he would have no intention to honour the bet. There's no social reason for them to meet, it could only have been because after the meeting with Cortez, Paulsie immediately contacted van Stahl to say unexpected funds were available. And another thing, just as important. Günter Koekemoor had dropped out by now, and van Stahl needed someone to front the buying of the explosives to keep his own hands clean. At the time they met no explosives had been purchased. For van Stahl this was always going to be a potential weak link, a necessary inclusion of outsiders from beyond the Simonez/Nathan and Paulsie/Voorstmann circle. Then, presto, along comes Cortez to replace Koekemoor. Problem solved, plus Cortez was paying so van Stahl could also pocket the Nathan/Simonez expenses. It was a great day for van Stahl. By the way, the leak to du Randt came from Koekemoor, not Paulsie as you suspected."

"That may be, but how could Gustavo have found the funds to make the investment? He does not have that kind of money," asks Honorita.

"You don't need that kind of money, but you have to have access to it. Someone else's money. I would bet that after you had asked him to investigate, Cortez had found out the reward fee for blowing up part of Barbate, which let's face it isn't that difficult. Thought he'd buy himself in, have a little play himself."

From the next office the telephone rings. Coronel Molistán looks annoyed and says she has to answer it, for them to carry on, but first she reminds Bo that "Teniente Cortez is a highly decorated submariner in the Armada."

They wait for her to close the door and Bo says, "Honorita, I'm sure in South Africa it would not be too difficult to raise that sort of money, given some time which he had, on a high risk gamble with good potential, especially if you were there, bored and rich like a lot of South Africans. All he would have to pretend to Paulsie, Voorstmann and van Stahl is that he was an investor gambler too, maybe he could say he'd made a lot of money in Spain and wanted a little action, some speculation, in South Africa too."

"But Bo, I know Gustavo, he would not do it, you see…"

La Coronel puts her head around the door, "Capitán Rosca, that call was that the departmental meeting has come forward, I'll see you there," and then to Bo she says coldly "and I'll see you tomorrow, with some explanations to these slanders from your side."

Bo stands and asks Honorita, "This goes on all day, this department meeting?"

"Probably, it's once a month, normally in the afternoon but it's always into the evening. We'll have to start again tomorrow like she said."

"But, I know, let's have dinner tonight, we can talk more there, talk of other things too," says Bo.

"No," she says hesitantly, "er, I'm busy tonight, but tomorrow morning."

"Too busy for a drink before dinner?" tries Bo again.

"For that too. But I have some other news for you,'" she says. Bo fears the worst, fears his own pre-emptive move has backfired and he was still fired, "I am to be the field officer in FP too, so whoever else goes, I go too. Adios, Bo, hasta mañana," and scooping papers and files she is gone.

28
Dateline 22nd

Hernán Eboleh tells his driver to wait, over there in the shade and keep the a/c on full, and he and Mike Tuffy jump out of the Cadillac Escalade SUV and up the steps into the lobby of the Bahia Hotel. Already, at only just after nine in the morning, it is humid and oppressive outside. He sees Claude-Michel Michaux waiting in a chair by the coffee shop, reading yesterday's Herald Tribune.

"Monsieur Gaillard," says Eboleh using Michaud's alias, " how good of you to visit us."

Michaux folds the paper and stands up. "Admiral Eboleh, thank you for seeing me at such short notice."

"My car's outside, I thought we could visit the cutter and you can tell me about the radar on board," Hernán says loud enough for all to hear. Michaux nods, they leave the lobby, brave the air and rush themselves back into the aircon heaven of the Escalade. On the way to the harbour Eboleh points out some features of Barbate: the main presidential palaces, the central barracks, the old colonial town square, now renovated by the UN as a world heritage site. After five minutes they arrive at the harbour, and see the US made Coastguard Cutter, FPN Nguru. The hostility of the tropics has already turned the cutter, gleaming white when delivered only two years ago, one shade to yellow.

Eboleh asks Tuffy to wait in the car, boards the boat with Michaux, dismisses the watch from the bridge, and when they are alone says, "Well now, it's a long way from Sussex Gardens, monsieur."

"I hope you don't mind similar precautions though?" asks Michaux.

"Of course not." They both pad down each other's clothes for sound, find nothing, smile, shrug, and the Eboleh says, "and just to make sure let's hang over the side, port side in the shade."

For a while they both stare at the fetid water, with its oil slick pollution and dead fish. Michaux take out a packet of Gauloises Blonds, offers one to the admiral, who refuses. Michaux lights up and says, "I've got a funny story to tell you. There's no other way that we will achieve our objective except that you are fully informed. Are you ready?"

"I'm listening," says Eboleh, now on full alert to the possibilities that might, just might, be falling into his lap.

"In five days Gustavo Cortez will arrive from Nigeria. You've heard of him?"

"Of course. It's the biggest news here for a while."

"It will be to our considerable advantage if he does not reach Black Beach."

"Why, what's he done?"

"You've heard of Jean-Baptiste Cygan too I suspect, the arms dealer, equipment trader."

"Well, I know he's French, based in South Africa, was the main sanctions buster in the apartheid days and now somehow is best friends with the new Mbeki regime. Quite a trick to pull."

Michaux flicks his cigarette end into the harbour, half expecting the sea to spontaneously combust. "Word around the campfire is that Cortez wanted to be part of the big bomb here, and approached Cygan for a loan. Not a very clever move, because Cygan found out what he could and told the SASS and, being at heart still a good Frenchman, our embassy in Pretoria. He declined the loan. Now we know that the SSAS knew anyway about this through Jacobus du Randt who was also working for your uncle here. Everyone knew that everyone knew, except the plotters of course. Cortez wanted to borrow a million US, and said he'd double the money. If the bomb had gone off he would have collected, assuming van Stahl paid up, a big assumption if you know anything about van Stahl."

"So now he's coming here, but wearing hand cuffs not hand grenades."

"Exactly, admiral. Now all the time he has been locked up in Kirikiri in Lagos this has all been kept quiet. We have managed to, shall we say, convince the Nigerians not to use this information which they have from the SSAS. Of course Cortez himself will not say anything. But now that he will be extradited everything

116

changes. To put it mildly, it will be a major embarrassment for France if he is subjected to African questioning, and if as expected he very quickly declines further questioning."

"But you say your Cygan did not invest, so what's the problem."

"No he didn't, but we did." Eboleh looks across with some surprise. "Yes I know, I know. But we wanted to find out what was happening, and that it was well worth the million dollars to do so, and if it succeeded to have an insider, Cortez, in our pocket. Of course this was anyway too small for Cygan to get involved with, and not worth his while at all if anything went wrong. So we arranged for a local hustler called Kellen to front it for us, which he did. Of course Kellen didn't know it was us."

"And….I'm thinking about what may come out under torture here, did Cortez know that the DSGE was involved?"

"Let's say he'd have to be pretty stupid not to have worked it out. He's had over a year in prison in Nigeria to think about where it all went wrong. He doesn't have to be a genius to work out that Cygan would have told us and that we would have set Cortez up."

"It's too sticky, let's go inside," says Eboleh. They slide back the bridge door and slide it shut again back on the cool and shade of the bridge. "So what do you want me to do?"

"You asked us for a favour, which we rejected, foolishly in my opinion. It's back on the table. In return we want you to use your family connections and influence to stop the extradition from happening. We have resources to back you."

Eboleh walks back to the refrigerator and offers Michaux some iced water, takes some himself. He does not have to think too long about the reply. "With respect Commandante, this is most unlikely to happen. My family view this as a major propaganda coup. No amount of money is going to change that."

"We realise that, Admiral. But there are other ways to influence events. The forthcoming UN investigation into oil corruption in West Africa could be very damaging for your country. The UN could insist on greater transparency. I'm sure your family could do without the aggravation, the limiting of future opportunities. France, being a major player in the region, is on the investigating committee. We could ensure that any irregularities need not come to a wider audience. Our view is that if you could find a wise council in your family to put these points to, the family will see that Cortez affair is one step forward, two steps back if one considers upsetting some of the more pious sensitivities at the UN."

Eboleh steps forward to shake Michaux's hand. "OK, we have a deal. My uncle Tomás is less excitable than his brother the president, more balanced. I will put the case to him. He is discreet, as I am too. I will say that this is my idea. But, Commandante, I have a far better idea."

"Which is?"

"I kill the bastard once he's here. After the celebration, but before the questions."

29
Dateline 23rd

Bo rolls over and checks his bedside clock again. Ten to eight, ten minutes to go. Mind you, she's always late. He thinks back to exactly twelve hours ago, the last time he rolled over and looked at the alarm clock, ten to eight this morning when the bedside the phone rang and woke him. It was Honorita then to say that today had been cancelled for both of them, she and the coronel had to go to the Ministry of Defence. Bo had immediately thought the worst, that they weren't going anywhere, just buying themselves a day in which to contact London and replace him. He wished he hadn't told them his theory about Cortez's bad cop activities; although he was sure he was right, and at the time the best form of defence was attack, he still had a horrible feeling he had only succeeded in offending their sense of military honour. He had spent the day in the Duc d'Alba's Hotel's Fitness Centre building up himself, but for more than his usual hour a day, and in the Internet café in the *Calle Nuevo Mayo* nearby building up his knowledge of the coup, and on the phone to Y building up profiles of Teniente Gustavo Cortez and Capitán Honorita Rosca. But she had, surprisingly enough, agreed to a date, and it was Honorita he was waiting for now.

At twenty five to nine, the bedside phone rings. She's sorry she's late, the driver had to go early and she couldn't find a taxi. Bo goes downstairs and sees a very different Honorita, *Honorita incognita*, in black slacks and Spanish leather boots, a red, white and gold silk blouse, and suede jacket, and for the first time since his arrival at the airport, make up and jewellery. Bo had made an effort too, having exhausted the suitcase he was living out of, with a new shirt and, coincidentally, new suede jacket. They kiss hello on both cheeks. She has made a reservation at *Los Farollilos*, in *Calle Istan* a ten minute walk away.

She orders *esparrogos a la plancha* followed by *pollo verde*

Almendrado, he orders *almejas con Manzanilla* then *cazuela de cordero,* a bottle of 1999 Velilla Gran Reserva Rioja and a bottle of still water, and they chat about the army and the coronel and Y, and chat about the CNI and MI6 and the CIA and the DGSE and the SASS and the NIS, and chat about their lives in Madrid, Rabat, Buenos Aires, London, San Diego, Tokyo and, in speculation, about Barbate. She does not mention his suspicions about Cortez and neither does he, although part of today's conversation with Y had convinced him more than ever that he was right.

"I haven't seen you wearing jewellery before," Bo says.

"It's a Service tradition from the Army, no jewellery for men or women on duty, and only Service issues wrist watches on active duty. It's just carried over to the CNI."

"And that little ring there, worn where we would wear an engagement ring..."

"We also wear our engagement ring there. This is my engagement ring," and she twists her hand up and shows the ring more closely to Bo.

"And have you been engaged for a long time?"

"For three and a half years."

"That's a long time."

"Not really for us. I suppose it is another Service tradition, maybe there was more travelling, more overseas postings in the old days."

Bo pays the bill and they leave the restaurant for the walk back to the hotel, she says she'll look for a taxi on the way. Bo decides against suggesting a night cap at the hotel; the talk of her engagement has altered the mood, his mood anyway.

"Do you always do that?" she asks smilingly.

"What's that?'

"Change over to walk on the outside."

"Oh that," he replies, "just a habit, I suppose in the old days people thought it was more dangerous to walk nearer the road, highwaymen maybe, I'm not sure, it just feels wrong for me not to be on the outside."

"How very chival...."

She does not have time to finish her sentence as they are both knocked off balance with a strong push each from behind. Bo stumbles forward and is kicked in the ribs as he falls. As he falls he can see Honorita already face down on the street and then he looks up to see three men run away, the last one clutching her shoulder bag.

"You hurt?" he asks, kneeling up.

"Not badly," she says coming to her feet, putting a shoe back on.

"Wait here!" Bo shouts and he is already off full sprint after the three muggers. Behind him he can hear Honorita shout "I'm with you too!" and the sound of her running footsteps in awkward shoes.

Bo is now only twenty metres behind the last one and thirty metres behind the first two. He is catching them fast. Before him he sees the night crowds part on the pavement as four men and one women sprint flat out along the street; all five are shouting, at themselves and each other. He rugby tackles the first one he catches, the one with the bag, and as they fall the mugger takes the full force of their landing. Bo untangles himself, and prepares to hit the man, who he now sees is a teenage boy, a gipsy or moor. As he does so he sees a flash of black leather to his left and then hears Honorita's foot land firmly in the boy's mouth. He squeals and clutches his bloody face, Bo punches him as hard as he can between the legs, the boy doubles up in agony, and he sees Honorita grab back her bag and straddle him on his stomach, disabling him in wrestling lock.

Without words Bo sets off after the other two, now nearly a hundred metres ahead. People are now watching from the opposite pavement, cars have stopped, others are hooting. The two boys ahead look round to see how far behind Bo is, as they do so they loose thirty metres of their lead. He hears one of them shouting, then pointing and they split. Without knowing why Bo instinctively follows the slower, the weaker. He sees the boy stop and turn sharp left into an alley. Bo follows him, now only twenty metres behind. The mugger tries to climb a fire escape, Bo arrives just in time to reach for his legs, drag him down and as he does so punch him hard on the nose. The boy's hands come up. Bo kicks him hard in the balls, and as he goes down grabs his right arm in a lock behind his back and trot marches him back into the street and along to where a small crowd have now gathered around Honorita and the first mugger. As he arrives, pushing the boy before him, the crowd parts and spontaneously clap. Bo can hear cheers from across the road and more car horns. He throws his mugger to the ground, and Honorita gets up from hers.

"It's better we leave separately before the police arrive," she says, "Interdepartmental questions are always tiresome. The Coronel will want to know why they're still alive!" Bo borrows a tie and belt from a spectator and ties the two together. Honorita kicks them both in the face again with a flash of leather boot. They hear the first stirrings of a police siren and leave the scene together. On cue a taxi arrives. Bo opens the door and helps her in. He shuts the door, and she holds up her shoulder bag from inside and smiles and nods at him, then blows him two kisses goodnight. The taxi leaves. Bo turns to see some vigilante justice happening to the muggers, and then a dispersal as louder sirens announce the arrival of the first police car. Bo himself stalks off towards the hotel, his new shirt ruined but he himself, in general, enamoured.

30
Dateline 24th

Hernán Eboleh always likes to visit his uncle Tomás, wishes he could do so more often. The eldest surviving brother of his grandparents' children, Tomás lived apart from the others, and because of this, and the natural respect for the elder tribal and family members, he was trusted as being above ambition, and wise in his years. Hernán knew from the moment Michaux suggested his side of the favour-bargain that uncle Tomás was the only one who could influence the Cortez extradition case.

Hernán's driver turned the Escalade into the dirt track and up to the sentry box. Inside a Moroccan guard barely looks up before waving them through. Hernán thinks again that one of the many first things he is going to do is to get rid of the Moroccan guards. His uncle Bolivar, the president, owed Morocco a favour for having backed his own coup in 1980, and had been overpaying back handsomely since then; all the politicians in the family used British bodyguards for their personal protection anyway, as he himself had Mike Tuffy. He looks ahead and sees uncle Tomás's Spanish ranch. That is another thing Herman likes about this uncle, some sense of style. Whereas all the others had hired Texan architects and interior designers and given them unlimited budgets and scope for vulgarity, Tomás, maybe because of having spent so much of his youth with the Jesuits in Spain, understands elegance, even their austerity.

"If you can live without air-conditioning, Hernán, we can sit over there in the courtyard, but if not...."

"No, no, uncle, it's fine, the courtyard will be fine."

They sit on the bamboo chairs, draped with deerskin, just in range of the fans high in the cloister ceiling. A boy in bare feet and bright white t-shirt and shorts brings a tray of iced tea. "Unless you would prefer something stronger?". Hernán assures him iced tea is perfect, and that he sees his uncle is still running his unofficial orphanage. Tomás gives the boy a kindly pat and sends him on his way. Hernán thinks 'no need for Michaux style shakedowns here', and smiles.

"What are you smiling at Hernán?"

"Kindness. Your kindness. It's not often we come across it nowadays."

They chat about family matters over the iced tea. "Guess how many nephews and nieces I have?" Hernán has no idea. "Forty four, and how many great nephews and great nieces?" Again Hernán can only guess. "Wrong, forty four as well, but not for long. I expect Lena will have another next month, and then I will be overtaken by the subsequent generation. But how are things with you, and Giselle? She is not too homesick for South Africa? First, more iced tea?"

Hernán holds his glass out gratefully. "I am fine, and Giselle is expecting in five months, so soon you will have another grand nephew or grand niece. From now on she will be homesick, not travelling so much now she is pregnant, but really she is fine. The life of an Admiral is stressful, but we are protecting the country's waters and keeping troublemakers out. Actually, it was about a country matter that I want to seek your advice."

"I thought you might have something apart from our extended family on your mind."

"You have heard of the Cortez extradition?"

"The Spanish terrorist due to arrive next week. Yes, it is on television a lot. Big celebrations are planned. Is there a problem with it?"

"Not as such, no. But as a result we will make a lot of enemies because we both know what will happen to him in Black Beach. The Spanish of course, because there will be a big fuss in Spain, one of their citizens treated like they used to treat us. The Americans because it draws attention to the region and to their blue chip companies' behaviour here, sanctimonious is an American not a Spanish word these days, uncle, the British because they have financiers involved whose other interests could be affected, the French because…"

"Yes, I see all that, but why the French, they have nothing to do with it, surely?"

"Well, because they want to extend the Francophone and are generous in that pursuit, this will reflect badly on our country.

This Cortez has been tried and convicted elsewhere, don't forget. There's something else. You know about this UN investigation into the oil exploration corruption scandals in West Africa?"

"What will they find?"

"Nothing new, uncle. Its mostly aimed at the Nigerians. But so far what has happened to our family as a result of oil is known to only those busybodies who take an interest. Mostly, who cares? But once there's an official UN report the whole world knows. Do-gooders, tree-huggers, greedy lawyers, it cannot do us any good. Best for us is no change, it is not going to get better than this."

Tomás looks into the distance for a while, then says, "I can see that to pursue Cortez is one step forwards, two steps backwards, but what can we do?"

"Your brother Bolivar will listen to you. He will not listen to me. You could tell him to cancel the extradition, but before we do negotiate with those who have most influence at the UN to neuter the report, at least the part of it that concerns us. The French will be the best bet. You could even say I would be a good person for that task."

"I could, but he would be suspicious, and I never play with politics. I could just give him the advice; you are right in what you say. But there is something you don't know, which makes all this most unlikely," says Tomás ruefully.

"What's that, uncle?"

"I was at your Aunt Marissa's last night. Your uncle Bolivar was there, and your cousins Augusto and Jorge. Bolivar says he is waiting only to eat Cortez's testicles. I don't think anything will dissuade him. He sees the power in eating his enemy's private parts as we have seen before."

"I remember, and the last time General Mingunni and his father-in-law were still alive when he ate their testicles, they had to watch the president boiling and eating all four of them, like an old tribal feast. Still just about alive, he took them outside and hacked them to death with an old machete, hands first, then feet, then arms, then legs. I think Cortez may expect something similar."

"Indeed. Many family members watched. I don't know if Cortez will be dead or alive, but nothing will persuade Bolivar, not even the UN, from boiling and eating Cortez's testicles."

31
Dateline 24th

Honorita has not been looking forward to today much; actually not at all. A summons from the formidable Coronel Molistán to join her shooting party could firstly not be refused and was secondly a competition that could not be won. Both of these annoyed Honorita equally; the non-refusal because she prefers her martial arts and cross-training and the non-winning because firstly the shooting with the coronel is always so competitive and secondly because she knew she was a much better shot than the coronel anyway. On top of these though was today's further complication: Coronel Molistán had insisted that she bring Bo along too. When she told him that he had to shoot less well than the coronel, even if it meant missing on purpose, Bo had replied "oh don't worry about that, I've never fired a shotgun in my life." She had groaned quietly to herself. Honorita's view of Bo had improved somewhat since the mugging incident, but Coronel Molistán's had not improved at all. She viewed the rescue of Honorita's shoulder bag as no more than would be expected, had been annoyed by London's encryption that 'no-one else was available in the timeframe specified' and still fuming about his slur on Teniente Cortez's character.

Honorita's driver had picked him from the Duc d'Alba on time, but they had waited for her outside her apartment for nearly half an hour, washing machine problems, and when she saw him in the back of the car she groaned again. He was wearing trainers, jeans and a cream leather jacket, and it was too late to change now. She was wearing fatigues and boots, and then when she had mentioned partridges and mud, he had said he thought they'd be shooting clay pigeons and said something vaguely unenthusiastic about hunting animals. The traffic through the suburbs had been horrific and on the way it had started to drizzle and now they were arriving the rain was driving hard at them.

They pull up at the shooting lodge gate. An army sentry signals them to stop. He recognizes Honorita. "Good afternoon, Capitán Rosca." It has just turned midday. "A message for you from Coronel Molistán. Go directly to the Mess, she will meet you there for luncheon." She notices he has the air of taking pleasure in reprimanding, if only by proxy, a superior.

Honorita says nothing but groans inside again: not only a wasted day, but also a dressing down at lunch too.

They wait in the Officers' Mess. At exactly two o'clock the coronel strides in, wet from top to bottom, takes off and hangs up her full length military coat and headgear and confronts them looking dry and refreshed. She nods them to a table, nods at a steward to come and serve them.

"It's shame you were late," she says sardonically. "I had an excellent morning. Bagged eight, winged four more."

"I'm sorry about that," says Bo, "my fault. Overslept unfortunately."

The coronel gives him a withering look. "I'm not surprised. I have to tell you Mr. Pett or Pitt or whatever you name is, I am less than impressed by your suitability for this job. Oversleeping is a pathetic excuse. Your appearance for a shooting expedition is frankly disgraceful. Any self-respecting partridge would be long gone by the time you arrive. I have asked London for a replacement, and have been refused. It seems we are stuck with you."

Bo says he's sorry to hear that, but re-assures her he "will be alright on the night".

"What night?"

"Oh, it's just an expression. Don't worry."

"Don't worry! Of course I worry. Who wouldn't?" The steward arrives and without asking she orders rabbit stew and water and for all of them. "We need to get a few facts straight. Do you know why you are here?"

Honorita feels Bo's foot tapping her leg under the table as if for help, then he says "yes, to spring Gustavo Cortez from Black Beach."

"Why?"

"Well, because he's one of us," Bo replies helpfully, hopefully.

"One of us. If he was just 'one of us' why do you think we

have let him rot in Nigeria all this time?"

"I wondered about that. Surely it would have been easier to spring him from Kirikiri than Black Beach?"

The stew, piping hot, arrives. The coronel waits for the steward to leave, then turns to Honorita. "How far has the briefing gone? Have you mentioned the hot potato 'A' word?"

"Aznar, yes coronel," Honorita replies. "Señor Pett knows all the background."

There's a silence while the coronel considers, into which Bo says "and if I know, Cortez must know."

"Now you are getting there," the coronel replies. "To put it bluntly, as you know so much," she gives Honorita a questioning stare "and you think you know so much," she gives Bo an even more despising stare, "about Teniente Cortez too, you should know the hazards ahead, and my deep concern about you personally. We are being blunt, Capitán Rosca and Señor Pett."

Honorita and Bo stop eating and look and listen.

"The reason we are happy to have Teniente Cortez serving time in Kirikiri is because as long as he's there that is all he is doing, serving time. No questions, no answers, just time, and one day he would have been released and everything forgotten. He would have his job back, plus a promotion. Nigeria has no desire to embarrass us as they have the British, but in FP we are in the same position as the British in Nigeria. If they start questioning Teniente Cortez in Black Beach I am not sure he will be able to remain silent. If he does not remain silent there will be an international incident. Spain is eager to maintain its image of being a good world citizen, more than a good citizen, an actively useful national member of the global community. Now we have a new government, socialist unfortunately, but these days we must all respect democratic decisions, we can say that the whole Aznar government's dalliance with Adolpho Stobo and a change of government in Fernando Po was ill advised; actually it was not ill advised, it was advised against, particularly by the CNI. At the moment the FP government has suspicions. We have kicked Stobo out of the country, but they still have suspicions. Suspicions, no more than that. But if Teniente Cortez breaks under torture, which is possible even for one of us, and reveals his true role and his government's involvement, there will be an international outcry."

"Excuse me interrupting," says Bo, "but my understanding is that Spain took no part in the plot."

She answers straight back, "A lawyer could argue that, but even so the fact is we knew about it and did nothing to stop it as our treaty obligations oblige us so do; so we are guilty by association if nothing else. But it's worse, because not only did we do nothing to stop the act, by sending warships to the region under the pretext of sorting out the Mbagne/Gabon mess at the same time as all this, we could be said to be anticipating its successful outcome and just 'happen' to have rescue vessels nearby."

Honorita leans forward, "Then it's really absolutely essential that our plan to rescue Gustavo is successful."

"That is what concerns me, and my blunt assessment is that Señor Pett is not man enough for the job. Worse, if he himself gets captured he will, in my opinion, crack under torture immediately and tell them not only of this assignment but the reason behind it, and we will be in twice the mess we are now."

All three resume lunch, chewing on the cooling rabbit stew and considering what to say next. Eventually the coronel says "I have already told Capitán Rosca that she will go, overtly or covertly yet to be decided, to FP – if only that we have someone there on the ground. Señor Pett, I will make a decision about you in the next few days. Capitán Rosca will be in charge of your training. I want him to go through an intensive training course, a commando course. I don't care if it nearly kills him, I want him to be fit and dangerous, and only when he is fit I will decide if he goes."

"Yes, Coronel Molistán," says Honorita quietly.

"Yes, Madame, Madame Coronel," says Bo, with acute mixed feelings.

"And now, you two," says the coronel pushing her clean plate away, "let's go kill some partridges."

32
Dateline 25th

Bo is lying on his bed in the Duc d'Alba, towel around his waist. The body is tired from the commando training Spanish Legion-style, the hotel sauna and steam room and then a hot blast shower in his bathroom; the mind is drifting in and out of his twilight zone, awaiting the arrival of Colonel Harding from London. Bo looks at his clock, it is 9.30 p.m. and he drifts in and then drifts out, back in, back out of wakefulness, then he hears the sound of the four taps, and a familiar voice "Room service, 108."

Bo opens the doors, apologises for his state of undress and reappears from the bathroom enrobed. "Thank you for coming over, Colon...Y, something from the minibar, or room service?"

"Better make it the minibar 108. Any plonk in there? No problem coming over, it's good to get out in the field again, even if a quick flight to Madrid and a night at the airport hotel is all I can manage these days. How are you feeling anyway, must be knackered?"

Bo unscrews a half bottle of whatever-there-is, and pours it carefully into a plastic cup. "Cheers. Knackered? Not too bad actually. I'd be dead if I wasn't fit already. No, I think I'm as fit as they are, haven't got the stamina yet and won't have in a week, but can run faster than most of them, might come in useful. I'm learning basic man-to-man stuff, even that's quite like the judo I did at school. Guns take some getting used to, that's the hardest part."

"What do they use?"

"Star M30s, Spanish made, I suppose they are alright but I've got nothing to compare them with. Seems that's what they plan to smuggle into FP so the idea is to get used to it. Hard not to be frightened of the damned things though."

"Nothing wrong with Spanish firearms 108, it's the idiots who fire them. Good hand guns the Stars, especially the M30, light and true. Listen, I wanted to come myself as this whole business had suddenly escalated."

"Oh?"

"Yes. British Gas, God help us, have just signed a seventeen billion pound supply deal with TransExplo Oil, and now BP are joining the next Mammoth consortium bid for Field 27; they've just won 26 and seem to know whom to play cards with out there. These people have clout 108, and FP, or at least the Gulf of Guinea, is on the Cabinet agenda for two weeks time. Security and stability are the words our masters want to hear. Your assessment, backing up the CNI assessment, of the fallout from Cortez squealing under torture we believe is bang on the money. There's something else. A little bird has told us that the French are snooping around this whole mess, we don't know what they are up to yet but it won't be to our advantage, it never is. We need you to succeed, 108."

Y finishes off the cup of wine, goes to his briefcase and lays out two dossiers on Bo's table. "As we discussed some background on Capitán Rosca of the First Mountain Brigade, and here on Teniente Cortez, submarinero in the *Armada Española*." He picks up Honorita's file first. "I have had young Spriggs dig around in the NATO files in Brussels. So, Capitán Honorita Cervilla Rosca, born 15th September 1977, two years after Franco's Spain finished. Military family, father a full *Teniente General* in the *Grupo de Operaciones Especiales "Tercio del Ampurdan" IV*, no less. Grew up in Toledo, went to the *Escuela Militar Combinado* until baccalaureate age, then to *Collegio El Rodoño Oficial*, a sort of Spanish Sandhurst. Then on graduation in July 1999 she joined the First Mountain Brigade, and was then seconded almost immediately to the NATO Operation in Kosovo, KFOR in December '99. Left there with her current rank of Capitan in January 2003, special assignment to the CNI."

"Mmm," says Bo, "she's quite a high flyer."

"Yes. Then we come on to Teniente Gustavo Blanchera Cortez. Five years older, born 18th September 1973, inside the Franco period. Father a full Fleet Commander in the Armada. Same school as Rosca, the *Escuela Militar Combinado*, then officer graduation at the *Escuela Naval Militar* in July 1994. Joined as a submariner, deployed on S74 Tramontana. Worked his way up to

Teniente, I'd say he'd be a bit disappointed by that, a Teniente is only a Lieutenant, and after 5 years he too joined, volunteered to join, we know not why, KFOR. Also left there in early 2003 to join the CNI." Colonel Harding folds up the dossier and puts them back in his briefcase.

"A lot of co-incidences, aren't there?" says Bo.

"Struck me too. Both families from Franco era military background, top level too."

"And from Toledo. Both Virgos."

Colonel Harding thinks aloud, "Hadn't thought of that. Would have known each other for sure."

"Same school, up to 18, although five years apart."

"Would have met in the holidays too in all probability."

"Yes," says Bo "then she's seconded to NATO, sent to Kosovo."

"If I'm right and his naval career wasn't exactly taking off, he then volunteers for KFOR. Spanish contingent was small. They'd have known each other there for certain, spent a lot of time together."

"Then both go the CNI. Together there for nine months or so, till he's sent to South Africa to look into Jacobus du Randt's report."

They are silent for a while, and then Bo says, "She's been engaged for three years. Says it's the normal amount of time for the officer class."

More silence, then Colonel Harding muses, "Are you thinking what I'm thinking 108?"

"Can we check it?"

"I'll get Spriggs onto it. Presumably the upper classes announce their engagements in the papers like ours do. If they are engaged I'll text you. Code word 'United'. And if they are not…"

"Code word 'City'.

"Very droll 108. With that I'll bid you goodnight." And Colonel Harding slips out of the Duc d'Alba as anonymously as he slipped in.

33
Dateline 26th

Honorita looks across the aisle of the CASA CN235 military transport plane to Bo sitting opposite. In the dim light she cannot see if he looks overly keen on the jump ahead or not. Mind you, she wasn't the first time, but now after several dozen jumps she has nothing worse than a slight knot in her stomach. The plane lurches forward from its stand on the apron and taxis over to the end of runway. Bo's instructor sits with his feet out opposite facing her, filling in a form on a clipboard. It's been quite a day, and it's still only early afternoon.

Honorita had only just arrived in her office when the telephone rang. It was her mother. Instantly Honorita knew something was wrong; her mother hardly ever called the office. Her neighbour and close friend Señora Cortez had just called, very upset. She herself had just been phoned by someone called Kellen, a nasty sounding man from South Africa. Kellen had said that her son Gustavo had been in business with him, had lost his money, that Kellen had been waiting patiently for his release from Nigeria but now he had heard that he was going to spend the rest of his now short life in Fernando Po in which case he, Kellen, would not get his money back. He had paid to track down the Cortez family, he wanted his million dollars back and if the family didn't pay him back things will get very nasty, very quickly. He had called it exposure, to Honorita it sounded like blackmail. What was Señora Cortez going to do? Now a widow, she did not have a million dollars, nothing like, and neither could she have her family's honour besmirched. What, Honorita's mother had gasped, are we all going to do? Honorita had said she should ask Señora Cortez round to talk it through.

As she was putting the phone down Coronel Molistán had walked through their connecting door. Was everything OK, you look shocked? No, just family problems, to which the coronel replied she was many times a day pleased she did not have one to give her any problems. Then she said that they had just heard that Teniente Cortez's extradition date had been set, for the thirty first, in five days time. How was Señor Pett shaping up? Honorita did not know exactly right now, but had not heard that he was hopeless which she would have if he had been. There's a plan, Coronel Molistán had said, drawn up by the *Unidad de Operaciones Especiales* themselves. Honorita was impressed: the UOE were the Armada's special forces. The UOE would co-ordinate Cortez's rescue from Black Beach from the sea, but they needed two good agents on the ground to create the diversions. The coronel said that it was better that Señor Pett was killed than captured. If she played safe by sending one of her own agents, and if anything then went wrong, it would be a political disaster from which none of them would recover; which was why they had asked for a proxy from London in the first place. She walked around the room for a while considering her next move, then she told Honorita to go to the commando camp and carry out her own assessment and then report back. Then they would decide whether to risk the British agent and hope for the best, or "halve the odds yet double the risk" by using a proper one of their own.

When Honorita had arrived at the camp half an hour ago, she had searched out the training officer. The Englishman was fit, he can fight with his body, but he's not the army type, cannot use a bayonet with any conviction and is still frightened of guns, still closes his eyes every time he fires one. He is slow to obey orders, not out of disrespect but he seems to have his own timeframe. No sense of urgency, especially on the parade ground. Always polite, good moral fibre, officer class but not officer material, not for us. He was about to do his first parachute jump. Oh, could she join him? Of course, we'll get you kitted out. Kitted out she had jogged across the apron to where the CASA was waiting, props turning patiently. She had jumped in, Bo had looked surprised, then had smiled and waved above the unsilenced noise of the two turbo-props.

Now as the plane accelerates into its short take off she looks at him again. He is looking straight ahead; in the unlit interior of the transport she cannot see his expression. So, he was right, it seems, about Gus's little business venture. Foolish. It would explain a lot, a lot she had preferred to place in a box marked wishful thinking. She looks at Bo again, trying to see him in action in FP, creating diversions, running riots at Black Beach, working with the UOE, but could reach no conclusions; she is wary now of wishful thinking. The instructor puts his clipboard down and talks into a handset to the flight deck, and holds out three fingers and makes a thumbs up sign. They can feel the plane level off and the engines throttle back, the nose lifts as the plane slows. Very slowly the rear cargo door is being lowered and fresh light comes into the hold. She looks at Bo and can now see him more clearly. The noise inside is louder than ever and she holds her thumb up, then down, at him. He smiles in return and moves his own thumb up and down from his wrist, pats his stomach and points at her, thumbs up the thumbs down? She nods affirmatively. The instructor moves between them, clipping Bo's line on first, then Honorita's and then his own. The cargo deck is now fully open. The instructor presses a large button by his shoulder. They wait, and wait, Honorita now centres on her own jump. A green light comes on by the cargo door. The instructor waves his hand palm up at Bo and then into the open air beyond. Bo looks at Honorita, pulls a mock frightened face, then rushes out through the cargo door. It happens so quickly that she is caught by the speed of his jump and she in turn almost rushes out after him. She looks down to see him waving his arms and legs around like he's trying to fly, then the always reassuring shot of white nylon from the backpack and the full shape that follows. She pulls hers, and feels the sudden tug up as the 'chute takes hold of the air. She looks down and across to see him pulling the lines to try to steer the parachute, but these training 'chutes are only built for an unexciting and safe descent. He lands ahead and is already back on his feet to welcome her own landing. He offers her his hand and helps her up.

"How was that?" she asks, brushing the earth off her uniform.

"Cool," he replies, and running his fingers through his hair, "but once is probably enough."

And that moment she knows that Bo, in spite of himself, would be coming with her to Black Beach.

34
Dateline 27th

Bo takes his seat at the rectangular table. Next to it him is a tall well-built man in a blazer that he has not met before, and opposite him is the full presence of Coronel Molistán and an empty chair for the late Honorita. On the table is a projector pointing forward to a screen at the end of the small basement room. Honorita arrives, only two minutes late, says she's sorry she's late, photo-copier broken. As she is sitting down Bo's mobile phone makes an irregular tone, he apologises, looks at the text message and turns the phone off. The message said 'United'. Bo wanted not to, but could not help, looking at Honorita and smile knowingly. She nods back to him with her eyes.

"Let me introduce you," says Coronel Molistán doing just that. "Here is Capitán Honorita Rosca, of the First Mountain Brigade, now with the CNI, this is Capitán Fabian Romero of the *Infanteria de Marina's Tercio de Armada*, now a Platoon Captain in the *Unidad de Operaciones Especiales*, the famous UOE, and this is Señor Beaumont Pett of MI6 from London. Regrettably Señor Pett is not of a military background. Señor Pett has been leant to us to provide discreet third country support in FP. Capitán Rosca will be travelling under UN, so diplomatic, cover with the express intention of interviewing Teniente Cortez on his incarceration. We do not expect any local resistance to her request to see him on his first day there. The media and propaganda value is more important to the goons down there than any further confessions. They know they can wait a day or two for that. We know we cannot. Our embassy there is working with the UN office and what passes for the local government for this access. Señor Pett might like to know that the UOE is running this assignment. They have now returned from Iraq, with considerably more operational success that your British equivalent, the SBS. Is that not so Capitán Romero?"

Capitán Romero looks across to Bo and says courteously, "That is what has been said, Señor."

"Congratulations," says Bo, as neutrally as he can.

Coronel Molistán reaches forward to turn on the projector. "We have exactly four days before the extradition. Teniente Cortez is expected to arrive in Barbate around midday from Lagos on a chartered executive jet on the thirty first. That is the schedule, heaven knows when he will actually arrive. The UOE will take operational command to free him and deposit him on safe ground. Safe ground will be an Armada submarine offshore, by a twist of fate it will be Teniente Cortez's old vessel, *S74 Tramontana*." For the first time ever Bo sees the coronel smile; he's not quite sure why this should amuse her. "Over to you Capitán Romero."

Next to Bo, the platoon captain unravels from his seat, he seems to go on forever. Bo sees the Special Forces leader is a tower of a man, yet calm and polite, used to command and control. He takes off his blazer and folds it neatly with his giant hands. A map comes on the screen.

"This is the island of Fernando Po, discovered by the Portuguese explorer Fernão do Pó in 1472. Portugal gave it to us in 1778," and looking at Bo "and then from 1827 to 1843 it was British, then it was ours again and since 1980 it is theirs, the Fernando Poans.

"These are satellite pictures and we will zoom in, and *in*, and *in again*, and you can see that the main town, Barbate, and all the activities are in the northern point of the island. The airport is *here* on the north-west, then just to its north-east we have Black Beach *here*, and heading further east the main harbour in this area *here*, and then on the north-east corner the presidential palaces, military headquarters, the one or two embassies.

"The plan is based on simplicity, on the proven reality that if things can go wrong with special operations they will. Timing and surprise are everything. I will lead a platoon of twelve heavily armed commandos in two high speed rigid inflatable assault craft onto the beach, Black Beach *here*, coming blind side from the far north-western peninsula *here*. S74 Tramontana will be three miles offshore just to the west of this slide. To the west of the peninsula point there is no habitation, and once around the point we will be exposed to view for only seven minutes at twenty-five knots, but the moon does not rise until ten that night. We will strike early in the dark hours. Barbate is more or less on the equator, so dawn and dusk are both at 1800. From debriefs by previous prisoners the CNI have given us the prison layout and schedule. Lights are out at 1900 in theory, but it's unreliable but certainly out by 1930. Our calculated risk is that on the first night the guards will be celebrating their new arrival with beer or their local hooch or smoke, and most or all will be drunk or drugged from 2100. Lastly by striking early in the dark hours it will make hiding in this inland bush area *here* after the prison closes easier for Capitán Rosca, whose exit will be with us and Teniente Cortez by sea. Any questions so far?"

"Yes, Capitán Romero, what is the schedule for Señor Pett and myself?" asks Honorita. Bo sits up imperceptibly. Following Y's advise he has not told his CNI colleagues about the Manchester United cover, or his night candles, SIM card and torch.

"You will both arrive, separately of course on the 30th," replies Coronel Molistán. "Capitán Rosca will travel on a Mexican passport as Attaché Mercedes Pitón from the UN Office of the High Commissioner for Human Rights. The West African office of the OHCHR is based in Lagos, Nigeria. For very good reasons, no doubt. She will arrive on the regular morning UN charter flight from Lagos. The Fernando Poans are expecting her to be there in her official capacity and they will not dare to refuse access to Teniente Cortez on his arrival at Black Beach. She will stay at the Bahia Hotel, this is the normal stopping place for UN visitors. Our embassy, which represents Mexico, will provide a driver."

Capitán Romero, still standing, takes over the briefing. "On the Teniente's first night, which we predict will be the 31st, after the prison closes for visitors at dusk, say 1800, she will remain hidden in this area," he points again at the aerial map still on the screen, "and at exactly 2100 she will set off a series of explosions. She will be fully equipped with a Rocket Propelled Grenade Launcher and two dozen grenades. This will create a diversion which will make any guards still on duty turn their attention inland, leaving the beach clearer, we hope completely clear, for our landing which will be at exactly 2105. She will fire the first grenades to knock out the generator, fire all the remaining grenades and then move in and shoot to kill any guards she can, as will we on our landing, assault, rescue and exit."

"And my persuaders?" asks Honorita.

"You will have a standard issue NATO RPG, the Type-7. The grennys are HEAT anti-tank. You'll have two Star M30 hand guns. You will be familiar with these I presume?" Honorita concurs. "You will arrive with them in your baggage, simple as that."

"And if it's searched?" asks Honorita.

"It won't be. Unfortunate misuse of UN privileges on our part, but it happens all the time," says Coronel Molistán. "And now for you Señor Pett. Your passport is in the name of Pitt?"

"Yes," says Bo, "Ernest Jasper Pitt."

"Pett, Pitt, why so close?" asks the coronel.

"Pure co-incidence. Makes it confusing."

"Mmm," says the coronel dismissively. "Your cover is a firework salesman, working for this Spanish company, Pyrotecsa," she shows the table some letter headed paper, "and we'll have our business cards ready in time."

"But I don't speak Spanish well enough," says Bo, "not well enough to represent this firework company, and all the officials there are fluent. And I will have a British passport."

The coronel looks cross. "Very well. Invent the name of a British company, and we will use that."

Bo thinks for a few seconds and then says "Big Bad Bang Firework Company."

Honorita and Capitán Romero smile, the coronel writes it down impassively, and Bo thinks he has no intention of using any such cover.

"And the address?"

"Guy Fawkes Lane, Rocket-on-Sea."

"Phone number?"

"0511 1605."

"Very well," says the coronel finishing writing down the details. "It will be done. Now, your luggage will include samples of fireworks, but of course they will not be what they seem." She walks over to the chair behind her and brings back a box which she unpacks. "This Catherine Wheel comes apart like this and is a catapult. The bangers are in fact high explosive small scale grenades," she unscrews the top from one and places it in the catapult. "You will also stay at the Bahia Hotel, for two reasons. First it will give you an innocent opportunity to liaise with Capitán Rosca room to room – 'yes please,' thinks Bo – should you need to, and secondly you will see the location," she points at the aerial photograph on the screen, "is near the presidential area and main military barracks. From the roof, with the catapult, you can create major confusion."

"At exactly 2100," says Capitán Romero, "you will engage from the roof. You will have sixty disguised small explosives, like your thunder flashes. Every twenty seconds for twenty minutes you will release an explosion on different sides of the roof."

"Then you go to bed. Simple as that. Your Iberia flight back to Madrid is on the first. Any questions?" asks Coronel Molistán.

"None, it all seems very straight forward," replies Bo, "I've always wanted to be a pyrotechnic, a hooligan with a catapult and a salesman, now I can be all three."

Honorita laughs, the UOE captain smiles, Coronel Molistán scowls, "Do try to act your age, Señor Pett."

Bo wonders where he has heard that before recently, the memory comes back to the briefing at Vauxhall Cross, the warning about Spanish gadgets and Miss ffinch saying 'do try to act your age, 108'. He says nothing about his obvious concerns: taking high explosives on the aeroplane, the certain dramas at FP Customs, the puniness of the catapult, the reliability of the mini-grenades, the accessibility to the roof, the twenty minutes exposure. He gives thanks and praise to Y and Miss ffinch for the Manchester United cover, the night candles, SIM cards and torch, and the warning about Spanish gadgets.

"Sorry, Coronel Molistán, it's the schoolboy in me. I will be fine on the night." He receives another look of contempt from the coronel, a discreet smile from Honorita, and a raised eyebrow from the Special Forces captain. "Really," he says to them all as reassuringly as he can.

"Very well," says the coronel. "One last and most important instruction. Your actions are interdependent. If any part of it is failing we call off the mission. We analyse your situation and we regroup. We do not go ahead if any of you are in trouble. Is that understood?"

"Yes, Coronel," agree Capitán Romero, Honorita and Bo in unison.

35
Dateline 27th

"Mama!"

"Honoritita!"

Mother and daughter kiss more formally than mothers and daughters in Spain usually do, and Honorita greets Señora Cortez even more formally. The atmosphere is tense, both elder women had been crying. They have known each other since Honorita was three days old, they were still planning to be mother-in-law and daughter–in-law, and her fiancée was her mother's godchild, yet there is no obvious sign of warmth or familiarity between the three of them.

Honorita looks around the ranch house in the military compound outside Toledo where she grew up. Nothing had changed, she smiles at the interior, like meeting an old acquaintance again. She sits on the upright chair her father used to use and asks both of them, "So tell me, what happened?"

Señora Cortez is distressed even before she starts to tell the story. "It was just a phone call, Honorita. Of course I answered it, the voice said Señora Cortez?, I said yes, who is that? And he replied 'my name is Kellen, you don't know me...yet'. He had a horrible vulgar, rough voice, threatening. He said Gustavo had gone into a business deal with him a year or so ago, had borrowed a million American dollars, yes a million dollars, and had said that he would repay it in three months but it would be two million and they would split it, and then Gustavo had been arrested and Kellen was waiting for his release and then he said that once 'your clever little boy is in Fernando Po he won't last long'. What does it mean, won't last long?" Now her head was in her hands, then she took in a deep breath and sat up again, "he said he had investigated Gustavo's background and he knew all about us, who we are. But how does he know?"

"It's not that difficult," says Honorita, "if he has a date of birth, maybe they may have a contract, any lead is enough, you hire a private detective, he knows someone in the *Oficina Data Civil*, then you can find the parents, then the family background. This is a high profile case, everyone knows Gustavo is in prison in Nigeria, but not many people know the full story. Except Kellen." And Bo, she thinks to herself. "And now he wants his money back?"

"If we don't repay him he will expose Gustavo, and his family," Señora Cortez pleads.

It was all starting to make sense for Honorita, unfortunate sense. In their time together in Kosovo, when they had fallen in love, Gus would talk for hours about his plans for life after the Armada; a life that could not come too soon for him. Gus and a military career were not a long-term relationship, they both knew that he just wasn't very good at it. When he left he wanted to go into property, he knew people, had heard of more people, who had made fortunes in the Costa del Sol property boom. He knew how to do it, he would be out of the army, his family debt of life paid, they would be rich, she could leave the army too if she wanted to. She didn't but went long with it, she liked to hear his plans, plans which included her. But now it seems, without any doubt, that he could not wait, that the get rich quick temptations of the Fernando Po affair, which had involved a worldly wise financier who knew how to distance himself, had also sucked in Gustavo who didn't.

"And what about the engagement?" her mother asked. Señora Cortez looked up too. "You have waited all this time he has been in Nigeria, we all thought he would be released and back at sea within a year from now, the grand marriage could go ahead, but what now?"

"I don't know what now, Mama, Señora Cortez. It seems the least important item we have to deal with, there's the extradition and now the blackmail to fight, my engagement can wait."

But Honorita knows to herself that she has been thinking about it often. She loves, loved, loves, she's not sure, Gustavo. He was her first love, her only love. Looking around this house, so many childhood memories. She a daughter, an only child, a substitute boy, a tomboy, a strict upbringing in the home, frequent beatings and constant scoldings, then a military boarding school where discipline was constant too, bullying, sport, cadet life, Officers' College. Gus had chosen to come to Kosovo to be with her, had been the first man she had met who was in the military yet had a life, and had dreams, beyond it. He made her feel feminine for the first time, she had made love for the first time. She had kept herself for him, had been pleased to do so, but for the last two weeks had known in her heart that he would never be released unless her rescue mission was successful. And then there was Bo. He made her laugh, feel happy again, he loves her, she thinks he loves her, and now she's not so sure about the certainty and uncertainties of Gus.

"Honorita!," her mother scolds, "You are day dreaming."

"Yes, Mama, sorry. I am leaving Spain on a mission next week, I shall be away for some days."

"Where are you going, with whom?" her mother asks.

"Oh just some military mission to Mexico. On my own. Then she walks over to Señora Cortez and kneels down in front of her. "Listen to me, Señora Cortez. You must not pay Kellen, it will certainly only lead to more demands. Next time he calls ask him to leave a number so that Gustavo's fiancée can contact him, say this fiancée is in change of all his business dealings, she has told you she will pay the debt. If he asks to contact me refuse. It is I who must contact him. He is greedy, and sounds arrogant, you will bluff him." Then she thinks that when she knows who he is and where he is she will arrange to have him killed, that would be the best solution for everyone. Then she thinks about Bo at the briefing yesterday, and chuckles quietly to herself.

36
Dateline 28th

"Welcome, welcome to our second home, Commandante Michaux."

"Oh, please, let's say Claude-Michel, and I believe the admiral is Hernán."

"I am. Good, and welcome to Dawn Avenue, Constantia. Second time in Africa in a week, hardly worth going home?"

"Well you know how it is. At least it's much easier flying to Capetown than Barbate."

"Of course. Come on in, this is my wife Giselle," and Giselle and Michaux shake hands, "and keep walking through, we are having the BBQ in the west garden." They walk through a succession of African Modern rooms. Michaux stops to ask about two of the paintings in the main living room, Giselle explains that she collects *vauge afrique,* shows him a sculpture in the same vein and they emerge into a paved area by a swimming pool surrounded by rhododendron bushes in full bloom. A gardener appears surprisingly out of the shrubbery. A maid appears with two very cold Castle beers and a glass of Chablis.

"This is very pleasant," says Claude-Michel approvingly, sweeping his hand around expansively.

"I like the outdoor life here above all. In Barbate we have an inside pool and inside BBQ. You may have noticed that it is too humid to be outside in the day and the night belongs to the mosquitoes and other flying friends; a small volcanic island in a big sea on the equator is bound to have the worst climate in the world, so we live indoors, just like in Québec they cope with their climate underground."

Giselle, remembering an inside chore, excuses herself. "If I may say, I am surprised that Giselle is not African," offers Claude-Michel.

"Oh, she is, as she will be the first to insist. You meant black

African. She is from the white tribe of Africa, English liberal clan. Durban is her family home. We met in Québec. Now we both have dual nationality."

"Useful."

"Indeed."

They sit and chat the evening away, Giselle rejoins them, commuting to and from the BBQ; how wonderful life looks from Dawn Avenue; the famous and infamous neighbours; the Eboleh family's love affair with the area; the impossibility of life without an executive jet; the price of oil; climate change, if any; the French *départements* in Africa; the north African invasion of France; the changes in South Africa; BBQ culture in South Africa; the schooling of Giselle and Hernán's baby; the name of Giselle and Hernán's baby; Claude-Michel's retirement plans; France's place in the world; the American hegemony; the Canadian view of the American hegemony; the Québec Libre movement; Madame Laforge. Giselle announces it is time for her to leave the boys alone; they stand to see her off.

After a while Claude-Michel says, "By your message from Madame Laforge, I gather the chances of extradition prevention are not too bright."

"No. Especially if you are Cortez's testicles."

"What do you mean?"

"Uncle Bolivar plans to eat them."

"My God, but how?

"I don't know, he just puts them in his mouth and chews I suppose."

"No, no, how does he prepare them?"

"Oh, I see, I imagine he just boils them, or has them boiled. I did not see him prepare them last time."

"Last time?"

"Yes, a coup plotter called Mingunni, some time last year. It's an old Esangui tribal custom, eat your enemies balls and you add their *doonti* to yours."

They both look into the distance. Michaux puffs out his cheeks. Eboleh stands, claps him on the back, waves the cook away from the BBQ and says, "come on Claude-Michel, lets pick at the remains. I can guarantee you there are no testicles, especially human testicles, on my BBQ."

They chat about cannibalism, ancestor worship, tribal customs, the afterlife before Michaux says, "You remember when we were saying good bye in Barbate, what you said?"

"Not exactly, what do you mean?"

"We were talking about Cortez. Silencing Cortez. You said a better idea was 'I kill the bastard once he's here. After the celebration, but before the questions.' Or words to that effect"

"Well it's the most obvious solution."

"And the offer still holds good?"

"It wasn't an offer, Claude-Michel. Just an idea. We had not discussed a price."

"Shall we now?"

"That's why we're here. Apart from your good company."

"Quite so. The last price you mentioned concerned wiretaps on three mobile phones. We can pay this."

"I'm sure you can. But the wiretaps were for something less than killing a certain embarrassment, and one in human form. I think a price increase is not unreasonable."

"Such as?"

"There is another wiretap as you put it. Plus some banking information. Two of the people with the mobile phones have bank accounts at the Bank of Central African States. I want to see their statements monthly and details of the incoming and outgoing transactions over $500,000."

"But that may be a little bit more difficult."

"It may be, but it is in the heart of Francophone, so not impossible."

"Yes, alright. I think so."

"And two more small requests. The president's eldest son Augusto has an apartment in Paris. I presume you already have it bugged. I would like to see those transcripts."

"And?"

"And?"

"You said there were two more items on your shopping list."

"Yes. The ones agreed, the mobile phone and bug transcripts, the bank account details, these are for agreeing to kill Cortez. The last item is deliverable after I have succeeded."

"And that is?"

"At some time in the future, probably within a year, I want you to agree to lend me twelve members of the *Commandement des Operations Speciales*. For no more than, say, ten days maximum. Undercover, under my command. They will be killing too. We can have no contract of course, only a handshake."

"Alright. You kill Cortez, you have the commandos, undercover, under command, for ten days. But it can only be a handshake, as you say."

"In that case let's do it the old Canadian way." Eboleh spits into his right palm, rubs his hand clean on his thigh, and holds out his hand. Rather uncertainly Michaux does the same. They look each other in the eye. They shake hands.

"The old Canadian way."

"The old Canadian way."

PART THREE

37
Dateline 30th, early morning

Bo feels the nose up and hears the power down; outside the early sun dips back behind the jungle tree line as the 747 touches down. Inside he is optimistic, impatient, nervous and excited. He had asked for his Business Class seat to be by the port window for the view of Black Beach on the usual southerly approach, but the prison was so close to the end of the runway that he had only a few seconds glimpse of it. It looked reassuringly like his briefings said it would, but with even less activity. Maybe it was too early. He looks out of the window at the jungle to the east; he can almost touch the humidity even this early. The Boeing almost stops, turns back on itself and now he can see a ramshackle old terminal with some rig supply helicopters, some coming and going, some waiting to, a few Twin Otters, a couple of other STOL jungle planes he does not recognise. The plane keeps moving and now he sees a strikingly modern steel and glass bungalow of a terminal with the words *Welcome to Eboleh International Airport* in large chrome letters along the top.

As the plane stops Bo gathers up his shoulder bag, feels relieved and guilty but not surprised about Miss ffinch's candles not exploding under his seat, has a final look at his Manchester United paperwork, tells himself there's no need, he knows his cover backwards, has another look anyway, puts the papers back, closes his case and tells himself to relax. The four engines whine down, the auxiliary kicks in, the doors open and the First and Business Class passengers board the bus at the steps. Bo notices, without comment, that all the First Class passengers are African and all the Business Class passengers are European, well American mostly. The short walk down to the coach is sticky and close, the aircon in the coach turned down African low.

Inside the terminal all the plane's front end passengers are given a laminated card with a number. Bo looks around at the other passengers. Most are regulars and know the form. They take their card and sit in one of the sumptuous leather armchairs. Bo follows suite. The regular regulars take out a light sweater or jacket against the cold. Most take out something to read as though preparing for a long wait. Bo takes out a copy of the soccer magazine Four-Four-Two. Outside he can see the economy passengers standing and sweltering in line.

"Seventeen!" "Seventeen!!" Bo looks up, sees everyone is looking around, checks his card and jumps up. He approaches the immigration desk. "Passport." Bo hands his passport to the shorter of the two agents. With a practised shake the agent turns it upside and the taller agent scoops up the $100 that falls out. Bo had been nervous about this ruse, in spite of CNI assurances, and is pleased he hasn't unwittingly upped the ante. "Reason for visit?"

"Football scout. I am looking for young talent. For Manchester United." Bo opens his shoulder bag and produces the headed letter. They do not look at it.

"David Beckham," says the shorter one, with a smile to the taller one, and then they both smile to Bo for the first time. "Gillette. *Ingles* shaving. Vodafone. "

"I am looking for new David Beckhams in your country."

"Many David Beckhams in FP." The taller one makes a swerving motion with his hand. "Bending. Ball. Goal!" They both laugh heartedly.

The shorter one takes Bo's passport and the Manchester United letter and photocopies them, hands them back and says "Barcelona *major*, Barca better." Bo tenses, he has a feeling that David Beckham now plays for Barcelona but he isn't sure, so he says "yes, Barca better", thanks them and leaves. He feels a hand on his shoulder as he passes the desk. Now the shorter one is glowering.

"Manchester United rich club." It is a statement, not a question. "FP poor country."

"Ah, I thought my visa fee was in the passport."

"That was entry fee. Must also pay staying fee. Same as entry."

The CNI had told him to keep loose mixed dollar bills in different pockets, and now he reaches into his left trouser pocket, the hundred dollar pocket, and lays one on the counter. Without looking up the taller one waves him along and shouts, "Eighteen!"

Bo walks on, looks ahead and sees two heavily unformed, and not lightly armed, men waving him to them. The sign above them says *Customs and Duties. Welcome to Fernando Po. Especially to Barbate.* He walks over, sees the open bags of his fellow passengers on well-ordered tables. He hauls his bag up and opens it obligingly. They look through carefully, taking out the top layer. As expected they find the flat $100 bill laid on top and with a magician's move the younger one scoops it into his palm and it passes to the older one. The latter asks, "What you do?" Bo tells them. "Wayne Rooney, ha. Big." Bo agrees, wanting to be polite but also minimal and on his way. The case is almost empty when they pick up the torch, examine it, are influenced by its shabby appearance, and just as Mss ffinch had predicted set it aside as worthless.

"What these?"

"Candles. Night candles. In case of power cuts." The older one puffs himself up, "no power cuts in FP."

"Not for FP," says Bo, "I am going to other countries afterwards."

"Then you must pay import and export tax," says the younger one quickly.

"Two hundred US," says the older one. Bo reaches back into the loose supply in his left pocket, feels two notes, folds them into his right palm, and shakes the older one's hand as the money passes between them.

"OK, go," says the younger one but as Bo repacks his bag the older officer takes a candle from the box and puts it in his pocket.

"No power cuts in FP," says Bo hopefully. "Please." He holds out his hand in a gesture. The younger one waves him along without looking at him, and Bo sees the older one already waving his next victim up to the inspection tables.

Bo wheels his bag out of the terminal and is immediately hit by a density of moist closeness, cloying heat and jostling taxi drivers. He is pushed to the taxi closest to the pavement, parked with one wheel on the kerb, the boot already open. He had been warned about this too and Bo throws the bag into the rear seat, climbs in after it and gives a little reassuring tug to his shoulder bag across his chest. Still there. Without asking the taxi lurches off. The aircon is noisy and struggling, the taxi smells of sweat and old plastic. Bo looks around. It's hard to tell what it is, or was; Bo's best bet is a ten-year-old Nissan or Toyota. Moments later they are at the airport entrance and a roadblock. The driver hands over a dollar note, Bo wonders how much it is, reckons on a 10, 20 or 50. The window winds up, there is no mirror so the driver looks over and asks *"Donde vas, gringo?"*

"Hotel Bahia, *por favor.*"

They drive towards town. The road is dual carriaged, as empty of cars as full of litter. Either side of the road are dirt tracks, barefoot children and scrambling chickens. Bo sees older villagers scavenging, loitering or just sitting in the early shade. In the listlessness the taxi driver converses only with his horn. After just ten minutes they arrive under a new and gaudy arch with Barbate in gold paint, already faded matt by the tropics, laid into it. Bo wants to open the window to catch some cooler air, then remembers the air con. They drive straight through the first red lights, then stop at some green ones as a large oil transporter drives through his reds. The streets are more crowded now, less lethargic. He sees his first white man. He sees another in a Stetson. Without warning the taxi lurches right, rides rough over three speed bumps and is in front of the hotel. The CNI had said it should be a flat $20 from the airport. Bo fishes out a twenty from his right back pocket. The taxi driver turns round and glares. "Cinquenta." Bo pulls out another $20, and lets it fall on the front seat. Without waiting he opens the boor and hauls himself and his bags out. The taxi drives off angrily, and the doorman tries to take his bag. Bo hangs on to it, and darts into the hotel lobby. The air is cold again, unnaturally cold, but mercifully dry. The lobby is almost empty but light; anodyne muzac is the only sound

"Yes," says the receptionist, bored already so early in the day, without looking at him. Bo sees an unsmiling young African woman in the bright red hotel uniform. She is very black; her lips are sticked very red; Bo wonders if it's a colour coded policy or coincidence, the matching red. He looks around the lobby, sees the usual collection of international detritus attracted to anywhere as unattractive as Barbate, notices two African men in American casual clothes watching him. One is chewing gum. Bo nods back in return, gives them a smile; they both wrap their eyes in sunglasses.

"Pitt. Ernest Jasper Pitt. I have a reservation."

She gives a print out a quick scan. "No reservation here."

Bo opens the shoulder bag and hands over a fax. "Here's my confirmation," he tries a smile, unreturned.

She glances at it. "This is not a confirmation from us. It's from you. The hotel is full." She looks away.

"I have heard that sometimes there's a cancellation, and if I pay their cancellation fee…" says Bo leaning forward, talking quietly.

"I could look," she says moving back opposite him.

Bo feels in his $100 left front pocket. He slides over a note and says, "It would be most helpful."

She puts the note in her jacket pocket, turns to look at the rack full of keys behind her, takes one at what to Bo looks like random, turns back to Bo and says "Here, room," she looks a the key, "836." Bo thanks her, she looks blankly and with some degree of loathing, back in his blonde direction. He takes the elevator to the eighth floor. The hotel is new. The lift obliges, mysteriously silent. The room is clean, spacious and very cold. It has a fine uninterrupted view, which becomes less fine on examining the shanty contents in the distance. Offshore he can see a rig throwing an untreated flame into the heat haze. Bo finds the safe in the wardrobe, works out the procedure, locks the candles and torch inside, re-checks the procedure, takes a shower, changes into a white shirt and blue shorts, takes the elevator back down to the lobby, notices the gum chewer nudge his mate, and heads out of the hotel for a first look around the streets of Barbate.

Bo has memorised the layout of the small town from the briefings in Madrid; anyway the fifteen storey hotel is its most distinguished landmark. Outside he puts on a baseball cap and sunglasses and tries to blend in as an anonymous white man. He turns left and left again towards the presidential area. There are more white men than the briefing photographs suggested. He is the thinnest and youngest. They all readily return his nod.

As he crosses the *Calle Tres Septiembre* he turns to see the two Africans from the hotel following him. He turns right, and at the end of the block left onto *Calle Principal* and sees the *Palacio Eboleh* at the end of it, four hundred metres away. He walks on, ambling naturally, nonchalantly. The humidity has already made his clothes damp and his skin stick and sweat. Two hundred metres before the Palace the streets become emptier. By the time he has scouted to within one hundred metres from the entrance he is the only person walking. He sees three palace guards stop doing whatever it is they are not doing, stand up and look up at him. Bo turns left and left again. He should be on *Calle Monrovia*; he is. On *Calle Monrovia* there should be the Baton Rouge Bar and Diner; there it is. Bo pushes on the door; closed. He cups his face in his hands and presses up to the window; inside is Louisiana, sweet home Louisiana. He sees it opens at midday, half an hour away. The air is no longer plain humid, but wet, hot and wet.

He walks away, completing the other side of a square and now can see the Hotel Bahia. He quickens his step towards the promised cool inside. On his way up the steps he sees his two followers reflected in the mirrored glass. Now they are both wearing sunglasses and walkie talkies. They are quickening their pace too. The doorman is sheltering in a shadow. A sign above the door says 'Make Yourself At Home In Welcoming Barbate'

38
Dateline 30th, midday

Capitán Rosca feels the nose up and hears the power down and opens her eyes just as the tyres smoke up outside her window. She has been trying to doze, unsuccessfully, for most of the journey and is annoyed with herself for having fallen asleep for the last five minutes and missed the view of Black Beach on the approach. But she can forgive herself. Nigeria would test the patience of a nun. Even the UN flight had a local thug as a seat blocker, and the $100 to shift him had been snatched from her hand as some kind of right. The half empty hotel in Lagos had been overbooked, West African style, that was another $100, and the taxi to the airport held up at gunpoint, a further $300, she was sure by a relative of the taxi driver who had been on his mobile phone as soon as they left the hotel. The policeman, or whatever that was in policeman's uniform, had demanded "dash" to park near the Executive Terminal, used by the UN, and the option of a further $100 or a long walk with bags in the heat and humidity. Considering what she had in her luggage, she forced a smile and paid. As they took off she vowed that she would never, ever, in any circumstances, even if her mother's life depended on it, ever return to the filthy, rotten, corruptocracy-cum-shithole known as Nigeria. She had given it one last shudder as Lagos disappeared into the smog below.

She is now awake enough to feel nerves in her stomach. She doesn't like to feel nerves in her stomach. She thinks back to the last time she saw Gustavo. They were in Madrid, at Barajas airport. He was about to fly to Johannesburg. They hugged goodbye. It would be four months till they were to meet again. It had been nearly two years. They had made love that last night, he had brought her breakfast in bed. She never ate breakfast, he said it was to get her used to South Africa where they only ate breakfast and barbecues. He would look older now. She is prepared for him to be broken; she likes to think she would never be broken. She thinks of Bo, if he is in the hotel, if he will be strong enough, if he will get out alive, if she will get out alive. Of course she will, she and Gustavo both. Bo too. She slips out her Mexican passport. She now feels back in military mode, she is wholeheartedly Attaché Mercedes Pitón from the UN Office of the High Commissioner for Human Rights. The West African office of the OHCHR is based in Lagos, Nigeria. She is here for three days to interview, and to ensure the welfare of, Teniente Cortez, a Spanish citizen. She is to instruct the local UN office and the Spanish Embassy to insist on weekly visits, to bring him food and the guards' bribes. Simple as that. She thinks of Capitán Romero, and his rendezvous with the *S74 Tramontana*, and wonders with which US navy carrier he is working right now. She looks at her watch; 12.30 p.m.

The white United Nations Dash-7 turboprop stops at the far end of the apron, and all 26 officials bow their heads through the cabin and stretch back straight down the steps. A clag of hot and wet air envelops them as they head for the terminal. Some run to enter the buildings as quickly as possible; some walk slowly so as not to sweat one more bead than they have to. Honorita Rosca runs; she likes the exercise after the cramped flight. Inside the terminal there are no controls in the walkway marked "UN and NGOs"; no immigration, no customs, no bribes, no scowls. She is thinking that she likes FP already; at least it's not Lagos.

"Snra. Pitón" the sign says clearly enough, and she walks up briskly hand outstretched, "I am she," she says. She is welcomed by the young driver from the Spanish Embassy. His name is Antonio Sobrano, he is surprised the plane is on time, happy she has had a pleasant journey, is sympathetic about Nigeria, had just been in FP three weeks himself, no – from Valencia, didn't think it was too bad here, is pleased how quickly the bags had arrived, wonders if hers is so heavy because it is full of bricks or books? She wonders how much he knows, knows he cannot know anything, and replies "Books and bricks". They load up the white Mercedes E200. The two big bags of launcher and RPGs take up most of the boot and she throws her smaller bag and shoulder bag onto the rear seat. They set off for the Hotel Bahia. At the perimeter is a roadblock. The sentry sees the CD plates and waves them through.

She asks if it is always this easy, he replies that it seems to be, they only hassle each other most of the time.

Outside the hotel, a man appears from nowhere with an umbrella while another approaches the boot. She tells him to leave the bags there, and tells Antonio we'll deal with them later. She takes his cell phone number and gives him hers. She will need collecting tomorrow, she's not sure when, she'll call him, and taking her to Black Beach. He says he'll be here.

At the reception desk she sees an unsmiling young African woman in the bright red hotel uniform. The Capitán notices her bright red lips and that they exactly match her uniform. The receptionist picks up a list and asks "UN?" Honorita confirms and is handed a key and gestured upstairs. A quick scope of the lobby reveals the sort of white riff-raff and black spooks she expected to find in an oil town with no bottom.

She unpacks and walks along the corridor to find a maid. She gives her $20. She wants to know in which room is Mr. Pitt. She offers to write down the name, the girl refuses, she cannot read. Pitt? Yes, Pitt. She point to her room, number 417. The maid disappears. Three minutes later there's a knock on the door. The maid holds up eight fingers, then three fingers then six fingers. Honorita gives her another $20, puts her finger to her lips, they smile as each other and the maid leaves. Honorita reaches into her small bag, takes out two of her four Star M30s and ammo and puts them in her shoulder bag. She leaves the room and walks up the five flights. More exercise. She approaches 836, slows down to make sure no one else is around and knocks on the door. Bo opens it, and gestures her inside. She reaches into her bag and pulls out the guns and clips. She hands them to him, gives him an involuntary playful smile, takes his hand from her shoulder, turns and leaves. Skipping back down the stairs, she is pleased with the mission so far, but cross with herself for that playful smile. She is here for the mission, and for Gustavo.

39
Dateline 30th, evening

Hernán Eboleh feels the nose up and hears the power down as he pulls back the wheel on the Gulfstream V. He senses he is a little too high, and the plane sinks more than it should and lands on the runaway with a heavy jolt. He spends a while annoyed with himself. He loves flying, especially the Gulfstream, best jet he's ever flown, and likes to think he's a natural pilot.. In the left seat the South African captain says "well done, sir, we're down," and runs through the taxiing checklist as Hernán applies the brakes, turns through 180 degrees and taxies back to the Executive Terminal. He turns round to look through the open cockpit door. The setting sun shines an orange beam through the port windows. Giselle is lit up, aglow, and waves, and Mike Tuffy, shielding his eyes from the rays, gives him a big nod and thumbs up. Ahead, just over the tree line, he can see the pylons above Black Beach and he thinks about his mad cousin Julio and the Spanish spy he is going to shoot. Right there.

One day he has promised himself a proper pilot's license, in fact at home he has brochures from any number of US flying schools, but they all need time, time he just does not have. An admiral's life is busy and there are much bigger fish to fry, a whole country to fry. In the meantime this way works out well for him. He hires the Gulfstream V and two pilots from Regal Aviation in Capetown. He swaps places with the co-pilot for take off and landing, does the fun bits and leaves the boring bit in the middle to the co-pilot instead. He watches a DVD or chats to Mike or Giselle. He does not drink, strict with himself about that. He always insists on the same pilot, Captain Mijs van den Hoojt, and has got to know him well, even had him up to the house in Constantia from time to time. Mijs used to be in the South African Air Force, then flew as a mercenary with Wickus Paulsie's air force and now flies exec jets for Regal. They shoot the breeze over a

BBQ; Mijs is the air force, Mike the army and Hernán the navy. Old times, new times, Hernán enjoys those evenings as much as any other in Capetown. Mijs has given Hernán private lessons in a Cessna 172; Giselle feels safe with Mijs as captain, even when her husband joins him on the flight deck. Mike Tuffy couldn't care less about feelings or safety. Hernán likes that about him. Mike doesn't know it yet, but one day his boss has big plans for him and a bodyguard corps of Brits in the new FP.

The plane stops, the engines die as the aircon auxiliary starts up. The co-pilot opens the door, lets down the stairs and leads them all out to the minibus. Mijs always complains about the climate in Barbate. Outside, even as the sun goes down, the humidity soaks them, and the aircon is either not enough, as in the minibus, or African freezing, as in the terminal. All five of them are staying with the Ebolehs tonight. They walk straight through – as usual there are no controls in the Executive Terminal. Hernán leads the way, followed by Giselle, Mike and the pilots. Two porters bring the bags. Hernán sweeps through the glass door and looks for the driver. No driver.

"Where is that fool?" Hernán asks nobody in particular.

"He's normally reliable," says Gisele in the direction of Mike and Mijs.

Mike holds up his mobile phone, "No reply from him."

Hernán darkens. "This better be good. Come on, let's take a couple of taxis." Outside it is almost dark but the heat from the floodlights adds to the clamminess. Half a dozen taxi drivers rush towards them. Hernán shouts at them in Fang. The first two open their cars; the others help with the doors and luggage. They set off in convoy and then slow down for the roadblock. The soldiers look inside, the sergeant recognises the admiral and waves them through. They stop the second car. Hernán orders his driver to stop, opens his door and shouts an order to the roadblock. The sergeant salutes and waves them along too.

Hernán and Giselle settle back on the rear seat. Hernán looks at the driver in the mirror. He looks like he is from the Kirange tribe, possibly from the Nomone district. Hernán likes to think he's good at ethnicity. He looks out at the spreading edge of Barbate, shanties. He's going to bulldoze them all, built proper townships like they have on Capetown. One day he might even be elected, they'd be so grateful. His daydream stops, he looks back and sees the driver smile and wink at Giselle in the mirror. He reaches into Giselle's bag and snatches out her Schnauzer .36 Saturday night special.

"You fucking heap of Kirange shit!" he is shouting at the driver in Fang and now pressing the barrel against his neck. "Stop the car!"

"I'm sorry boss, wha…"

Herman has his arm round the driver's neck. "Do you know who I am?'

"Boss, I…"

"Obviously not you fucking cockroach!" the car has skidded to a stop across the road. Hernán kicks open his door, and with the gun in his right hand opens the driver's door with his left. "Get out!"

A few people from the shanty are gathering around. Behind them the other car stops. Mike is already out and running towards them and now throws himself at the driver. They scramble in a cloud of dust on the ground. Moments later Mike stands up with the driver's head below his left boot. The driver is holding his stomach and wincing. The small crowd is becoming larger. Hernán points his gun at the driver's head. He walks up closer so his gun is only six feet from the driver's head. The driver is whimpering, begging. Hernán puts his gun down, and nods at Mike. Without a word Mike kicks him in the back of the head and jumps into the driver's seat, flicks it into gear and both taxis speed off again. Giselle asks her husband if he is aright. He says he is. She asks Mike if he is all right. Her husband replies that he is.

They pull up outside the Casa Fortuna, Hernán and Giselle's home. In the drive they see the Escalade parked at an angle. It doesn't look right. Hernán throws open his door and prowls round to the front of the car. The right front end has been smashed, smashed badly as if against a tree or post. The right passengers glass is broken. There is some dried blood on the passenger's side floor. Mike and Giselle, and now the pilots join him. He says to Mike, "find this bastard, Mike" and to the others "come on, let's go in and party."

40
Dateline 31st, 09.00am

Gustavo Cortez feels the nose up and hears the power down as the old Air Nigeria 737 touches down with a perfect landing. There are only seven of them on board. The two pilots, three Nigerian guards, the Nigerian minister, and himself. And now his stomach ache joins them, and for the first time in nearly two weeks the old familiar pain in the gut makes him bend double. From his place in the jump seat he can see the pilots occupied at the controls, and how he wishes for their life now. Purposeful, intelligent, and out of here within the hour. He wonders if he will ever get out of here. The Nigerian guards are still asleep, sprawled across the business class seats, still wasted from their in-flight session. The minister has been preening himself for the last half hour, and is now brushing his shoulders. One of the guards stirs and wakes the others. Another one looks over to Gustavo and with a finger makes a slicing action across his throat, and the others laugh.

He thinks back to the send-off in Lagos; dawn, an empty airfield except for some photographers and TV cameramen. He had expected something of a full state occasion, brass band, dignitaries on podia, important speeches. Gustavo was aware of the photographers and aware that the pictures they were taking now would be spread all over the world. His 24 hours in the sun. He had tried to show dignity, to hide his inner dread. Physically he wasn't feeling too bad after the fattening up in hospital. As he clambered up the aircraft steps he did not know whether or not he should turn and give them a final wave; he hardly felt he was leaving in shame. He decided to walk straight in, uprightly and decorously.

The pilots, Australians or New Zealanders – he couldn't really tell, had given their safety briefing and flight schedule as though this was a regular flight. They had been airborne for less than five minutes before the minister made a retching sound and Gustavo smelled sick on the floor behind him. He looked around and saw the minister emerge from his knees, almost pale, and rush off to the toilet. Gustavo almost pointed out that the Seat Belt signs were still on, out of habit from normal flights, but thought better of it. As soon as he was gone one of the guards had produced a joint from his top pocket and lit up. The others took their share. One of them went to offer it to Gustavo, but withdrew it teasingly before Gustavo had a chance to refuse. Another guard took a hip flask out of his back pocket, and they passed that around too. The minister returned, and they made some sort of effort to hide the flask; they could do nothing about the acrid smell of burning bush. The minister pretended not to notice, or did not care. After an hour the guard who had produced the joint dug into his rucksack and brought out a bottle of Johnny Walker Black Label. They were swilling straight from the bottle and becoming aggressive. Gustavo walked up to the flight deck, tapped on the open door, and invited himself to sit in the jump seat. They cleared him some space. He settled down, and after a while commented that there did not seem to be much radio chatter. The co-pilot answered that he cannot understand them when they do reply, but it's OK because there's hardly any traffic up here anyway. The pilot says South Africa is OK, but even that's going down the toilet, the rest of it you can forget. Gustavo sensed someone behind him. Then he saw the minister leaning over him and tapping the captain on the shoulder. The minister pointed to Gustavo and indicating that he wanted to sit there. The captain told him to fuck off back to his seat. Gustavo asked if that is not dangerous, talking to a minister like that. The captain replied no, on the ground he can tell me to fuck off, but up here I tell him to fuck off. Africa. The co-pilot asked if they should close the cabin door. The piloted replied no, they had better keep an eye on the little monkeys. Gustavo warmed to them and their banter, though back to Big-K and that he would approve. Big-K. Kirikiri. If only.

Now, landed, Gustavo sits up and sees the door opening. Dense hot moist air fills the cabin in moments. From the top of the stairs he sees readiness of ceremony. Three new white Toyota pick-up trucks are waiting, as are some men in suits or uniforms under umbrellas. To one side a military band is playing a tune from a Hollywood musical. *Those were the days*. Gustavo wonders if there is any significance. He walks downs the steps. The minister is following him, the guards and pilots watching from the plane. An officer directs him onto some makeshift steps leading on to the back of the middle pick-up. The steps collapse as Gustavo puts his weight on them. He pretends politely that nothing has happened. The minister jumps up behind him, then one of the men in suits joins them. He introduces himself as Alfredo Eboleh, the Minister of Justice. The Nigerian minister from the flight introduces himself too, but Gustavo does not catch the name. He notices a digital display on the shiny new terminal: it is 0915; it is the 31st; there are 32 degrees Celsius, there is 89% Humidity. Minister Eboleh waves the convoy to go forward. The pick-up in front of them stalls, then tries again, lurches forward and is then moving ahead but erratically.

They drive around the back of the terminal and Gustavo is surprised to see an even larger convoy waiting for him at the front of the terminal. From the shade half a dozen motorcycle outriders make a formation in front. Just behind him a new Mercedes van with a half a dozen enormous speakers on the roof starts playing music at a blaring volume, the sound so distorted as to be unrecognisable. They drive out through the perimeter and onto the road into Barbate. Now someone is speaking into the speakers, but it is still impossible to hear anything distinguishable above the noise and distortion. All along the road crowds gather. They wave at him, smiling. He wonders if they think he is an astronaut, or cargo cult divinity, if they have any idea of who he is or why he is here. He waves back, sheepishly at first, then with greater conviction. The crowd become even more emboldened and soon all three, Gustavo and the two Ministers of Justice, are waving all around them. They are soon in the middle of Barbate, and in a square with a sign *Plaza Conchita Eboleh* in front of a Palace the convoy stops as abruptly it has started. Gustavo is aware of TV crews now too. The local Minister of Justice next to him is handed a microphone, and begins to speak into it. It doesn't work. Someone jumps up and flicks a switch. It works. Gustavo cannot distinguish what he is saying, but there is no mistaking the cheering. He hands the mike to the Nigerian minister. Gustavo cannot understand what he is saying either. Looking around, amongst the swamp of black faces he notices a young blond white man watching him intently from the steps of the old church thirty or so metres away. The blond man waves discreetly. Gustavo nods back, slowly as to remember his face; he does not know why. Then he has the mike in his hands, everyone is looking at him, and he is being gestured to speak. He says how happy he is to be here, he has always wanted to visit FP. It feels foolish as he says it but he cannot think of what else to say. He hears more clapping and cheering, and feels a friendly pat on the back from one of the Ministers of Justice. All around is the activity of due ceremony, African spontaneous due ceremony. Not far away he hears an explosion, it seems to come from high in the office block to his right; no one else seems to notice. He looks around for the young blond man on the steps. He is staring up towards the office block too. Now he is leaving; no one else seems to be leaving.

41
Dateline 31st, 11.00am

In the old square, *Plaza Conchita Eboleh*, watching Cortez in the back of the pick up, Bo had been reminded of the scenes of the tumbrels in *The Tales of Two Cities*, had had the impression that the cheering crowds had meant that Barbate was a tropical eighteenth century Paris, full of heaving masses, drunk on raki and emotion, unpredictable and horrific, but once out of the square there were no masses at all; it was as if the few people that are in Barbate had all congregated together to give the impression of many. He had left when he heard the explosion; it seemed to come from a first floor office open window, he wasn't sure why he had left then, but he had done enough, caught a good look at Gustavo, as much as Honorita's lover as his mission target, and had confirmed the candle drop locations he would use later in the square. And he needed another shower, more fresh clothes. The streets back to the hotel were empty, hot, tired and midday sleepy, the hotel entrance unattended, even his followers must have gone to see the Cortez show, the lobby deserted.

Back in the room Bo flicks on the TV. In spite of the *Channel Guide and Video Choice* card on top of the television there are only two channels, both local. Bo wonders what the Texan oilmen watch. Channel One has the news in Spanish, Channel two a local programme, possibly a soap opera, in what Bo presumes to be Fang. He switches back to the news. The 12.00 o'clock news is just starting. His English Spanish is struggling to keep up with the African Spanish, but the pictures tell the whole story. They are reporting the morning's events: Cortez arriving at the airport, Cortez in the back of the pick up, Cortez with a local suit, now identified as Alfredo Eboleh, first cousin of the beloved president Bolivar Eboleh, then another suit, sounds like the corresponding Minister of Justice from Nigeria, Bo couldn't catch his name, then Gustavo's cortège leaving the airport, then Cortez waving to the crowds on the road into town, Gustavo, Bo observes, now looking confused rather than concerned, and now Cortez in the *Plaza Conchita Eboleh*. Bo moves closer to the TV, recognising the shots, all near where he was standing. He sees himself in the picture, recognisable only to himself by his Bahia Hotel baseball cap, otherwise anonymous enough. He sees and hears some speeches, the happy crowds, the happy ministers, a not unhappy Gustavo, a speech from him about the pleasantness of FP, and then Bo hears, unmistakeably, the sound of a small explosion. He heard it then and he hears it now. He can see Cortez heard it too, cocked his head up to the building to his right, then went back to smiling and waving. Bo does not see himself leaving. He gets up from off the end of the bed, kicks his sweat-damp clothes off and jumps in the shower. He stops mid-wash. The candle! Maybe the explosion was the missing candle. Bo had thought at the time it was a strange place for an explosion, up there in the offices, and now sees that an accidental explosion makes more sense. He speeds up the shower, then quickly rinses off and, still wet, heads for the safe. Time to get to work.

He takes the twenty-three remaining night candles out of their two packets and lays them out on the bed. Although only five centimetres high they will fill both his cotton jacket pockets and camera bag. He is aware that he will be the only person wearing a jacket. He puts six in each pocket and the rest in his camera bag. He dresses. He pulls the chair up near the window and looks out, running through the plan again. The square; the TV station and museum; the barracks, especially the barracks; the Tourist Office; the Ministry of Immigration and Permits building; the bus station. In that order. Twenty minutes. Back here before siesta is over. He pauses, runs through his route again from the beginning, pre-tracing his city tour, just as he had planned and researched it so often in Madrid. He goes back to unlock the safe, sees the guns and taser and slips one gun and the torch into the camera bag.

He leaves the room, skips down the fire stairs and out into the street. The now familiar route left and left again, straight on for two blocks to the old square. He walks up to the first statue and waits for another foreigner or straight looking local. A Texan appears. Would he mind taking Bo's photo, against that statue would be fine? Of course not buddy. Bo walks backwards against the statue and quietly slips a candle behind its feet on the plinth. Another one? No that's fine, thanks. Bo doesn't want two candles together, one setting off the other. He walks over to another statue and repeats the procedure. There are two more statues; Bo will make these the last two drops, on the way back to the hotel.

He leaves *Plaza Conchita Eboleh*, heading north on *Calle Once Noviembre* towards the TV station and further along the *Museo Nacional de la Descubrimiento*. On each he enters the building, asks for someone fictitious and while being told he is lost, plants an appropriate candle. On his way out of the TV station he sees an old foot rest, he bends down the re-tie his laces and plants another. At the junction at the north end of the road, where it meets the *Avenida Cristóbal Colón*, he sees two large skips and tosses a candle into each as he walks past, not in the plan but two less to worry about. Ahead of him now lie the barracks, his main target, the *Cuarteles de Generalissimo Francisco Franco*. The main entrance, fully guarded by Moroccans, is half way along and dominates the *Avenida Cristóbal Colón*. He turns right along the unguarded sleepy westerly side street, *Calle Mandrosa*, and drops a candle on each of the four filthy window ledges. He turns left onto *Calle de Maceo* and repeats the process, chucks his empty jacket into another skip, and repeats it once more by turning left onto *Calle San Sebastian de Torres*.

Clear of the barracks he turns right again to the top of *Avenida Cristóbal Colón*, then left into the *Avenida de la Independencia*; he is now heading back towards the hotel. On his right is the National Tourist Office. He wanders in, asks for a map, is given one grumpily and wanders out and studies it in the shade of the portico outside. Another candle is dropped in between the arches outside. Opposite, just next to the *Palacio de la Familia Nguru Eboleh*, he sees the Ministry of Immigration and Permits. He enters to enquire about opening hours, leaves a candle held under the desk with chewed gum and two more outside on the back of each column as he studies the map. He reaches into his camera bag and feels five more candles. He heads south to the *Plaza de la Revolución* and the bus station and leaves two in dark corners under benches while he takes a rest and one on the ledge behind the ticket office grating.

Back in the *Plaza Conchita Eboleh* he finds another two oilmen to photograph him against the other two statues. All the candles have been placed. Bo walks back to the Bahia.

"Hey, you, stop!" Bo looks around. He sees a smartly dressed young African in open neck check shirt and pressed trousers. "What you doing?"

Bo opens his arms in English body language. "I'm sorry, what do you mean what am I doing?"

"I've been watching you in the Plaza here. I have seen what you are doing."

"Well, that's fine, and who are you?"

"You cannot photo in the Plaza."

"Oh really, I'm sorry, why not?"

He is up close to Bo now. Bo is relieved to smell beer on his breath. "Open your bag."

"OK," says Bo, "but let's get in the shade." The man nods him over to a fully shaded side street, and now takes Bo's elbow as if to frog march him. Bo resists the temptation to shake him off, not wanting to attract any attention. Once in the alley, Bo pushes him away and flips open the top of the camera bag, whisks out the gun and points it at the man. The man recoils; Bo signals him to turn around against the wall. As he turns Bo pistol whips him and frisks him even as he is falling. He finds only several dozen dollar notes in his pockets, doesn't look to see what they are, and stuffs them in his pocket and leaves. It's all over in seconds; as Bo thought, the man's a hustler, not a spook. Bo puts the gun back and takes out the torch. He holds it against the nape of the man's neck and turn on the taser. "Next time I'll kill you," he hisses, not wholly convincingly, but the man has gone limp and Bo worries that he has killed him. Time to leg it. Back in the hotel he takes another shower and puts the gun and taser back in the safe. There are no candles undeployed in Barbate. He thinks back to Miss ffinch and smiles, wishes she and Colonel Harding could see his good work. He hopes the hustler is alright, more or less.

42
Dateline 31st, 12.15pm

"Are you all right there sweetie, you seem a little tense, something on your mind is it?" asks Giselle as Hernán prepares to leave for lunch.

"Yeah, I'm fine, I'll be back soon. Come on, Mike, let's go and see what it's all about. We'll have to take the Corvette." In fact Hernán had been feeling more than tense ever since the phone call at breakfast, just as he was saying goodbye to Mijs and the co-pilot. It had been one of Uncle Bolivar's nephews; his so called Chief of Staff, Ernesto Eboleh, a weasel sneak of a man whom Hernán, and all other family members, distrusted. Would Hernán report to the Palacio for an interview with the President at 1.00 p.m.? Hernán could not say 'no', that much was clear. But why? Why did his uncle want to see him? On a Sunday? Without his family? Should he be in naval uniform, smart in a silk lounge suit, or BBQ casual? Ernesto said it didn't matter, a sure sign that it did. How much did he know? Had the French betrayed him? Possible, but they would have to have bought Cortez in some way and clearly hadn't. But how? Didn't make sense. Had his calls been intercepted? Possible, but unlikely, he was too careful. Had the South Africans bugged Constantia? Even if they had he had never plotted indoors. Had he? No, and why would they ditch him? Everyone wanted Bolivar out, his own family, well the second circle of his own family, and all of Africa, all the world pretty much.

"Use the East entrance Mike", he said as they approached the Palacio.

"You expecting trouble, sir?" asked Mike.

"You know what I'm like about the unusual, Mike, Stay close to me."

At the gate the car is stopped; unusual. They are asked for papers; again unusual. Hernán speaks French to the older

Moroccan who then waves him through. The Moroccans! Maybe the French have blabbed to the Moroccans who blabbed to Bolivar? Unlikely, but something is wrong, or as worrying for Hernán, unusual. Inside the Palacio entrance are four more Moroccan guards. They stop Mike from going through; Hernán nods him to wait there, but he knows he himself has to go through. Inside the vast reception hall his footsteps echo across the marble floor and stone walls, even up to the vaults. The room is empty, cold, and gold. The walls were bare of paintings, or decoration, but covered entirely in gold. In each corner stood an identical abstract sculpture in silver; their main purpose to impress in quantity what they lacked in quality. An elaborate setting of plastic flowers are in a silver font in the centre of the hall, with a fountain spurting over them. Hernán shudders at the Texas Vulgar style, a superiority he had readily embraced in his time in Canada. No time for that now, though. He walks towards the door on the far side of the hall and once close enough can hear the sound of voices, many voices inside the east parlour room. He opens the door and inside sees all the members of the immediate family. On a chair in front of the window, his hands tied behind his back is Gustavo Cortez. On the wall a large flat screen is showing the news, re-running the procession from the airport and the celebrations in the square. Cortez is looking at the screen; he is also looking very frightened. Hernán feels a massive swell of relief sweep through him. His uncle is laughing in the centre of the family circle, and now notices Hernán enter.

"Admiral! Welcome, welcome! It's a happy day today!"

"Yes, uncle President. But so much security here today."

"We cannot be too careful now we have our prize. The colonialists want to snatch him from us we can be sure. Here he is," the president says pointing to Cortez, who now looks over, helplessly, towards them.

The president walks him over to the prisoner. The others follow. With a tone of mock respect, when the room is silent, the president says "You tried to kill me, you tried to ruin everyone in this room. Everyone. Their families too. But it is you who will be ruined, my friend, not your wealth, not your status, not your mission as God's trustee, none of these valuable purposes in life.

No. When I say you will be ruined I mean you will be ruined. Your body, ruined. Your mind, ruined. You have a week before you commit suicide. Most unfortunate, an accident in Black Beach, isn't that so, Julio?" For the first time Hernán notices his mad cousin Julio, now turning a leering crease across his face. "But first, a confession. Tomorrow morning I will personally oversee your confession. Your last week can be one of pleasantness, even boredom, or continuous agonising pain. Julio here wants to skin you strip by strip, but I am sure that will not be necessary."

"Why wait, father?" his son Manuel asks, "why don't we flail him here, now, it will be more fun."

"You young people only think of fun. I am the President, I have to think about our friends and enemies outside. That is why the Moroccans are busier today. No, events will come to their internationally approved conclusion. A suicide in prison, not unknown.

"And this time next week you will all be invited back here. For my special celebration. Do you know what that is Señor Cortez?"

Cortez shakes his head slowly.

"Your balls, I need to eat your balls. Want to eat your balls. Your *doonti* will be my *doonti*. In the old days they would do that while the assassin was still alive, but we are more civilised now. But for you, the clocks of civilisation will be reversed."

The room falls silent. Hernán knows he must make his move tonight. He looks at Julio. His old friend Julio. His mad cousin Julio. The idiot governor Julio. He'll leave Mike behind. Tonight.

43
Dateline 31st, 1,00pm

"Good afternoon, Antonio."

"Good afternoon, Señora, you have to give that door a little pull, there. A new Mercedes too. I trust you have recovered?"

"Yes, I'm fine thank you. We are going to the Black Beach prison, you know the way?"

"Of course, it's famous around here, it's only a few minutes away right by the airport, then down a long track. Not the sort of place I ever want to visit."

"Quite a busy morning in Barbate."

"This man Gustavo Cortez, yes. We watched it on television from the Embassy, Senora. He is a Spanish citizen. And were where you?"

"I was in the *Plaza Conchita Eboleh* along with everyone else. That's whom I'm here to see, Gustavo Cortez, at Black Beach."

"Yes, I presumed as much. I'm just the office junior and part time driver, but it's not every day a top UN official arrives, not from the High Commission of Human Rights. So what will happen to him, to Gustavo Cortez? I know he's one of ours, Spanish, probably makes it worse."

"I can only set up the visiting rights, try to keep him in the public eye, get the correct NGOs involved. But I wouldn't like to be in his shoes that's for sure. What's that?"

"That's a white-headed vulture, there's three more over there. Frequent visitors to these parts. That would have been a dog. This is a good road for them."

"Dogs?"

"No, senora, vultures. This is the only decent road in FP, and you've seen the speed they drive along here. The dogs live in the villages either side of the road, and the way they drive they never slow down. I've even seen one swerve to hit a dog on purpose. Like kicking a football. Ah, here we are, we turn right here."

Honorita looks ahead and sees a track off the road to the right. Antonio slows right down and the Mercedes bumps its way along the dirt, dust billowing up behind it even at this slow speed. She can now see the pylons above the prison. They crest a small hill, but when they have the view in front of them again she sits straight upright and gasps. There is no cover. She looks around at the burnt shrub, recently burnt too, which is why the satellite photos seen in Madrid still showed the thick shrub land. They drive slowly on, now only four hundred metres from the prison gates. They view is uninterrupted, and they pass the exact spot where she was to have hidden with the RPGs and guns, now not a hiding place at all. Plan B. What plan B? She is thinking fast. She will have to involve Antonio, use the car as an attack vehicle. She can tell him the minimum. What if he panics? Acts like a civil servant; he is a civil servant. Better get it out in the open now.

"Antonio?"

"Señora."

"Slow down for a while. Look, things are not what they seem. I was planning to ask you to drop me and the luggage off just back there on our way back to Barbate this afternoon, and to tell you it was just some UN surveillance station and I'd make my own way back later."

"OK."

"Not OK. In the boot, the bags. They are not surveillance."

"No?"

"No, they are rocket propelled grenades, a launcher and a couple of STARs, which I was, am planning to fire into the compound later in the darkness."

"Oh."

"But there's no cover, you can see all around us, there must have been a bush fire. Are you and the car available later tonight?"

"No, Señora, there is a dinner dance at the Norwegian Embassy. I have to drive the Ambassador and his wife, and attend myself."

The car stops outside the prison gates. "Maybe if you ask him..." Antonio suggests

"I can't do that. I shouldn't even be talking like this to you, but I need you and the car later if there's no cover to hide in here."

"Will I get into trouble for doing this?"

"Only if we are caught. Which we won't be. You need to drive in just like we did now. Stop just over the crest. Just back there. There'll be no moonlight. No car lights. Drop me and the RPGs off and drive away."

"RPGs?"

"Rocket propel…"

"Grenades, yes, sorry. But why, why are you firing these rockets?"

"You don't need to know that. A minute later all hell will break loose, but you'll be on the airport road back to Barbate by then. We need to think about the Ambassador though, what to tell him. But how about you, Antonio, are you ready for this, well, irregularity?"

Antonio swallows hard and grips the wheel. "I am worried we'll be caught. Black Beach is famous, I don't want to be in there. But I want to help."

"I cannot guarantee to keep you out of there of course, but I can guarantee that if, when, we are successful your career will benefit directly. That I can promise you. The main beneficiary of this is not Cortez, but Spain herself."

"But how, how…?"

"Too many questions, Antonio. Are you with me?"

"Yes, Señora, I am with you."

"Good boy. Now I must go and see this famous Gustavo Cortez."

The blazing heat and stickiness hits Honorita as soon as she is out of the car. She approaches the guard at the main gate. "Here are my papers, I have come to see Gustavo Cortez."

The guard looks back at her listlessly, distractedly. She thinks he must be drunk or drugged. "He's not here."

"What do you mean 'not here'? He left the Plaza two hours ago."

"Don't know. Not here."

She looks in her file. "Then I'll see Governor Julio Eboleh."

The sentry wipes his nose on his sleeve, "Not here. Maybe they together. Don't know."

"Well can I wait in the Governor's office, it's too hot out here?"

"No, can't come here. Maybe this them," he nods behind her to a trail of dust. She turns and sees a small convoy of cars approaching. They pull up in fogs of dust, and as it clears she can see Cortez standing in the back of a pick up truck, the same one as was on in the Plaza, his face red from the sun, his clothes dusty and damp. He is looking down at the floor. The door of the limousine at the front of the convoy opens, and the guard shouts over something in Fang, nodding towards her. A chubby African in a tight fitting shirt, floppy belly and wearing a leering grin comes over to her.

"Illustrious Madam, we are expecting you. Always pleased to see the United Nations, you are very welcome in my humble prison. I am Grand Governor Julio Eboleh," he says taking her by the arm and leading her towards the gate. Then he turns around and orders "Bring him in. I'm sure that Señora United Nations wants to see that Señor Terroristo is in perfect health in our five star hotel." A few seconds later, for no apparent reason, he starts laughing convulsively to himself.

They enter the cool and shade of the office. A prisoner in rags is on the floor, handcuffed to a side table. Julio kicks him sharply on a leg, laughs and pulls back a chair for her, and orders her some water, and a beer for himself. Moments later, Cortez is pushed through the door. She looks up to see him, her fiancée, for the first time in nearly two years. He looks thinner and waner, but worse he looks frightened and despaired. He is a ghost of the man she knew for all these years. She knows she has to get him out of here. He doesn't recognise her, is not expecting to see her. Then he does, sees her and recognises her at the same time, and seeing her tries to give no clue about recognising her. She can see he is thinking fast too. She stands up and says, "Señor Gustavo Cortez, I am Attaché Mercedes Pitón from the UN Office of the High Commissioner for Human Rights. I have just arrived from our offices in Lagos. I am here to ensure your well being. Is that not so, Governor Eboleh?"

Julio ignores them both, looks up and laughs again. "*Grand* Governor Eboleh, Attaché. Well being. Being well. Well done. Done well. Everyone here is done well, well done," and he sets himself off cackling again.

She says to Gustavo, "I have a message from your family in Madrid. They would like to see you again soon. All nine of them, will be thinking of you tonight. Please think about them too, that way you can help each other in these difficult times. The first night is always the hardest, think well of all nine of them tonight."

Julio now stands up. "I must show our privileged guest, Señor Terroristo, around the hotel. You will wait here Señora United Nations. It is no place for ladies. You will be safe in here. Out there, savages. Animals, some of them. But we will be back soon, wait here, make yourself at home." He chucks some magazines in front of her. Porn magazine mostly, hard porn, blonde porn, and some on hunting and some gun magazines too.

44
Dateline 31st, 2.00pm

"So, my friend Señor Terroristo, welcome to our five star hotel, no I make a mistake, it is not a five star hotel. It is six star." Julio stops in the passage just outside his office, looks over to Gustavo with mock seriousness and then bursts into laughter, doubling up and coughing with the effort. The two guards join in as obliged. Gustavo manages a smile. But he is only thinking about Honorita and her message about the family. 'I have a message from your family in Madrid' He has no family in Madrid, she must mean the CNI, and why else would she be here, and under UN cover? 'They would like to see you again soon. All nine of them, thinking of you tonight.' Nine of them tonight? Nine *combatientes*? Why nine? Sounds like too few or too many. Nine, nine, nine o'clock. Must mean nine o'clock. 'Please think about them too, that way you can help each other.' Can only mean be ready at nine tonight. 'The first night is the hardest.' Yes, nine tonight. Then he thinks back to the blond man on the steps, the one giving him a small acknowledgment. Who was he? Must be part of it all. Julio pulls himself upright from his laughter and slaps Gustavo on the back. "Come on, let me show you to your room, your double de luxe room. Double de luxe! Ha ha ha!"

Out of the passage and air-conditioning they pass through a door; a door straight into Gustavo's idea, anybody's idea, of hell. Without being able to see, his eyes not having yet adjusted to the almost total darkness, he is hit by the air, the foul smell of acute decay, of open sanitation, of rot and despair. His ears are next to tune in; the occasional clank of irons on floor reminds him of Kirikiri, but this is far worse. There are not even any moans, or sounds of any life from the cells. Now the air is full of the sounds of Julio. "Honoured guests!" he is shouting, his voice echoing around the walls. "We have a new arrival, a terrorist. A man who would terrorise a god, a living god. A relative of mine. Yes, guests, friends, I am a relative of God. But you know that already, ha-ha. Who has room in their bedroom for the terrorist?" There is even less noise than before, in fact none at all. Gustavo senses all the prisoners have ceased all signs of life, as if to have him share their cell will bring even greater hardship on them all. Julio is shouting again, "come on, come on, someone must have a spare bed?" Gustavo's eyes are used to the dark now and he can see inside the cells, just make out figures slumped across the bare floor. The stench is all around him and inside him. "If I have to find some space there'll be party games!" Julio is now yelling, the yells bouncing right back off the ceiling. Gustavo can hear a few manacles moving across the concrete, and now one or two groans. "Very well, cell six." One of the guards pushes him up to the cell. There is no door, just floor to ceiling bars, and no wall, just more full-length bars on either side. There is a space of three metres by two metres, and six filthy bodies lying across it and on parts of each other. "See, there's plenty of room in there," Julio is telling them, then looking through to the cell next door says "I did not hear you say you had spare beds in your room. You have, but you tried to cheat our new guest. Guards, party games in cell seven tonight. The sound of breaking bones. Snip snap. Snip snap, ha ha ha!" Gustavo looks through at the bodies on the floor, too desperate to care any more about what else could happen to them.

"Come with me Señor Terroristo," says Julio. "I hope you like your new bedroom. You will find your fellow guests most entertaining. Full of conversation. You can see how much fun we all have here. But sometimes we need to ask our guests some questions, even in the best of hotels." He is laughing aloud again, and rubbing and patting his flabby and wobbling stomach. They follow him out of the door at the far end of the passage. The relief of the heat and humidity is enormous after the rankness of the cellblock. Soon they are through another door, and into a cooler and well-lit room. As the door closes Gustavo sees a man hanging upside down from a rafter behind it. Blood is finding its way down his legs towards his stomach. He is naked and breathing heavily. On a table next to him is an old farm trough full of what looks and smells to Gustavo like sick and urine. "Everything alright, Mr. Chimwainie? Quite comfortable?" Julio walks over towards him, he instinctively tries to wriggle away. Julio kneels down so that his head is next to Chimwainei's and Gustavo sees the two African faces, one upside down and agitated the other the right way up and leering. "You see Señor Terroristo, when our visitors have gone and we have the place to ourselves again we can play party games in here." He picks up two electric wires from the floor. "Zzzzzz, crackle, zzzzz, they go, don't they Mr. Chimwainie? Like to have our little screams, don't we Mr. Chimwainie? Still won't tell your favourite Uncle Julio all our little secrets, will we? I'm sure Señor Terroristo here is more sensible," he leers then puts the two wires together. He gives himself a shock, jumps backs and yelps, dropping the leads. He takes a wild kick at Chimwainie's head in return; it catches the prisoner on the temple. "More fun later, we need to make the room free for our new guest, so lots of talkies tonight if you please, Mr. Chimwainie." he says with mock courtesy.

They walk back through the cellblock at a brisk pace. As they pass Gustavo's cell Julio shouts "getting ready for the party?" and starts laughing again. Soon they are in the office. Gustavo sees Honorita standing by the window looking out as they walk in. "Please everyone be seated," says Julio. "More water, Señora Pitón? Señor Gustavo? Good, two bottles, and a beer for me," he orders. "I have shown Señor Cortez around, and everything is to your approval I trust. We would not like the UN to be concerned about any of our guests."

Gustavo looks at Honorita. He hopes his sense of desperation is reaching her. "Yes, everything in this hotel is wonderful. I hope all nine of my family members will be envying me here."

"Yes, all nine will be in their own time," Honorita replies. "Everything is a question of time. I am sure their prayers will start this very night. In the meantime you must know that the full force of the United Nations is behind you. Señor Eboleh, I must say that this so-called hotel of yours does not enjoy they most salubrious reputation with foreign governments or NGOs. Fernando Po has signed up to the relevant UN treaties on prisoner treatment and respect. We expect that they will be honoured."

"Have no doubt, Señora. Now you will see we will start by asking the prisoner doctor to examine Señor Cortez. This is for his protection and ours. We do not want any infections or diseases coming from outside to our sanitary conditions inside. You and I will stay here and discuss life's conditions while the doctor examines Señor Cortez's condition." He is laughing again, being his most genial. He stands up, opens the door and shows Gustavo out, then tells a guard, "Frederico, a nephew of mine", to take him to the prison doctor for "thoroughly thorough examination." He laughs once more, and Gustavo sees him go back into the room with Honorita and hears the door lock click shut behind him.

45
Dateline 31st, 3.00pm

Bo is, he has to admit, unexpectedly bored. In all the preparations in London and Madrid the one factor he had not built in was boredom. He was bored with push-ups, had nothing to read, the TV was junk and time passed minute by minute. Outside, all the candles had been planted. Well planted too. Honorita had arrived. Cortez had arrived. Capitán Romero and his men would be offshore, maybe kicking their heels like him. Six hours to kill. He wonders if they are above water or below. Honorita should be at Black Beach right now, or maybe she has just left. He tries to picture her in the thick shrub land just behind the prison, setting up her side of the assault. He sees her crawling in the heat, on her stomach or all fours, keeping her head down, burying or covering the RPGs for later. Then the long wait. She had never complained, not even jokingly like an English agent would have done, but she had been given the tough part of the assignment. But they were not equal, he had to remember that. She is the professional, a highly trained covert agent; he is the amateur with whom they are doing their best, reluctantly doing with him at all. Anyhow, aside from that, the fact is that here he is, resting restlessly in five star air-conditioned hotel while she was out in the bush surrounded by a small arsenal and waist high scrub protected only by nature's overgrowth. Snakes, scorpions. Later there would be insects. Insects could be the good news out there. Still, there was nothing he could do about it, that was the plan. "They also serve who only stand and wait," he says aloud to himself, aware that at that very moment far from standing he is lying, lying naked on the double bed. But he is waiting. He looks again at the time on his phone, only five minutes since the last check, 1510 now, 1505 then.

When he first sees his photograph on the TV, a muted flicker in the corner of the room, it does not register for at least half a second. Then he sits sharp upright, feels a lump in his chest, then a weight in his stomach. He slowly eases himself off the bed and for some reason he wonders why even as he is doing it, wraps himself in the hotel robe before reaching for the remote. By the time he zaps off the mute his picture has gone. Now a voice in that heavily accented Spanish is saying "....citizens are requested to be vigilant and report any sightings to the police. He entered the country yesterday from Madrid. The officer who was injured spoke of his good luck. He lit the candle in his office while the terrorist Cortez was being paraded in the Plaza below, then went to take some water before it exploded. He remembers the suspect well from his arrival at the airport, he is working for Manchester United, the English football club. The police are now searching the capital." Then the image changes. Now a new face is talking. Under this new one is the caption, Francesco Eboleh, Director National Security. "This is clearly another coup attempt. The guard around the President and his family has been doubled. On the very day we have one foreigner behind bars another one emerges. Be not alarmed! These events are not connected. Compatriots! Be vigilant!. We will capture this plotter too and he will join his fellow cockroaches in Black Beach!" Now Bo sees his photograph again. It is the one on his visa, photocopied at the airport, blurred by enlarging. But clearly him. He leaves the TV on as the channel switches subjects to a visit by another Eboleh family member to Angola to discuss something or other.

Bo sweeps through the bedroom throwing his clothes on, grabbing the mobile phones, swapping the SIM card from the shoe, putting the shoe back together again, wondering why he had not done all this before, telling himself to hurry, telling himself to slow down, whirling through the safe, collecting the guns, the taser torch, his money and passport. He stops. Tells himself to breath deeply. Maybe the best place to stay is here, right here in this room. No! He put Bahia Hotel on his entry card, and where else would they look for a foreigner anyway? And there's a TV in the lobby. For sure that surly cow would have seen it even though she hardly looked at him. He is sure he has been reported by now anyway. The taxi driver, the doorman, the hustler if he's still alive. Murder, they'll do me for murder too. Maybe not. Now ready to leave he has a final check, breathes again against his heartbeats, and opens the room door and waits. Collects his thoughts. He has the phones. Nothing else matters but the phones. Those candles have to explode. He pats a trouser pocket to recheck. He has one phone in there. He looks again in the camera bag, sees the other phone, the guns, and the taser. He hears a clamour from the landing, from the lifts area around the corner and the sounds of shouting. He shuts his door quietly and sprints to the fire exit door. He makes sure it closes quietly too. Crouching low, he raises himself just high enough to peer through the bottom of the glass. Half a dozen uniformed police are banging on his door. He has seen enough. He sprints down the stairs three at a time, counting the floors, then loosing count on the way. Tells himself it doesn't matter.

Suddenly the stairwell is dark, he is now below ground level. He has trouble seeing. He slows down, feeling his way now by the banister. It is cool down here, and quiet and dark. He pauses, carefully opens the fire door onto an underground car park. He can hide here till dark. He looks at the camera bag phone; no signal down here, but he can let the candles off from the ground floor. Anywhere. But it's dark down here too; so dark that Bo can hardly see. He looks around, there are just some plain light bulbs giving off what little light there is. He walks up a ramp. He is becoming concerned now, there should be light from the street outside. There is no light from the street outside. There is no way out except through a drive-through security door. He walks up to the base of the ramp and looks at and feels his way around the keypad. A number. What number? He has no idea what number. He can hide near the door and run out when the gate is raised. That will do, that will get him out of here. Then a further thought: there are hardly any cars in here. What if none leave before nine tonight? He squats and waits behind a pillar. He's safe for now. Then he hears a dog, now dogs, bark from the floor above.

46
Dateline 31st, 3.30pm

Honorita hears the door lock and sees Julio walking around behind where she is sitting. Now his hands are on her shoulders. Under the table she clicks her fingers around her knuckles. She feels his sweaty palms on her shoulders, now squeezing them in turn.

"You know something?" he is saying smoothly. She does not reply. "In prison it is helpful to have the governor on your side." He laughs. "And then again, most unhelpful not to have the governor on your side."

She feels his right hand slip down towards her breast, fumbling to reach inside the bra. She can hear his breathing replace his laughter. "I mean, you are here to ensure the comfort of the prisoner Gustavo Cortez. He could be comfortable, or he could be uncomfortable. You know what I am saying, Madame United Nations?"

New she feels his hands move from her breasts to under her arms and lift her up so that she is standing with her back towards him. Against the small of her back she feels the hardness of his erection. Now he is rubbing himself up and down against her. In spite of her disgust she lets this happen, all the while thinking of Gustavo. Suddenly she is spun around and facing him, her head held from behind in his hand and her lips pushed up to his. She smells the beer and sees the slobber.

She wriggles her head to one side and now instinctively pushes him away. He walks over to the table and with one violent sweep and a curse clears all the magazines off the table. The chair with her jacket hanging off the back of it goes flying across the room and lands with a clunk. A porn magazine lands on the floor in between them, open on a full glossy page of a blonde teenager with a black cock in her mouth. She sees him look at it then look at her, then look at her mouth. Her arm is pulled over to the centre of the room and now she is being pushed onto the table.

With a whir she changes from victim to victor. She reaches down and takes hold of his testicles. For a moment, a brief moment, he is smiling again, then she sees him squirm as she tightens her grip. She head butts him ferociously on the nose and as his hands come up to his face she uses the movement of his arms to roll him off her and the table and onto the floor. She straightens up her clothes, and looks down on him writhing on the floor.

"Governor Eboleh. You have made a major mistake. I will be back early tomorrow with a full delegation from my office and the Red Cross. I will also insist on the appropriate government ministers from your own family being present. We will inspect prisoner Gustavo Cortez. If one hair on his head is missing, if he even slept uncomfortably, I will personally make sure that your position becomes untenable. Is that clear?" He doesn't reply but is now kneeling on one leg as she struggles upright. "Untenable," she hisses again, and kicks him back down to the ground.

She picks up her jacket from the floor, puts the chair back upright and unlocks the door and closes it behind her. "Better leave him for a few minutes," she says to the two guards who smile leeringly at her. One rubs his crotch, and says "how about me too?" then laughs out loud. She closes that door too and walks out of the gates to the Mercedes parked in the shade.

"Let's go Antonio."

"Are you alright, Señora?"

"Fine, Antonio and a lot better than the governor."

They drive out up the dust track more quickly than they arrived. They pass the spot at which she should be dropped off, her and the RPGs and guns in the boot. She is running through Plan B in her head. She has an assault vehicle and a driver; she's with them both now. There's a problem with the ambassador and the Norwegian reception; they will be wanting the assault vehicle and driver too. All she has to do is stick to the plan, as long as she fires the grenades at nine she will have done her part.

"What time does this gala at the Norwegian embassy finish?"

"Around midnight I suppose, why what have you in mind?"

"Nothing really," but she is thinking fast. "I was thinking that you could take the ambassador and his wife, make some excuse, I could be part of the excuse, then go back and....No there's too much to go wrong. It's better if I have no contact with anyone except you."

They come to end of the road. "Where now, Señora?"

"Its four o'clock. We need to loose five hours. Where can we go that's quiet?"

"Well right here in the airport, there are cars parked, and only one roadblock in and out. Around the island there are many roadblocks. They are expensive. Anything can happen at them.."

"OK, let's wait at the airport. Gives us time to think of a good excuse for your ambassador. You could just say the car has broken down."

"But it's a new Mercedes."

"So, they're shit these days."

"How about we are delayed at Black Beach? I am meant to be your driver after all?"

"But he will know it closes at six, or thereabouts. We'll just say I have asked you to collect another UN VIP from the airport and you will be there just after nine, which you will anyway."

"OK, but I don't have a phone."

"No problem, use mine," she reaches into her jacket pocket. "Oh hell!"

"What is it?"

"The phone, my cell phone."

"And?"

"It must have fallen out of the pocket when my jacket hit the floor."

"Why did your jacket hit the floor."?

"Too many questions again, Antonio." But she is thinking through not having a phone. No contact with Bo, no contact with Capitán Romero. No contact with Madrid. "We deal with what we deal with," she says as they pull into some shade in the airport car park for the long, and now lonelier, wait. But she worries quietly to herself about being incommunicado.

47
Dateline 31st, 4.00pm

Gustavo has been waiting outside the doctor's office for what seems like an hour; he has no way of knowing. He is beginning to doubt there is a doctor, and that the office he is waiting outside is an office at all. At least he's in the shade, even if still standing in the shade. The guard won't let him sit on the ground, he has to "stand up for the doctor."

But what has really been on his mind has been Honorita. Honorita locked in the room with the fat thug governor. Honorita here at all! Honorita and the number nine. Honorita and the Mexican cover. Honorita and the UN. He had no doubt she could look after herself if he attacked her, that he'd be flat on the floor within half a second. The number nine must be nine o'clock, especially now she kept mentioning time. But above all he has the confirmation that this makes sense. What he had never been able to talk about in Nigeria, about being with the CNI, not even to Elisa or Big-K, he had always hoped somehow would be his rescue out of this mess, somehow, some time. The CNI must have known the risks of him confessing; what he had not figured on was an immediate covert rescue mission instead of what he predicted would be a mixture of diplomacy, pressure and bribes. The Americans own FP, and they owe Spain a big favour for Iraq; in his mind he had become this big favour. Now, standing here at the edge of hell, part of him was disappointed he was not this big favour, but a far greater part mighty relieved about getting out of here before it had even started. He looks down at the guard, squatting in front of him, and reflects on the strange twists of fate that means he, Gustavo, is subjugated to the ignorant savage starring blankly from nowhere into nowhere. Never again, he tells himself, if he gets out of here, will he even set foot in African again.

"Cortez! Hey, Cortez!!" the guard springs up and without necessity shoves him hard towards the office block where the governor Julio is calling him. Gustavo just stops himself from lashing back behind him. "What did the doctor tell you?" Julio is asking, and before Gustavo could answer adds, "We have another visitor. Come."

Julio walks back into the air conditioning and back into Julio's office. He sees the Minister of Justice who was on the back of the pick-up with him. He is smiling warmly at Gustavo and extending his hand. "Alfredo Eboleh, Minister of Justice, and very pleased to meet you again." Gustavo shakes his hand and smiles back. "And these are representatives of the local and international media," he announces grandly and spreads his arm in the direction of two photographers and a video cameraman, all busy now with shots of Gustavo and the Minister shaking hands and the minister smiling. Julio walks around behind them so that he is standing in the centre of the shot and puts his chubby arms around both their shoulders. Alfredo is annoyed and removes the arms around him, and scowls at Julio who backs off. Like a pack of dogs, thinks Gustavo, as he continues to try to smile.

Alfredo pulls back a chair, and gestures for Gustavo to sit in it. Alfredo puts himself in another chair. He checks the cameras are working, and says to Gustavo, "We hope your stay here will be a pleasant one. Although this is a prison, and you are to stand trial for some crimes, alleged crimes, you are innocent until proven guilty. This is justice FP style. Here you will be well cared for. My cousin Julio is the governor and he is a family man, a religious man too. You will be in the care of my officials from the Ministry, and your trial will be soon and fair. Would you like to say a few words to the world media?"

Gustavo looks blankly for a few moments, then sits upright and says directly to the camera "I greatly appreciate being in the care of two members of the illustrious Eboleh family, and look forward to the fair trial which will prove my innocence. Thank you very much."

"Good, good," says Alfredo, gathering up himself and his media. He says a few words, friendly words, in Fang to Julio and is gone as quickly as he arrived. Julio and Gustavo are alone in the room.

"So many visitors," he says, "and tomorrow morning more to

come. You must be very famous. Well, I know you are very famous, on television all morning. Tomorrow that woman from the UN is coming back with some others." Then suddenly he stops the ingratiation and puts his face up close to Gustavo. "But one day they will stop coming," he hisses, " and then we will have a party. A party in your honour."

"Governor, may I make a suggestion?"

"A suggestion? A suggestion?" he is holding his stomach fat in both hands and looking at Gustavo incredulously. "A suggestion. Let me see. We let you go. That would be a suggestion! I give you a beer, that's another suggestion! We buy some new flex before we wire you up, we fill the bucket up with fresh shit before we dump you head in it. Suggestions!" he is shouting now, "suggestions! You want a box for your suggestions like on American TV?"

"No, governor, my suggestion is to your advantage not mine." Julio sits up and listens. "I sleep here tonight, on this floor, right here."

"Why?"

"Because if all theses international VIPs are coming in the morning it will be better for you, and for me I admit, but better for you if I am in good shape and not smelling like I've slept in the cells you showed me earlier."

Julio thinks for a moment. "Not a bad suggestion, but not in here."

"I can just sleep on the floor."

"I know you can sleep on the floor, you will always sleep on the floor. Like a dog you will sleep on the floor. There are some new women prisoners today too, two girls," he rubs his crotch and winks, then remembers his and Gustavo's status. "No you will sleep in the doctor's office."

"But there is no doctor."

"Then you will be in his office alone. Locked up over there. A good idea, good, our suggestion. You won't hear Chimwainie or the girls scream from over there, you'll be fresh tomorrow for your VIPs."

Julio stands up and walks over to behind Gustavo's chair, and now his chubby hands are around what is left of Gustavo's neck, loosely, and shakes his neck slowly, playfully. "Frederico!" A guard comes through from next door. "Take our friend Señor Terroristo to the doctor's office, lock him away. Give him water, some bread or whatever we have."

48

Dateline 31st, 5.00pm rewrite danger

The dogs' barking is becoming more insistent, more determined. Bo feels in the camera bag for the gun, feels its reassuring shape around his left hand. He swings the bag over to his right shoulder, then feels it even better with his right hand. He puts the taser in his left and climbs into the back of a pick up truck. He hears more than one bark, but has no idea how many dogs or handlers he is going to have to shoot. Part of him knows he has never killed before. Surprise will be everything. Let them come onto him. He'll shoot the handlers first, then the dogs, then back up through the stairwell. He makes himself a shooting space in the back of the pick-up.

Bo hears a new sound behind him, a whirring mechanical sound in the gloom. Then he sees a tiny chink of light, spreading slowly horizontally upwards. The garage door is opening, opening slowly, inch by inch, but opening. He throws the taser back in the bag and leaps out of the truck, gun still in his right hand. The dogs and shouting are now a step louder, they must have opened the access door. He sprints behind the pillars towards the opening car door, staying in the shadows. In the new light he can see the dogs straining their handlers to get to where he was before, on the opposite side of the opening door. They are there within ten seconds. He holds his breath and completely still squeezes the gun in his hand. Then they pick up his scent that leads to the truck, and are heading away from the door. The door is now high enough for him to roll under, but the car is now moving forwards and he has to wait. As soon as it is through he darts out into the sunlight. His eyes hurt for a moment, readjust and he sprints up the ramp to a service door on the right. It is open. Inside he looks back. He can no longer see inside the garage but can hear the dogs and sees the door closing again. Slowly. The slowest door in the world. Now the door is below handler height, now below dog height. He's free, but they won't be giving up. He needs to be out of there quickly.

Out in the heat of the street Bo puts on his baseball cap and sunglasses and tries to blend in with Barbate. Be slow and inconspicuous, walk in the obvious places. He meanders on his familiar route, left and left again into the *Plaza Conchita Eboleh*. A tourist couple, they sound like they are from China, ask him to take their photograph against one of the statues. He obliges slowly, then walks behind them and sees a candle tucked away where he left it. He is aware of some men running in different directions, and now a police siren on a large American sedan heading for the Bahia. He carries on ambling. He is heading, but not too earnestly, for the Baton Rouge Bar & Diner. He crosses into the *Calle Monrovia*, and skips back over into the shadier side of the pavement.

"You! Stop!" Bo hears a shout from the other side of the street but walks on without looking around. Now he hears it again louder. He looks across the road. A tall African man in policeman's uniform is holding his hand up. "Stop! Wait!!" Bo points to himself, the man shouts back "Yes, hold it!" Bo backs into a door off the pavement and sees the man jogging over towards him.

"Your i/d?" Bo hears he has a slight American accent.

"Who are you? I don't just show my i/d to anyone."

"Listen. Shut up! It's you who need to prove your i/d. Your i/d, hurry."

"Well," says Bo "I can't hurry. I don't have my i/d on me. I don't need to have it here, just walking around?"

"Today you do. Where you staying?"

"It's called the Bahia. The Hotel Bahia. Bahia Hotel. One of them."

The man reaches onto his belt for his radio.

"Wait." says Bo. "I can show you something."

"What?"

Bo reaches into his camera bag and holds out the taser, and rummages around in the bag. The man takes the bait.

"What's that?"

"It's just a torch. Look, I'll show you." Bo flicks the back switch and holds it up to the man's eyes. He turns the torch on. The man staggers back and collapses as a dead weight. Bo pulls him to the back of the portico, takes the radio from the belt. At the back of the belt are the handcuffs. Bo hauls him further over and chains him to a railing. Bo stands back, sees the truncheon and gun. He puts the gun and clip in to his camera bag, takes the truncheon from the holster, says "thanks for these" and smites the man hard on the side of the head. "Sorry about that, officer, needs must."

Bo continues his walk, slightly more urgently than before, as he reckons by now they will be picking off any young white man. He turns right back into *Calle Principal* and sees the Baton Rouge sign sticking out a hundred metres down on the right. He walks up to the main door, hesitates, then on a hunch that he'll be among friends enters through the two glass doors.

Through the first door Bo is aware of entering a different world, a half way house between African West and the American South. Through the second door and he is in Louisiana. Relief and apprehension sweep over him in equal measure. Still wearing his baseball cap and sunglasses he walks up the bar and orders a coke. He looks in the mirror running along behind the bar. Everyone else has a baseball cap on too, and half are wearing dark glasses. Country music is playing on the jukebox, soppy country music too. There are four televisions: three with different US programmes, he can see CNN and then a couple of sports channels and the local news channel. The barman gives him a coaster, coke and a stirrer. "Hey, buddy, I'm Phil, you new in town?"

Bo puts on an American accent, "Sure am."

"Canadian?"

"Boston. Boston, Massachusetts. Nice bar you got here."

"Yep. My brother lives in Boston. Mill Park. Where you from?"

"Ah, I'm not from there I'm afraid, from Cambridge," says Bo hoping the only town near Boston he has heard of is, in fact, near Boston.

"No need to be afraid, boy," he laughs. "Most us folks is from Louisiana, some from Texas." Bo notices the oilmen on either side are listening in, and now joining in. Everyone is friendly, enormous, drunk but not drunk-drunk, off duty, wishing they were somewhere else, but makin' do here at the BR. "BR?" "Baton Rouge, boy, Baton Rouge." More laughter. Bo buys a round.

"You not drinking?" the roustabout on his left asks.

"Not today, antibiotics, makes me queasy in the heat."

"Queasy!," he laughs and gives Bo a mighty slap on the back. "We guys do a week on and a week off. And in our week off we have our own week on." Everyone joins in the well-worn joke.

"How long you in town?"

"Just a few days. Till Tuesday, then off to Cameroon. Looking for soccer kids," says Bo wishing he hadn't said it as he had.

The giant on his right joins in. "To hell with soccer kids. We need soccer mums! Widders preferably. Ain't seen no white women here for months, then they with some UN bull-shit."

"Yeah, this place truly sucks," says Phil, "Barbate I mean, not the good ol' BR Baton Rouge. I bought this bar three years ago. Hey, boy you wanna buy a bar?"

The others collapse laughing, don't touch it, don't ask to see the books, ask him where he keeps the cash, ask him how much he pays the gooks, ask him where he keeps the 'hos, ask him how much piss he puts in the whisky, tell him to scrap my credit, you could get some new tunes on the jukebox while you're at it, don't tell his ol' lady about his black squeeze.

"Hey, boy, you famous!" another voice booms from a bar stool. He is pointing at the local TV screen. One by one they all turn to look. There is the same copy of a copy photo, but even under the baseball cap they can all see it's Bo.

"Hey, Phil, turn that fuckin' shit down!" The barman points one zapper at the jukebox, holds down a key and the music slowly dies; he turns around and points another zapper at the TV, the sounds slowly builds. "....asks for vigilance from compatriots. This new coup plotter is armed and highly dangerous. A full-scale search is in motion. All units have been alerted. Anyone seeing the foreign plotter must contact the authorities. A reward is in place. The Minister...."

"Minister of Lining His Fuckin' Pockets! Turn that bullshit off, Mike."

Phil changes channel to another US sports programme and says "you stay safe here, boy, ain't that right, men?" Along the bar glasses are banged on the counter. "Too fuckin' right," the one on Bo's left says. "Shithouse dump. They way they treat their own niggers is disgustin'. So you plannin' to blow this fucker up, or what?"

"Well, I can't say really. But it is a patriotic cause, if you get my drift."

"CIA? Sounds good to me." Phil stands on his beer crate behind the bar and shouts above the chatter and music, "and now, if y'all don't mind, I suggest we change the fuckin' subject!" More cheers. Bo feels a glow of relief. Bo buys another round.

49
Dateline 31st, 6.00pm

"No you stay here and look after Giselle, Mike, I'm only going to check something on the boat, it'll be fine." Hernán skips over the door of the Corvette and guns it to the end of the drive, leaving a billow of dust. Mike disappears in that dust and then into the house. Hernán turns left out of the drive and stops again to put the hood up and screw the silencer onto the end of his Martin Hassler .45.

He looks at his watch, just after six o'clock. Dark in less than an hour. He is not sure if he's going to kill Cortez as soon as he gets there or later. Or how. He is going to see how the land lies. If he gets a chance he'll take it, but he reckons it's unlikely. He knows the regime at Black Beach. Lights out soon after dusk, in fact the lights more or less hardly come on. Then Julio and the guards get drunk, not every night, but most nights and for sure tonight. He'll hang around, pretend to get drunk with them. There should only be two guards on after dark, the others go home. Plus Julio, at least to start with. He has seen Julio in one of the three nightclubs in Barbate but not till later. Maybe he'll have to kill Julio and the guards as well as Cortez. Who knows? But he's ready, President-self-select Hernán Eboleh is well and truly ready.

He is halfway there now and sees an executive jet take off a kilometre or so away. He can't make out what it is. Would like to have done. Thinks again he might have been a pilot in another circumstance. Now he'll have to settle for president. He smiles to himself, checks his face in the mirror. Young man, not yet thirty, plenty of time to enjoy being one of the richest men who ever lived.

He slows down for the right turn onto the dirt track down to Black Beach, swings the Corvette onto the dust road and floors it for fun. An almighty cloud of dust fills the rear view mirror as the rear wheels break away and the car snakes down the track. He crests the hill at rally speed, looks down and smiles at the speedo showing eighty miles an hour. The prison is ahead of him now. He is always amazed that there aren't any fences and sentry posts, how it always looks like someone's farm house. But he knows the prisoners never leave their cells, and are too weak to get far anyway.

He parks the Corvette in the shade, and walks into the front guardroom.

"Hey, Frederico, how is life?"

"Fine thank you, Uncle Hernán."

"And where is my favourite cousin?"

"He's inside uncle, but you better not go in. He is interviewing."

But Hernán and Julio are more than cousins. They grew up together, same age, same house. At school Julio and Hernán were always bottom and top of the class, and they sensed some sort of balance with each other. Julio made Hernán laugh, Hernán made Julio confident. They lost their virginity on the same night in the same gang rape, some Kirange virgin Julio's elder brother had thrown into the back of the truck on her way home from school. Lately they had not been so close as they grew up and apart; they had nothing really in common nowadays except the shared childhood and family bonds. An interview wasn't going to stop him barging in now.

"Hey! Julio! Still action man!" A girl in new prisoner's clothes is spread face down across the table and Julio is standing behind her with his trousers around his ankles and his naked buttocks pumping in and out. Her head is turned away from the door.

"Hernán. Wait there! You can have her next," he says hurrying up.

"No thanks, not after you've given her God knows what pox."

Julio giggles, climaxes and withdraws, and throws the girl onto the floor. He kicks her and tells her to get up. "You can have that one if you like," he says throwing his hand in the direction of a chair behind the door. For the first time Hernán notices another girl in the room. She is squatting on the chair with her head hidden behind her knees. Julio walks over and grabs her hair forcing her head up. He wipes himself on her clothes. "Not bad, eh? I was saving her for later, but for cousin Hernán, I give her to you first."

"Maybe later. Why don't we play cards for her? How about a beer."

"Good idea. Hey, Frederico!" he shouts through the door.

The door opens, the boy says "Yes, Uncle Julio."

"You can have this one now. You before your brother Daniel. Keep this one fresh for your uncles later. And two beers."

Frederico grabs the girl by the arms. For the first time Hernán sees her face. She is quite pretty, well would be if she didn't look so traumatised. Better than the other one. Both Kiranges though. Julio! He'll never learn.

When they are alone Hernán asks, "This Cortez, cousin, when can we have a bit of fun with him?"

"No party tonight. Not for Señor Terroristo. We have visitors in the morning. Yes, VIPs from the UN to make sure he's in good shape. But when they go we can torture him to death. I don't care if he talks or not."

"Well I do. I'd like to find out the truth. It will be more helpful, don't you think? I mean no parties, no need for a party, it could be if we just sit him down here, just the two of us, get him relaxed, share some beers, tell Frederico and Daniel to go to a bar, tell him we'll help him if he helps us. I'm sure you know what to say, cousin, you do this all the time."

Julio laughs and bangs the table. "Never. I just get them screaming, that's what I like. Why would they talk if they're not screaming like virgins first."

"Because, my dear friend, you make it worth their while. I'll show you."

Julio slaps his tummy. "You've always been the smart one Hernán. I'm ready to learn. So after dark, we send Frederico and Daniel away, get Cortez in here, be nice to him, he will tell us the truth. If you say so."

"That's it. Think about it. We are still trying to prosecute the ringleader, the moneyman, through the British courts. The case is stalled for lack of inside information. Uncle Bolivar would love to have this information. So we get it, and then we go to Uncle Bolivar with the information. First we loosen his tongue with some blackmail, raise the stakes, I don't know what, say accuse him of spying, a more serious charge. Then you can torture him for a week. Then our uncle has his balls in the barbecue, his *doonti*, and the truth about the terrorist and his plot."

"Ok, we try it your way tonight. And then we fuck that other one," Julio is laughing again and rubbing his crotch.

"Sure, we play cards for her. Whoever wins fucks her first. Even if you win, I still fuck her later."

Julio doubles up with laughter. "You should come and visit us here more often. Much more often. And until then?"

Hernán considers. "I'll be back around eight thirty, nine. After dinner. I've got some work to do on the boat."

"Good. An admiral working on his boat. I like it. I'll try to keep my trousers on till then."

"You better! Until then!"

50
Dateline 31st, 6.30pm

"Gustavo Cortez, Teniente, you most definitely need to find a way out of here," he says aloud to himself. He has no idea what time it is, but he knows he is still only half way through the most important day of his life. If Honorita and the CNI are coming for him at nine, no when they are coming for him at nine, there's no point in him being stuck in this so-called doctor's office where they'll never find him.

He hears a noise outside, stands up and walks over to look out through the bars. It is nearly dark. An African man is starting up his American sports car, reversing out of the shade, and leaving noisily with a whirlwind of dust behind him. Then Cortez sees the two guards from the office dragging two girls over a sand dune. They must have just come up from the beach. One of the girls is in tatters, the other unharmed. Gustavo wonders why they have both raped one and left the other alone. He has one of his Africa shudders and says aloud again, "Gustavo Cortez, out of here."

He looks around more seriously. There is no light bulb, and there's scarcely any daylight left. He examines the door. The lock is old and rusty, but stiff and solid, almost certainly from the Spanish days. The key is in the lock from the other side. He looks around the room for anything to open up his side of the lock. The room is completely bare. As far as he can see there is not even a splinter of wood. The hinges are from the same period as the lock but even more eternal. He looks on them with frustration. An old lock and two old hinges and he can't find anything with which to budge them. He feels around the door. The centre panel is much thinner than the surroundings. He taps it quietly. It feels thin and soft. He bets that it is forty years old too. He bets he could smash it with his fist or elbow or shoulder. He bets the key will still be right there too. But betting is a gamble. What if he leaves it to nine tonight, then tries and fails? He walks over to the window. It is getting darker all the time. He pulls and pushes each bar in turn. All solid, no movement at all. It's the door panel, the door in the darkness, or nothing. He starts practising some fist clenching, tries a kick box, but the panel is too high.

There is a sound at the door. A gruff sound and a whimpering sound. He hears the key move in the lock, the door swings open and a girl is pushed in. She stumbles against the wall. The door locks closed again. She sees him and gasps, holds her clothes tightly around herself. He sees it is the girl from the dune, the unmolested one. What is she doing in here? He speaks to her in Spanish, quietly, softly, telling her not to worry, he is a prisoner too, not about to harm her. She stops whimpering and breathes more easily, but does not say anything. Gustavo tries to talk to her in English, asking her about herself, telling her something about himself; still no response, just a frightened stare at the wall.

He thinks about how this has changed his situation. She must have been thrown in here for use later on. So at some stage that door is going to open again. He can grab the guard, knock him out, escape. But then what? What if it's too early before nine? Where does he hide? And how will he know when it's nine anyway? There'll be noise at nine. So what does he do till then? The beach, hide on the beach? There doesn't seem to be a fence, or many guards outside, not that many inside. Maybe everyone is always locked up. And now the girl? Does he help her out too, or leave her to these savages? Can she help him?

"Can we escape from here?" He looks up surprised. She is speaking Spanish, quite good Spanish.

"That's all I'm thinking about. But how come you are here?"

"I know who you are. I saw you this morning on the TV at the police station. This morning they arrested my father. He is a doctor in Baku, on the mainland. We are Kirange. They took my sister and me here. I don't know where my father is."

"And your mother?"

"She is already dead. Last year she died."

"And your sister?"

"First the fat one raped her in the office. I was there but could not watch. Then the two boys raped her on the beach. She is only thirteen."

"And you?"

"Fifteen."

"No not your age. Why didn't they rape you?"

"They say they will later. The fat one and his cousin in the office, then the one who left." Gustavo thinks back to the sports car and the dust. "They will play cards for me. Then the boys will rape me too." She is sobbing now, a small wail of despair. Gustavo squats beside her and puts his arm around her.

"Savages. I will help all I can. They will kill me anyway. We both need to escape." He looks at her again. She is frail, too small and weak even before today to be of any physical help with the guards. But she could get them to open the door. When they come for her the door will be opened, but when will that be? He wants to ask her if she knows when she is going to be raped, but stops himself. Still a Spanish gentleman, he reflects, thanking God.

"Timing is everything," he says.

"What is that?" she asks.

"Nothing, just talking to myself." If they come for her within the first two hours of darkness it will be too early. He needs them to fetch her at five to nine, but knows that's impossible. If they have not taken her by then she can somehow get them to open the door. Otherwise he has to smash down the door once the noise starts. His thoughts are going around in circles, he is angry with himself.

The door opens again, too suddenly for him to react from the floor. With a whirl the other girl is thrown in. She falls straight into the arms of her elder sister and they cry and wail together in the near darkness. By the time they have quietened down it is dark outside, and the sound of the crickets now becomes louder than the sound of the girls.

"The fat one, again," the elder one says to him in Spanish. "They will come for me when the cousin returns." Her voice is a whisper in the black room. Gustavo stands up and feels the door panel, pushing at it in different places. But he still doesn't know how he is going to escape, only that he is. By God he is.

51
Dateline 31st, 7.00pm

The bar banter suggests that the president isn't as popular as Bo thought he would be. Bush, that is. They all hate Bolivar, goes without saying, not that he's personally screwed any of them, just by being responsible for the hell hole they've all chosen to work in. Can't save a bean here either, what with the Baton Rouge and the alimony. Bush they don't like either. Iraq. We should either have left them alone, sand niggers and towel heads the lot of them, left them alone to dump on each other, or we should have dropped the big one, made it safe for our boys *before* they went on in.

Bo is against the war too, thinks Blair is a lying prig, and twice nearly joins in the conversation as a Brit. He's aware they think he's CIA, agrees the Agency got it wrong on WMD, but then says they warned the neocons not to invade; a statement he's not quite sure is strictly speaking accurate, but they seem to buy it.

Bo feels safe here for a couple of hours till it's candle time. Now getting out of Barbate after that is something that is starting to occupy him. Then Bo's phone rings. Surprised he whisks it out of his pocket and looks at the screen. Madrid. Looks like more problems. He slides off the bar stool and walks to the quietest corner.

"Si."

"It's Molistán. Is the Capitan there?"

"No, I haven't seen her."

"Don't' say her. Think."

"Sorry."

"Don't say sorry."

"Sorry."

There's a pause. "She is not answering. An African sounding man is answering."

"Ah."

"Don't just say 'ah'"

"Sorry."

"Good God. You don't know where s- it is?"

"No, why, what's up?'

"A postponement. Exactly, exactly twenty four hours. Offshore troubles."

Bo looks around, thinks of his current predicament. "Difficult. Difficulty on the ground here. Delaying may not be much of an option."

"Why?"

"Better not to explain."

"OK. But still, no matter how difficult you will delay twenty-four hours. There is no choice without a sub. Can you get the message to your partner?"

"I don't know where it is. The fun starts in two hours."

"Then go find your partner. You have time. Are you in a night club, what's that noise?"

"Difficult is too an easy a word. It's a bar."

"I am giving you an order. You will attempt, no, you will find your partner. You will both delay. Repeat your order."

Bo is aware of turning heads looking at him, also aware they cannot hear him. He smiles into the phone. "We are to postpone for twenty four hours. I am to find my partner and tell it. Shall I call you back?"

"Of course," she hisses, and cuts him off.

Bo needs some time to think. He carries on an imaginary conversation into the handset. He cannot postpone, he needs to get out of FP quickly. Even before Coronel Molistán called his best hope was to get down to Black Beach and leave with Gustavo, Honorita, Romero and the boys. Exactly how he hasn't quite worked out yet. Well, that's no longer on the cards. And Honorita; there is no hope, absolutely no hope in the pitch darkness of finding a well-hidden special agent in the scrubland around the prison. He can hardly go round with a megaphone shouting "Capitán Rosca, Capitán Rosca, delay for twenty four hours". And the candles; some of them could easily be discovered in the next twenty-four hours. He will somehow get down to Black Beach, let off the candles at nine as planned, he presumes Honorita is going to fire her RPGs then too, they'll get Cortez out of there, and hide somewhere for twenty four hours until Romero shows up. Hide where? Bo gives himself a shudder. It's the least bad option. He decides to disobey orders.

"All OK?" says Phil, as Bo stalks back to his bar stool, "by the way, never caught your name?"

"Phil, can I talk to you alone?" Bo slings his camera bag over his shoulder.

Phil looks at the others with small air of triumph and importance. "Sure, let's go to in back."

Phil leads Bo through a swing door behind the bar into a stockroom. He springs forward to stomp on a cockroach. There's no aircon, it's sticky, with mosquitoes too. "Sorry about in here. What's up?"

"I can't say too much Phil, but I need your help."

"If I can."

"You got a car?"

"I got a truck."

"I need to get to Black Beach. Near Black Beach anyway. In an hour and a half, say an hour, time to get you back here safely first. Are you likely to be stopped, driving round?"

"Never have been. Everyone knows me, but if they're looking for you? I don't know. It's out of town, off the airport road, right?"

"Right. That'll be the problem won't it? The airport road will be blocked. Is there another way?"

"Not that I know," says Mike, "not by road."

Bo gives him a big smile. "Good thinking, not by road. Can you get me down to the port?"

"Sure, that'll be easier, it's only half a mile from here, I go there all the time to the warehouse."

"Can we go from here now? Just slip away?"

Phil takes out his phone and dials a number. He walks up close to the crack in the doorway and peers in to see Pete at the bar pick his phone up. "Pete, it's me, I'll be gone for half an hour, can you mind the bar for me? Yeah, no me neither, Ok buddy, thanks." And to Bo he says. "Done, let's roll."

Bo snuggles down into the footwall of the new Chevy pick-up. Mike throws some old towels on top of him. After less than a minute Phil says, "You certainly got this town jumping."

"Why? What's up?" says Bo.

"Activity, boy, act-iv-it-y. Police cars, foot soldiers. Here's someone stopping me, stay still." Bo stays as still as he can, thinking about the candles in just over an hour. Maybe it's not such a bad thing they are not all fast asleep, maybe more chaos, maybe better. Now he can sense the air change as the window comes down and hears Phil talking. "No, man, ain't seen nobody like that. Just come from the Baton, not there either. Drop by some time, we'll have a beer. Good luck." Bo hears the window wind up and the noise and air change, and feels himself unwind. "Fuckin' arseholes," Phil is saying. Then a few moments later, "we're at the port, what now?"

"Is it all clear?" asks Bo.

He sees Phil look around. "All clear."

Bo slides up the passenger seat. "That's better. I need a boat."

"You want me to go take a look?"

"No, Phil, thanks man, you've done enough. I'll just slip out here, there's bound to be one I can nick."

"Nick?"

"Steal."

"Hey, check this out?" Phil nods towards a small dinghy just entering the harbour. "It's small, though." Bo can see it lit by the only floodlight on this side of the quay. There are two men inside it, and no room for anymore. "It's big enough," says Bo, "and an outboard. No locks and keys."

They sit motionless in the dark of the cab and watch the two men climb out, tie up, take their gear out and walk off along the quay. No one says anything in the cab. After five minutes Bo picks up his camera bag, holds his hand out to Phil; Phil shakes it and says quietly, "Good luck, buddy, whatever your name is."

Bo walks over to the quay and without looking around slips down into the dinghy. He shakes the tank on the floor. Nearly full. He looks around in the gloom. There's a solid floor and a Honda four-stroke engine. It starts first time. He unties the painter, pushes off, engages the gear and as quietly as possible, hugging the shadows, leaves the harbour. He sees lights come on, Phil's headlights, sees them swing around and disappear. Now he is outside the harbour.

The night is as dark as Capitán Romero said it would be. Bo takes a few seconds to orientate. The airport lights glow above the jungle just inland. Black Beach should be just under the lights, just over a dune. He looks at his phone; still a signal, but only half bars, should be better near the airport. He looks at his watch. Nearly eight. He's only a mile off the beach. He kills the engine and drifts nowhere in particular. It's quiet, apart from the lapping water. It's dark, apart from the yellow glow over the dune. He feels alone. And nervous. Coronel Molistán. Stuff's gone wrong. Honorita. An African sounding man. Capitán Romero. 24 hours. He checks through his bag. Two guns, some clips, the taser. His eyes are getting used to the darkness, but there's still nothing to see; nothing to do except wait, wait and drift, wait and drift and think about the options. Except there aren't any except to carry on and hope for the best.

52
Dateline 31st, 8.00pm

"One hour to go."

"You're not bored are you, Antonio?" suggests Honorita. "We could always go back to Black Beach and rescue my telephone if you need a bit of excitement."

"No, Señora, not bored, not at all, just anxious. They'll be at the Norwegian Embassy now. I'll go anywhere except to Black Beach to rescue your telephone."

"Antonio, where's your sense of fun! It would be easy. I drive you up, you go in and tell the nice governor that the UN lady would like to have her telephone back. He's a charming man, I'm sure he would just give it you there and then! More fun than the Norwegian Embassy. Come on Antonia, admit it, you wish you were on Norwegian soil now too, don't you?"

"Yes, of course. You're not cross?"

"Why should I be cross? I'm only grateful Antonio. It's the waiting that's getting to you. You'll be fine once the action starts."

"Here comes some action now," he says, and Honorita follows his eyes. They see a series of fast moving blue flashing lights heading into the airport compound. Now they can see what is happening more clearly, three large American police cars rushing in, and now they can hear the sirens. A full-scale commotion. The cars turn in to the road behind them and pull up sharply outside the terminal. Antonio is watching in the mirror. Honorita slides down low in the seat and asks him what's happening.

"They're all out of the cars and running into the terminal." She notices his knuckles whiten as he grips the steering wheel. "Now one is coming over here, not in a uniform. He's walking up to the car." Moments later there's a tap on Antonio's window.

"What you doing here?"

"Just waiting for an arrival, sir," says Antonio.

"OK, we're looking for someone. You're lucky he's not

Spanish with this CD car. Either you two seen this guy?" He hands a fax through the window. Antonio looks at it, says no, sorry and passes it to Honorita. It is Bo. It's a fax of a photocopy but for sure it's Bo. "Sorry, me neither," she says handing it back.

"He is a coup plotter. Maybe the ringleader. British, name of Pitt, Ernest Pitt, works for Manchester United. If you see him let us know. There'll be a big reward." He peers into the rear of the car. "Open the boot."

"There's only my luggage in there," says Honorita, showing him her UN i/d and Mexican passport. He seems unable, or unwilling to read.

"I said open the boot."

"I am afraid you do not have that authority," says Honorita firmly. "This is a CD car. I am a UN official travelling on a diplomatic passport. There is nothing significant in the boot, but that is not the point. This is a question of international principle. A question of procedures. Protocol. Protocol is important. Everybody must observe protocol."

The officer stands up straight so they cannot see his face. Then he leans down again and says, "Wait here."

"Certainly, sir," says Antonio, and the officer walks back to the terminal. "What was that about?"

"I don't know, Antonio, sounds like a coup attempt." Honorita is thinking fast. "We need to get out of here before someone tells that ape he doesn't need any authority." So, Bo is in trouble. On the loose, hiding somewhere. At least he's not captured. God help us all if he's captured. And what's all this about Manchester United? What happened to the firework cover? She half expected something like this, using an amateur. The coronel will go ballistic. Let's assume no thunder flashes from the roof, so no diversion. Just me and the UOE. The stakes are higher now, especially as the place is now on full-scale alert looking for Bo. Why do they think he's a coup man? Probably a cock up. And a ringleader? What's going on? But the thunder flash diversion was always jam on the UOE bread and butter. Or was it? Then she remembers Coronel Molistán's specific instruction to all of them: if everything is not 100% between the diversion, the RPG attack and the UOE landing, abandon the mission. Abandon the mission.

That seemed fine in Madrid, but here and now she wants to go ahead. She'll be fine with Romero. Bo could be a distraction anyway. She needs to call Madrid. Her phone is somewhere in that fat slug's office.

"Antonio, can I borrow your phone?"

"Sure, Señora."

"Do you mind leaving me alone for a few minutes?"

"Of course not, but you cannot dial international on it. It's an Embassy phone, with call barring, just for local calls."

"The airport. There are phones in the terminal?"

"No, Señora, there are only phones in old buildings here in FP. It's all too new. People only use cellphones here."

She thinks again. Bo is out of action, so no diversion. Romero's boys are less than an hour away. She's in a car full of RPGs. Cortez is in prison. He needs to be out of there tonight. Coronel Molistán does not know about Bo, or that she, Honorita, knows about Bo. There's no reason not to go ahead that cannot be explained away later. She looks at her watch. Half an hour to go.

"What's happening out there?"

"Nothing, they are all in the terminal. Looks like one of the cars is leaving."

"OK, we'll leave too. Just make it look like we are re-parking to start with." The car moves backwards through ninety degrees. No sign of the troublemaker. "OK, Antonio, let's go. Nice and smoothly."

They drive out of the airport unchecked. She tells him to turn left onto the track down to Black Beach and kill the lights. There are clear orders to abandon the mission. There are clear reasons not to. She decides, for the first time in her military life, to disobey her orders. She finds discomfort in her conundrum, uncertainty in operating out of orders, and worry about Gus and Bo in equal measure.

53
Dateline 31st, 8.30pm

"Hey! Hernán, I've been waiting for you. A beer?"

"Perfect cousin, thirsty work out over there on the boat."
Hernán walks over to the other side of the table and sees five or six
empty San Miguel beer bottles in the rubbish basket.

Julio burps and focuses, burps again. "Hey! Frederico, Daniel,
anyone there?"

The door opens, Daniel says, "Yes, uncle?"

"Two beers, cold ones."

"You two boys want a beer?" asks Hernán.

"Yes please, Uncle Hernán."

"OK, bring us our two beers, then go to town for a few drinks.
Be back by ten."

"First get Cortez in here," says Julio looking pleased with
himself.

"Can we take the BMW?" Daniel asks.

"Bring us the beers, and Cortez and then you can fuck off in
the BMW!" slurs Julio.

The boys are moving a bit more quickly now. Within a minute
two fresh San Miguels have arrived. Hernán sends Daniel back for
four more. Julio asks, why four? Two for Cortez, two more for us.
Julio looks puzzled, then approves. The door opens again, this
time it is Cortez who enters, slowly at first, then pushed through
by Frederico. Daniel arrives with the fresh beers.

"So, Señor Cortez, I must introduce myself to you. I am
Admiral Hernán Eboleh of the Fernando Poan Navy. Would you
like a beer with us?" Hernán pushes a San Miguel across the table.
"Spanish beer, to remind you of home, maybe of happier times."

"And he is my cousin," blurts out Julio, already with the beer
to his mouth. "As well as being our admiral."

From outside they can all hear the sound of Julio's BMW 640
being fired up and driving off.

Cortez is looking better than Hernán expects. Maybe the prisons in Nigeria are more like the hotel Julio keeps telling everyone he runs here. Cortez looks wary, and has not reached for his beer. Now he does.

"You know, Señor Cortez, I wanted us to have this friendly chat to see if there was some way we can help each other. You probably think this is some good cop – bad cop routine, but it's nothing planned like that. I am not going to promise to release you, or anything I cannot deliver. But there are some specific details about the financing in London that we need. Inside information that you will know. It's a simple proposition. You sign an affidavit which incriminates Sir Mungo Nathan, one that we can use in a British court. Your profile will be raised internationally, which in itself will protect you. You will still have to serve your time in here, but we can make that time symbolic or punitive, and if symbolic in some degree of civilisation, civilisation that a punitive custody would not necessarily encourage."

"What are you two talking about?" Julio burps and slurs slouching down in his chair.

But Hernán is aware that only one of them is talking. He looks at Cortez, now swigging on his bottle. Hernán does the same, but he notices that whereas Julio's is already empty, both he and Cortez are just pretending to drink.

Julio stands up and unbuckles his belt and gun and holster, and puts them on the window ledge. He stands there looking out through the bars down towards the dunes. Not that he can see anything on this dark, dark night. Hernán notices Cortez noticing Julio. Hernán feels against this right pocket and the solid feel of the gun.

"You are not very talkative, Señor Cortez," observes Hernán.

Julio snaps out of his daydream. "That we can fix, cousin. You want him to talk, I can make him talk."

Hernán leans back in his chair. "I'm sure you can, Julio. But Señor Cortez here has the chance of redemption. In Canada my girlfriend was a film buff. She said all great films were about sin and redemption. I said they were about cars and girls. But you have sinned, now is your chance of redemption. But let's not be too noble about this. We are only talking about your self-interest. I mean, what do you care about some Jew in London? What does he care about you?"

"Shall we get the girls in?" asks Julio, leaning forward on the table.

"Later cousin, later. First we want to give Señor Cortez the chance to help himself. But so far he does not seem so inclined."

"To hell with that," says Julio, "I'm going for a pee." He staggers up and heads for the door leaving it open. Moments later they can hear the sound of him relieving himself outside.

Hernán looks at Cortez. Now is his chance. Shoot Cortez now. Right now. He feels in his pocket and puts his fingers around the gun. Then shoot Julio with Julio's own gun, still on the ledge, when he rushes back in. Put Julio's gun in Cortez's hand. Say when he, Hernán, was out for a piss Cortez must have snatched Julio's gun from the ledge and shot him. He, Hernán, rushed back in and shot Cortez before Cortez could shoot him. No witnesses. The perfect crime.

And yet. He can stage this at any time. Julio's going to need another pee soon. In the meantime he, Hernán, has thought of the *coup de grace*. If he could get this Spaniard to open up there would be even fewer questions about the shootings and he, Hernán, would have the evidence Bolivar wants so much. A win/win as the American oil men always say. If not, he'll shoot them both anyway. He looks at Cortez again. He thinks the Spaniard is lucky to be alive, and that he, Admiral Hernán Eboleh, can kill him whenever he likes. Julio walks back in. The moment, and the opportunity have passed. Hernán regrets it as it happens, he's just lost his fail-safe moment for ever, regrets it again as Julio makes himself comfortable, but now has no inclination to look within, only ahead.

54
Dateline 31st, 8.45pm

Gustavo Cortez watches the prison governor slump back in his chair. What a disgusting pig of a man. But this other one is different. Apart from Eliza the only bright black he has met. Cold eyes. Gustavo can't see him raping and drinking with his cousin. Maybe he does. Gustavo looks around. Julio's gun is still on the shelf, as if they were daring him to go for it. Julio is bored. This Eboleh is not drinking either, like him just swigging for show. Now Eboleh is standing up. Gustavo notices the profile of a pistol in his right pocket. Now Eboleh is standing behind him, now with a light touch has his hands on Gustavo's shoulders. Gustavo looks at his left wrist. A chunky diamond emboldened Rolex says it is ten to nine. He needs to keep this going for ten more minutes.

He sees Eboleh sit down and again Julio lean forward. "Well, cousin, what do you want to know?" asks Julio.

"I want to know if Señor Cortez here has any connection to the Spanish government."

Gustavo bristles inside. What can he know? Is he just guessing? Trying to raise the stakes? So far he, Gustavo, has not spoken, has not had a chance to speak. All his training is telling him not to say anything. Name, address, next of kin; he knows the score. Now they are both looking at him. If he talks now he can keep them here for the few more minutes, but in spite of himself his CNI discipline keeps him silent.

"Come on now, Señor Cortez," says Eboleh, "it is just a yes or no question. Do you, did you, work for the Spanish government?"

Still he remains silent. "Let's throw him back in the doctor's room" says Julio.

"Very well," says Eboleh. Gustavo can see him reaching inside his pocket for the pistol; he can't be sure what is going on, but whatever it is he needs it to go on a little longer.

"No."

"Ah, you see Julio he can speak." Eboleh and Gustavo look directly at each other; both knowing a line of defence has been breached. Eboleh reaches for his beer, and Gustavo sees that for the first time he is drinking some. His hand comes out of his pocket. "I only asked because if you were working for the Spanish government the crime is much greater. But of course you know that. You look like a sensitive man, Señor Gustavo. There are two girls here…"

"He knows that, there were in the doctor's room together," says Julio.

"Ah, very well. One has been molested already. She is of the Kirange tribe. A cockroach. Do you know what that molestation means?"

Gustavo shakes his head.

"It means that her life is worthless now she is not pure. She will not find a husband, at least not one who is a good man. But to her, her life still has some worth. None of us want to die. Her friend though is unmolested, and can walk free out of here with her life in order. I will make you a proposition. You confess to work for the Spanish government as well as Nathan, and the girls go free. If you deny it I will kill them both, of course after my cousin here and our nephews and I have taken a few well established liberties with them."

Gustavo turns to see Julio laughing and now staggering up, smiling as he pulls his trousers back up over his belly. "Good, this is more fun. I will go and get them."

"You see, Señor Cortez, we all have choices to make in this life. On the one hand we have the two girls. On the other your honour. And your comfort. If you admit to being a spy, even if are not one, as well as the Nathan operative we both know you are, the girls go free unharmed, but you will be tried for espionage. The sentence will not be death, not in today's world full of busybodies. But you will have ample time here in Black Beach to reflect on your good deed, knowing that however much you are suffering two girls will be women, and one will be a wife and mother. Probably a grand-mother by the time you are free. Nathan will be dead of old age by then too. If you deny being a spy and a stooge, even if you are both, then we kill the girls after utilising them again, and your time

215

here will be shorter, but spent in despair at their fate which you have decided."

There's a rush at the door and Julio pushes the two girls into the room. They fall on to the floor.

"Shall I fuck her now?" asks Julio.

"That's up to Señor Cortez," says Eboleh. Gustavo looks again at Eboleh's watch. Five more minutes. Easily enough time for Julio to rape her. What now? If he signs that he's a spy and knows Nathan and Honorita does not come he will be in worse trouble, much worse trouble. So will the CNI, and so will Spain. If he refuses she is raped but will live if Honorita and whatever she is planning happens in five minutes. Not only raped but a ruined life. It all depends on Honorita. Julio is standing over her now, undoing his belt and buttons. The girl is whimpering, shaking with fear. Gustavo wishes it was just three minutes later. It isn't. God help me Honorita; Honorita help me God.

"OK, I'll sign."

55
Dateline 31st, 8.57pm

Bo's eyes have now adjusted to the night and, lying flat in the RIB, he can make out palm leaves against the sky to his left. The only sound is lapping water on the rubber side balloons. He reckons he is only a few hundred feet offshore. He looks at his phone, presses a key for the backlight and sees 2057 and a full signal. Nearly candle time. He reaches back and pulls the string to start the little Honda outboard. He engages 'F' for forward and heads off to his right towards the glow of light from the airport still mostly hidden by the dunes. Within a minute the trees themselves at Black Beach are visible, and so is the white of the surf line. He cuts the engine as the stern is lifted, tugs on his shoulder bag and swings his right leg over the starboard balloon. The stern hits the sea bed and he swings out of the RIB onto the sand. He grabs the painter and pulls the RIB up out of the surf line, far enough up the beach to stop any third waves floating it off, but close enough to be pushed back to sea in a hurry. It is still almost pitch black behind the dunes.

Bo crouches up behind a bush on a dune. He undoes the camera bag and takes out both guns, checks they are loaded again, puts the clips in his pockets and waits. He holds his phone up to the glow from the airport and can just see 2059, without having seen the numbers change. Less than a minute to go. Bo can fell his heart pumping, but it's as if it belongs to someone else. He dials 999001, the backlight comes on and he waits for the numbers to change, and when they do go to 2100, he presses the green Send. Nothing happens. What was he expecting to happen? Sound takes a while to travel a mile. The phone has a message: Error in Connection. Fuck. He tries again, same message. The number looks wrong; try a nought. He redials 0999001. Send. Wait, listen, nothing, shit, boom! It works. Thank God! He presses 0999002 Send, 0999003 Send, 0999004 Send, 099 and a fierce flash from behind the prison and a much louder explosion startles his attention away. Keep dialling 9005 Send. Honorita! Late as usual, but at least she's in town. He smiles, he's not alone, huddles back down behind the dune and keeps on dialling.

56
Dateline 31st, 9.01pm

"Good man, that's what I like to hear," says Honorita aloud to herself as she hears the steady muffled blasts from the town. Bo may be on the run, but she knows he's on the Bahia roof catapulting thunder flashes. She is pleased for him and pleased for herself in bringing him. She picks herself up from the ground, stumbled there by the recoil from the first RPG. She finds some better ground, flatter ground, aims a little to the left and tries again for the generator. She sees the grenade trail hit the prison, but the lights stay on. She cannot see the generator, and is aiming for the spot where the briefings said it should be. In the distance she hears Antonio rev the Mercedes, turns to see the lights go on as he joins the main road.

She is not happy with her shooting ground but it was the best they could do with no headlights to find some level ground at all. She had been leaning out of one window and Antonio the other, peering into the black of night. She did not want him to leave the track and get stuck and so add more complications. She had been looking for flat ground nearby, had found some, but now feels it is too far away and she wants to be more to her left to get a better angle for the grenades. She reaches down to the grenade bag but even before she tries to lift it she knows it is too heavy. She picks up half a dozen grenades and feels five metres to her left. She finds some better ground, braces her weight evenly on both feet. Down the sights she can see some activity in the prison, reacting to her first two hits. She aims into a corner where a red object is lit up. She hopes that is the generator. She pulls the trigger, the grenade traces off, she sees a big flash and the lights go out. "Bullseye!" she shouts to the darkness.

She reaches down and picks up another, and then four more grenades, and fires them off quickly. Running back to the main supply she is aware that the blasts from the town have stopped, Bo must have used up all the thunder flashes. At least his job is done, and done well, even if he is on the run. She thinks for an instant about how she can help him, but immediately snaps back to the mission and meeting Romero and the UOE boys.

57
Dateline 31st, 9.02pm

"Mike, what the fuck is happening?" Hernán Eboleh shouts into his phone. He waits for a reply. "No stay there, look after Giselle. No, I am on the boat."

"What's happening, cousin?" asks a frightened little voice in the darkness. Julio.

"The town has been hit too. Must be a coup. That English guy Pitt," replies Hernán. He remembers his own mission, and reaches for his gun, but he cannot see Cortez in the new darkness. He can hear movement around the room, but cannot tell if it is Cortez or the two Kirange girls or his cousin. It's not his cousin, he can now hear him crying. He pulls the safety catch off his gun and starts firing blindly at the noises. None came back.

58
Dateline 31st, 9.05pm

All Gustavo Cortez wants to do is stay alive. The rescue is on. First he heard some explosions from Barbate, small but explosions and now he was on the receiving end of a full-scale attack. They must think he is in the cells, their plan must be to blow the rest up and release him and all the prisoners. He is ducked down behind an upturned table. The clever one, the admiral is firing his gun in the darkness. He himself is lying flat on the floor, as flat as he can squeeze himself down with his hands around his head. He is surprised the girls are quiet, either dead or terrified. Suddenly there is a much louder hit, the roof, now rafters come down and one is alight. He can see in the room again now around the table. A rafter has landed on the admiral and knocked him to the ground, now some masonry falls on top of him too. The fat governor is cowering in a corner with his hands over his ears. The girls? He feels something beside him, startles and sees them both there hiding next to him behind the table.

He needs to tackle the admiral, now stirring, and get the gun off him, knock him and the governor out with a rafter. He stands up and hears the incoming in the same split second. He throws himself down again, lands on top of the girls. The office is under direct attack, RPGs are his guess. He wishes whoever it were firing at them would fuck off and rescue them instead. Falling debris lands on him now, and he struggles to get free but is pinned down by sheer weight.

59
Dateline 31st, 9.05pm

Bo is now lying flat behind the dune nearest the prison entrance waiting for Honorita to finish off her RPGs. He is pleased his candles all went off, says a thanks to Miss ffinch, sorry about not acting his age, and can only imagine the scenes of confusion back in Barbate. He peers over the dune, and sees another flash and explosion. He thinks she will be weaker after the launching, then remembers, hopes, that she is Honorita, tough and trained. Handsome too, shut up Bo and concentrate. He has lost count of the RPGs, but it must be nearly twenty-four by now. He peers over the dune again and sees another explosion and more flying bricks, and that a fire has now started, now three or four fires, including what looks like the main block. He thinks about the prisoners inside, what they must be feeling, he thinks about Cortez in there, at least a trained special agent, and wishes she would finish firing and he could go in, but another grenade crashes into the flaming debris and he hears for the first time a howl, and a human howl, from inside. Then the RPGs stop. He waits a few seconds, a few more seconds, pulls himself forward, and prowls off towards the burning building with a Star M30 in each hand.

60
Dateline 31st, 9.08pm

Honorita throws down the launcher and takes a deep breath. She had not realised how much firing twenty four grenades consecutively and quickly, especially in the dark and on loose ground, would have taken out of her. She peers ahead at her handiwork and smiles at a job well done. The prison is comprehensively damaged, lit only by fire, three or four fires. She imagines Romero and the boys on the beach waiting for this moment, the moment when her grenades stop and they assault. She reaches down to pick up her hand guns, her favourite STARs.

The ground between her and the prison has been cleared by the shrub fire, so at least crossing it is easy, then she sees the dirt track in the flames and runs along it towards the entrance. Reaching it in fifteen seconds, she pauses with her back against the wall, spins round and sees Bo stalking in to the prison gate from the dunes and ocean. He must see her shadow from the flames at the same time because suddenly he swings his handguns towards her and drops to one knee.

"Bo! No! It's me! What are you doing here? Where are Romero and the boys?"

Bo puts his guns back down by his side and they rush to meet either side of the open gate. "Romero's not coming, not tonight, twenty four hour delay."

"So how...?" she starts.

"Beats me," she hears Bo say, "Let's get Cortez out first."

"Yes, sir," and, smiling broadly, she waves him in ahead.

61
Dateline 31st, 9.10pm

Hernán Eboleh regains consciousness, brought back to his senses by pain, a burning pain in his left shin from one of the rafters. He kicks it off. He has no idea what is happening. The only light is from the burning building. Smoke and ashes are settling in the room. Slowly events come into focus. There is an attack on Barbate and now an attack here at Black Beach. Who? Why? Must have something to do with the Spaniard Cortez. Or that Englishman on the TV, Pitt. Then he remembers, he is here to kill Cortez. Where is that bastard Cortez? There's no one in the room except Julio. Julio is whimpering in the corner, begging for mercy from who knows what demons. Hernán props himself up on an elbow, assesses his scalded leg in the flickering flame light and curses the pain. He tries to stand, cannot stand and thinks his leg may be broken too. He finds his gun just by his right hand, picks it up and aims in the direction of the blabbering Julio, says "shut up you stupid moron!" and fires loosely towards him; Julio obliges him immediately by dropping stone dead onto the floor. Now the room is quieter, just the crackle of burning wood. He falls back from the recoil and effort. Coughing from the ashes and dust, his eyes stinging from the wood smoke, he knows he needs to get out of there before what's left of the roof falls in.

The light from the flames is fading and now he hears a noise from behind the upturned table behind him. "So, Cortez my friend," he says aloud, "That's where you thought you could hide, is it? Hide from Hernán Eboleh. Your good friend Hernán Eboleh." He tries to turn himself around, but the pain from his leg slows him down, then stops him. He puts the gun down to roll over onto his other side and to shoot through the table from there. He yelps in pain as he rolls over, and now with his left hand reaches for the gun and looks ahead to the table.

61
Dateline 31st, 9.12pm

Bo kicks in what remains of the office door, and sees a dead fat African slumped in a corner with a swamp of blood around him, another African on the floor with a gun pointing at a table. He hears Honorita follow him in. The African on the floor looks around in surprise and slowly brings his gun around to point at Bo and Honorita. He sneers, "Who the fuck…?"

Bo pulls his trigger first and the bullet rips into the African's stomach, "…are you?" says Bo. "Gustavo, you in here too?" he shouts.

A voice for behind the table says, "Si, si, don't shoot!". From behind him Honorita rushes forward and pulls the upright table flat onto its top. Under it Bo sees Cortez and the two girls. "Who are they?"

"Gustavo, are you OK?" pleads Honorita.

"Honorita, I'm so, so pleased to see you."

Bo snaps in, "No time for that now, we got to get out of here, fast." He leads them out, he and Honorita coughing from the smoke and Cortez still in shock. "Listen," he tells them, "take my RIB over the dune on the beach. There's only room for two. I'll make my own way out somehow. There's a full tank of petrol. The UOE will be here at exactly nine tomorrow night. Hide the boat and yourselves at the end of the peninsula over there," Bo points over to the north west of the runway. "It's unpopulated, you'll be safe there till they come. I'll get word to Romero to pick you up from there. OK? Go!"

62
Dateline 31st, 9.15pm

Gustavo is recovering. He holds Honorita, and thanks Bo, "I needed to get out of there. I really needed to get out of there."

He follows Bo to the dune to help him relaunch the RIB. It is dark as soon as they go down the far side by the sea. From the top he peers at the dark ocean, and Bo points into the void towards the peninsula.

"Come on Honorita, let's go. We'll be safe where he says. Thanks again, I don't know your name?" he asks Bo.

Honorita steps forward, "His name is Pett, Bo Pett. No Gus, you go, I need to help here." She is looking at the young blond Englishman.

"But Honorita…"

"Quick Gus, you must hurry," she replies.

He says, "Wait here," and runs back inside. The room is even thicker with smoke now the fires are dying down. His throat and eyes sting as he climbs over new rubble into the office. He cannot see Bo and Honorita move closer together on Black Beach. The girls are still huddled in each other's arms behind the table. He grabs the eldest and implores her to follow him. Moments later he comes back to the dune with the two girls. One is holding onto the other who is holding onto Gustavo. They look, are, terrified. He takes them down into the darkness by the sea, picks them up and puts them down gently in the boat. Then he jumps in himself as Honorita and Bo push them afloat. He pulls the string and the little Honda starts again.

"See you in Madrid, I love you." he shouts over the waves to Honorita.

"Good luck, Gus," she says, and then he sees her turn and run back over the dune with this Bo.

64
Dateline 31st, 9.18pm

"Thank God that's over," says Bo.

"Now the hard part starts," Honorita replies. "We've got to get ourselves out of here, out of FP too. Whose car is that?" she says pointing towards the Corvette.

"Must be one of the guys in there. Neither of them will mind if we borrow it. Looks like a Corvette. Cool, can I drive?" he asks and without waiting for a reply jumps into the driving seat. "Bollocks, no keys."

"I'll get them," she replies, " and my mobile phone while I'm at it." She runs back inside the burning building.

Bo sees a brief case on the floor in the passenger's foot well. He lifts it up and opens it. A minute later Honorita slides in besides him and hands him the keys. "In his pocket, and the phone in the other guy's pocket. I've just pick pocketed two dead men." Bo notices she is enjoying herself more than at any time he has known her. It's infectious. He fires up the car and hands her the briefcase.

He turns on the headlights as they drive up the dirt track onto the main road. He sees the dying flames and blowing smoke in the rear view mirror as she turns on the reading light and goes through the briefcase. "Looks like you bagged yourself an admiral, Bo," she says with a smile. "Admiral Hernán Eboleh. Eboleh, now we're really in the shit."

"No need to sound so chirpy about it."

"Wait. Slow down. I think I've found his boat keys. Well, there are keys with the ship's papers. Fernando Poan Navy Cutter Nguru. Has to be in the harbour. Can you drive one of those?"

"Can't be that difficult if we have the keys," he says, fearing it must be a lot more difficult than just having the keys. They reach the end of the dirt track. "Must be left."

"Must be. Look at this lot," she says and ahead they can see a series of flashing blue lights heading their way. "Black Beach."

"Black Beach. You see what I see?"

"Roadblock."

"Roadblock."

"With luck they'll recognise the admiral's car and wave us through. Better slow down. Bo, better slow down. Bo!"

"No time for that," he says as he floors it through the wooden pole which crashes along the top of the Corvette's roof. They see uniforms scatter and shout as the roar through. They hears shots and duck down and the rear window shatters as they speed away.

"Oh, boy," she says. He is not quite sure what she means.

They drive along the main road overtaking everything in sight, then swerving back to miss the oncoming traffic. A bicycle without lights wobbles onto the main road in front of them. Bo holds down the horn and keeps his foot flat on the floor. They miss him by inches. Less than a minute later on the outskirts of Barbate they see more blue lights ahead in the city.

"Good candles those," says Bo.

"What candles?"

"Proper candles, British candles, I'll tell you later. Here's the sign for the port." He slams on the brakes, all four tyres squeal and smoke as they drift past the turning. Before they have stopped he has the lever in reverse and the Corvette jolts backwards for ten yards and stops sharp with another jolt. He throws it into forward, swings it left and blasts it down to the port. They come to a stop in a trail of rubber and look around the floodlit harbour.

"There's only one naval boat here," Honorita says, "That must be it over there."

"Must be," says Bo and launches the Corvette off to the gangplank on the dock on the far side of the harbour. They both jump out with STARS in each hand and spring up the stairs to the deck, and then up another flight to the bridge. The door is unlocked, they go in and flick the light switch; there is light. Honorita puts a key in the only lock and turns it. A series of red lights flash on the console in front of them. There are two red Start/Stop buttons underneath the red lights. Bo pushes one and from deep below they hear the opening rumble of a diesel. The other button repeats the process. Ahead are a steering wheel and two levers, with Forward, Neutral and Reverse written helpfully next to them.

"Well they make that pretty easy," he says. "Can you go and cast off the lines and flick off the lights?"

"Lines?"

"Ropes, chuck them all over onto the dock."

"Si, Señor Capitan!"

A minute later she is back in the darkness on the bridge next to him. He pushes the levers Forward and the boat moves ahead. He steers through the harbour entrance and out to sea, accelerating and disappearing in the darkness.

65
Dateline 31st, 10.00pm

"Romero was right about the moon. There she is. We could go and look for them," says Bo.

"We could," agrees Honorita half-heartedly, snuggling close to him, her arm around his waist as his is around her shoulder.

"But then again...," he says after a while.

"Nah, they'll be alright." she says. He looks across to see his two favourite dimples smiling back at him.

He slows the boat down, steers towards the moon, flicks a switch that says Auto and says that the admiral's quarters are bound to be more comfortable than standing here on the bridge. She agrees with this too, and he leads her off in that direction as smoothly as the cutter heads out to sea along the moon's shimmering silver reflection.

Epilogue

Bo managed to contact Coronal Molistán and arrange for Cortez and the girls to be collected by Capitán Romero and the UOE twenty-four hours later. Cortez returned home to a hero's welcome, counter blackmailed Kellen about his French involvement, left the CNI and tried and failed to make his property fortune. Señora Cortez brought up the two girls in traditional military fashion. Honorita was not so fortunate; she was suspended by the CNI after Coronal Molistán worked out she had disobeyed orders and would take no excuses She left the service and was recruited by a private security firm and is now angry and well paid in Iraq. Krause van Stahl is back in Constantia, his bank balance boosted further by Sir Mungo's hush money. Sir Mungo continues to thrive, but not in Fernando Po, and Simonez died of stomach cancer. The Eboleh family continue to cream off the US oil companies benevolence. Bo returned to San Diego and was then sent to Kenya, at the Kenyan government's request, to stem the illegal poaching of wild animals for the Chinese vitality market. Unfortunately other parts of the Kenyan government are not so well disposed, and indeed the triad gangs and certain tribal chiefs are not too well disposed either. Colonel Harding is keeping his eye on his protégé.